HOUSEBROKE

TITLES BY JACI BURTON

Riding the Night
Riding to Sunset
    (an eNovella)
Riding the Edge
    (an eNovella)

STAND-ALONE NOVELS

Wild, Wicked, & Wanton
Bound, Branded, & Brazen
Housebroke

ANTHOLOGIES

Unlaced
    *(with Jasmine Haynes, Joey
    W. Hill, and Denise Rossetti)*
Exclusive
    *(with Eden Bradley and Lisa
    Renee Jones)*
Laced with Desire
    *(with Jasmine Haynes, Joey
    W. Hill, and Denise Rossetti)*
Nauti and Wild
    (with Lora Leigh)
Nautier and Wilder
    (with Lora Leigh)

Hot Summer Nights
    *(with Carly Phillips, Erin
    McCarthy, and Jessica Clare)*
Mistletoe Games
    *(*Holiday Games, Holiday on Ice,
    and Hot Holiday Nights *in one
    volume)*

ENOVELLAS

The Ties That Bind
No Strings Attached
Wild Nights

HOUSEBROKE

~~~~~~

JACI BURTON

BERKLEY ROMANCE · NEW YORK

BERKLEY ROMANCE
Published by Berkley
An imprint of Penguin Random House LLC
penguinrandomhouse.com

Library of Congress Cataloging-in-Publication Data

Names: Burton, Jaci, author.
Title: Housebroke / Jaci Burton.
Description: First edition. | New York: Berkley Romance, 2023.
Identifiers: LCCN 2023006160 (print) | LCCN 2023006161 (ebook) |
ISBN 9780593439593 (trade paperback) | ISBN 9780593439609 (ebook)
Subjects: LCGFT: Romance fiction. | Novels.
Classification: LCC PS3602.U776 H69 2023 (print) |
LCC PS3602.U776 (ebook) | DDC 813/.54—dc23/eng/20230216
LC record available at https://lccn.loc.gov/2023006160
LC ebook record available at https://lccn.loc.gov/2023006161

First Edition: December 2023

Printed in the United States of America
1st Printing

Book design by Elke Sigal

This book is dedicated to animal rescue organizations and anyone who has ever rescued, fostered, or cared for a dog, cat, bunny, bird, snake, lizard, goat, horse, cow—well, you get it. Thank you for loving and caring for animals.

Please adopt—don't shop.

HOUSEBROKE

CHAPTER ONE

*H*azel Bristow lined up all her babies, preparing them for their early-evening walk. Today she waited until almost dark because even though it was late summer in Orlando, it was still muggy, and just chasing after these hellions all day inside was a sweat-inducing activity, let alone taking them on a long walk.

Of course as soon as she dragged the harnesses and leashes out, there were excited tail wags and butt wiggles. Even from Gordon the pug, who at twelve years old couldn't make it more than two blocks but gave it his best effort. Which was why she always brought the stroller along.

She got all five dogs hooked up and prepped the stroller, and they were out the door, Lilith the Chihuahua leading the way, even though she was the smallest of the pack. But Penelope the golden retriever was too busy sniffing every blade of grass in the front yard, and Freddie the dachshund had to pee on every bush they passed, and they hadn't even gotten off the property before Boo the pit mix parked his butt at the end of the driveway, refusing to go any farther.

"What's wrong, Boo?"

He looked up at her with his sad eyes, pulling on the leash to head back toward the house. She frowned and studied him, trying to figure out what the issue was. Then it hit her.

"Oh, right." She looped the leashes around the stroller, knowing they wouldn't go anywhere without her. "I'll be back in a sec, kids."

She dashed inside and found Boo's stuffed bear by the front door. She grabbed it and hurried back outside to find all five dogs waiting ever so patiently for her, though Lilith looked like she was ready to bolt any second and take the rest of them on the walk by herself.

"I'm so sorry for the delay, Lilith. We can go now."

She handed Boo his bear. He gently took it in his mouth, and now they were ready to roll.

The dogs always started out at a brisk pace, especially Boo, who was the youngest and full of energy. Which suited her just fine, too. Even with the heat, she enjoyed walking.

She loved this neighborhood with its nice homes and amazing trees in every yard. It had always felt friendly and homey to her. She was so grateful to her friend Ginger for letting her crash here, even though the house was currently for sale. And empty. But it was a roof over her and the dogs' heads, and she'd find something else soon. She'd promised her friend it would only be a short stay, and she'd keep the place superclean, which she had. And since Ginger and Greg had already moved out, Hazel felt like she was providing a service by keeping an eye on the place.

Plus, Hazel didn't have a lot of stuff, so it was easy enough to pack up and vacate whenever Ginger alerted her that the real estate agent was coming by to do a showing. Fortunately—or maybe unfortunately for Ginger, there hadn't been any activity for the past few weeks. Which had worked out well for Hazel, though she knew she was going to have to find another place to live soon. But right now? It was awesome, and she liked to imagine she and the dogs actually lived in the house.

As was typical, Gordon's tongue started hanging out after about fifteen minutes, so she scooped him up and placed him in the stroller, where he promptly turned in a circle, curled up, and went to sleep. The rest of the dogs kept up the pace, though after thirty minutes she could tell they were hot and ready to head for home. So was she.

They made their way back to the house, and she unhooked the dogs from their harnesses. Everyone ran for their water bowls to hydrate while Hazel put everything away, then she went to the fridge for the pitcher of water, pouring herself a glass. She drank the entire thing, breathing out a relieved sigh when she finished it. She washed and dried the glass and put it away just in case someone wanted to come look at the house. She never left dirty dishes or anything lying out, because just packing up the dogs and their things made it enough of a rush to leave.

Not that she had much.

She changed into her swimsuit, then opened the back door and all the dogs ran outside.

The best thing about this house was the pool. It was screened in to keep the bugs out, an important thing in Florida, so she could swim anytime of the day or night. It was also great therapy for Gordon, whose arthritis had gotten bad in the past year.

She grabbed his swim harness and put it on him, smiling as his tail swept back and forth.

"You ready for a little dip, baby?" she asked as she walked over to the steps and waded into the pool.

Gordon followed her to the side of the pool. She reached for him, and his short legs were already pumping before she set him in the water. She walked around the shallow end, letting him swim while she held on to the harness for support.

"You like the water, don't you, Gordon?"

Gordon didn't answer, of course, but she could tell from his goofy pug smile that he loved it. Because when Gordon didn't love something, he let you know with lots of grunts and whines.

So did Boo, who jumped into the deep end and swam around for a while before making his way to the steps. He got out, shook the water off, and lay down under one of the shade trees.

"You've got to have some Labrador in you, Boo. You just love your swims."

Boo rolled over on his back, stuck his feet up in the air, and went to sleep, ignoring her praise.

Typical. She continued to enjoy the cool water, though at times she wished she could swim laps. Sometimes she did, late at night, after the dogs were all asleep. She'd come out here and slice through the water, remembering the times she'd have a late-night swim in her own pool, at her own house, enjoying that quiet. Before her marriage went to hell and she lost everything.

Well, there was no point in reliving the past, was there? That part of her life was over. There was only now, and now was pretty great.

Temporarily great, anyway. This wasn't her home.

Not wanting to overtire Gordon, Hazel kept track of the time. Gordon would spend all day in the water if he could.

The other dogs would swim on occasion, but not every day, preferring the copious amounts of shade over in the grassy area of the yard. And it was getting late, so she scooped Gordon into her arms, unzipped him from his harness, and placed him on the ground, letting him shake off the water. Of course he'd dry in no time, so she grabbed a towel and dried herself off, put on her T-shirt, and headed into the house to get dinner ready for the dogs.

They all followed, knowing the routine.

She stood at the kitchen peninsula, prepping their food, the dogs sitting and waiting patiently nearby. All bets were off once she set the bowls down and told them to eat. Then it was slurping and crunching and Hazel should probably think about making her own dinner.

Except she needed to make a plan. She had the foster dogs, and the agencies she worked with paid for their medical care and provided a stipend for their food, which was great. But as far as income? She had mostly . . . Okay, she had nothing. And that wasn't going to put a roof over her head and gas in the car.

She took odd jobs here and there to pay the bills, but long term it wasn't ideal. And she was dipping into her meager savings more than she wanted to.

She sat on the fold-up chair and watched the dogs eat, realizing she was going to have to come up with something more permanent and soon. Living day-to-day and sometimes hour to hour just wasn't cutting it.

For her or for her dogs.

*L*incoln Kennedy pulled into the driveway of his next project, a nice four-bedroom in a prime location in Orlando. He turned the engine off in his truck and wished it was still daylight so he could take a look at the outside of the house, but that would have to wait until morning.

What a shit day. Shit month, actually. He gripped the steering wheel, wishing he'd had time to take a long vacation to somewhere tropical and shake off the dregs of his breakup with Stefanie.

It had all boiled down to the money. His money. Once Stefanie had found out how much he had, she'd changed. He thought the two of them had a chance at something, but she'd turned out to be no different than any other woman he'd ever had a relationship with. He'd been judged by his wallet, and once a woman found out his was fat, she saw him differently. Wanted things from him. Planned a future based on his income.

So he'd ended it, just like he'd ended all his other relationships.

Whatever. Girlfriends were too much trouble. And he needed to get to work.

He grabbed his bag and the keys that the Realtor had overnighted to him and walked to the front door, then slipped the keys in the lock, noting the lockbox was still on the door. He made a mental note to contact the agent in the morning so it could be removed.

As he opened the door, he yawned. The flight from San Francisco to Orlando had been long and exhausting, but such was the nature of his business. Not that he was complaining, since he loved the travel, and he was excited to start this new project. At least this would give him something to get jazzed about.

He dropped his bag at the front door, then paused, certain he'd heard a noise. He waited a few beats listening for anything else that didn't seem right. When he didn't hear another sound, he headed straight to the kitchen.

From the photos he'd seen of the place, he knew that's where he'd need to do the most work, so he might as well take a look.

He was about to hit the light switch when he caught movement out of the corner of his eye. Something was headed toward him, and he caught whatever it was in mid swing, his heart pumping triple time as he figured he was about to get blasted on the head by a tire iron or something equally skull smashing. In what felt like hours but in reality was probably only a few seconds, he had the offending weapon in one hand and the intruder wrapped around him in the other.

"Hey, hold on there," he said, realizing whoever it was trying to kill him was a lot smaller than him. And lighter, since he'd grabbed his or her arm and their weapon, which was a . . .

Cast-iron skillet?

He held the squirming burglar against his chest and leaned back to fumble around the wall for the light switch. He hit the switch with his elbow, which bathed the kitchen with light.

Okay, this was unexpected. He quickly let go of the intruder, and they made a hasty retreat to the other side of the room.

Linc had figured maybe a teen, or a small man. But never in a million years did he figure he'd come face-to-face with a gorgeous woman dressed only in a T-shirt and underwear, along with several glaring sets of eyes directed at him. He quickly counted—

Five dogs. And they hadn't even barked.

"What the hell's going on here?" he asked. "What are you doing in here?"

She tugged the T-shirt over her flowered cotton panties. "I think I should be the one asking the questions here, since you just broke in."

He shook his head. "No, I own this place."

"You do not. I'm friends with the owner."

"You mean the former owner. I closed on this house three days ago."

She frowned. "Prove it."

He frowned. "You prove it. Who's the owner of this place?" He wasn't about to give her a lead.

"Ginger and Greg—"

"Powell," he finished for her.

Her eyes widened. "They sold the house?"

"Yeah."

She lifted her chin, a defiant look on her face. "I don't believe you."

Now that his heart rate had come down to a more manageable level, he could think a little more clearly. And since whoever this woman was seemed to know the former owners, she was likely scared, too. Which was so not his problem since she was the one squatting in his house. "You should call her. Now."

She grabbed her phone off the corner of the peninsula while she eyed him warily. She pressed a button and waited.

"Ginger. It's Hazel. I'm at your house and some guy just came in and said he bought the place."

She listened, still staring at him.

"It's okay. I just didn't know. I would have left if I'd known."

She listened some more.

"I'm fine, honestly. Nothing happened other than both of us scaring the hell out of each other."

Then she laughed, and it was such an amazing sound. Light and easy.

He didn't care how she sounded. Why would he care? His first objective needed to be getting her the hell out of there.

"Yeah, I don't think either of us would want to see pics of what just happened. But we're both okay. No harm, no foul."

Linc motioned to her. "Mind if I have the phone for a second?"

She hesitated. "Uh, Ginger? He wants to talk to you."

She listened, then gave him the phone. He put it on speaker and laid it on the counter. "Hey, Ginger, how's it going?"

"Linc. I am so embarrassed. For some reason I had it down that you weren't coming in until next month. And then with our move and everything going on, I totally spaced and forgot to tell Hazel that the house had sold. This is all my fault. I'm so sorry to both of you for this."

Linc looked over at the woman, who still had her arms wrapped around herself but seemed a lot less terrified than she had a few minutes ago.

"Hey, it's okay. We both survived the scare. Is Greg there?"

"Oh, he's here, trying not to laugh."

"I wasn't laughing," Greg said. "Glad you didn't get arrested, bud."

He saw Hazel cock her head to the side. "Greg and I know each other."

"Oh. Okay."

"I'm so sorry, Hazel," Ginger said.

"Me, too," Greg said. "But it's still Ginger's fault."

"Hey, you could have called Hazel, too," Ginger said.

"I could have. My bad."

"It's all good," Hazel said. "Love you guys."

"I'll call you after this project, Greg," Linc said, "and we'll get together for a round."

"You got it," Greg said.

Hazel clicked off. "Okay, apparently you're legit. Ginger didn't tell me. She told me she'd let me know when they accepted an offer so I could clear out before the new owner arrived. I guess that's you."

"And I guess you're not a burglar."

She slanted a look at him. "Do I look like a burglar?"

He gave her the once-over, from her wildly tousled dark hair to her tanned bare legs. "Not any burglar I could ever imagine."

"Do you mind if I put some pants on before we continue this conversation?"

Actually, he did mind. She had amazing legs. "Sure, go ahead. And while you're at it, you can pack up whatever things you have so you can leave."

Her eyes widened. "Oh, right. Sure. I can do that. Sorry."

The look on her face was one of utter dejection. Linc would not feel sorry for her. She wasn't his responsibility, and he had things to do to this house that did not include a woman and five dogs.

"Come on, babies," she said, and just like that, her dog entourage followed behind, but he could swear that little beige Chihuahua gave him a dirty look before leaving the room.

Finally, Linc had a chance to exhale. And put the skillet on the stove.

The woman—Hazel—was talking upstairs. He should follow and make sure she didn't do any damage. And while she might be friends of Ginger and Greg, she wasn't his friend. In fact, he didn't know her at all. He'd known of squatters who kicked in drywall or did any number of things to screw up property before running off. He had his investment to protect, so he quietly made his way up the steps, stopping in the hallway when he heard the sound of her voice just inside the bedroom.

"It's okay, babies," she said, her voice low and trembling. "We'll figure something out. We always do, don't we?"

He peeked his head inside the door to see a blow-up mattress and an oversize backpack. Was that all she had? She'd put on a pair of shorts and wound her long, dark hair into a bun on top of her head.

"I promise I'll take care of you. You won't be homeless. We won't be homeless. I'll make this work. Somehow." The pit bull came over and laid his head on her thigh, and Hazel dropped her head to her chest and her body shook.

Dammit. She was crying. Linc turned away and made his way back downstairs.

This—she—was not his problem. He didn't even know her.

Hazel came downstairs a short time later, her eyes swollen and red rimmed, but she had a smile on her face. The dogs all followed her, then sat at her feet like little statues.

Weird little fuckers.

All she had was the remnants of that mattress and a couple of bags. Was that all she owned?

"I'm really sorry about nearly crushing your skull with the skillet. We'll get out of your way now. I have a chair outside—oh, and my skillet. I'll just put these in the car and be on my way."

She headed toward the front door, the dogs following. It was the most pitiful entourage Linc had ever seen.

Fuck.

"Wait," he said.

She stopped and turned to look at him.

"It's late and you obviously don't have anywhere to go. You can stay in the guesthouse for a day or two until you figure something out."

Her eyes lit up like bright round diamonds. "Really? Oh my God, thank you so much. I'm Hazel Bristow, by the way." She held out her hand, so he did the same.

"Lincoln Kennedy."

She gave him a look. "That's very . . . historical."

"I go by Linc. And my mother's a history teacher. She named all of us after historical figures."

"All of you. So you have siblings."

"Two brothers."

"I see. So you're moving in?"

"Sort of. I mean, not really. I'm renovating this place."

She frowned. "Why? What's wrong with it? It's a great house."

"It needs some updating before I sell it."

"Oh." She chewed on her lower lip for a beat. "So you're one of those people."

The way she said that told him she wasn't a fan of his livelihood. "You mean people who invest in homes, fix them up and make them better, then sell them and improve the neighborhood?"

He didn't miss her derisive snort. "Yeah. House flippers. You come in, do some cheap modifications so you can make a quick profit, then turn around and sell and then you're off to the next house."

"Well, when you say it like that it does sound bad. But that's not what I do."

"Uh-huh. Sure."

"And what do you do, Hazel?"

Her gaze shifted down to her dogs. "I foster dogs."

"Is that what those are?"

"Yes. Sort of. Mostly."

That was vague. "And you're staying in an empty house because . . . ?"

"It's complicated. Say, are you hungry? I'm hungry. I was going to fix myself some dinner. Would you like something to eat?"

She was avoiding the question, but he was hungry. "Sure."

"Awesome."

She seemed relieved not to answer the question about what she was doing staying at the house, but Linc supposed the answer to that question could wait.

At least until after dinner.

CHAPTER TWO

*H*azel was happy to have a reprieve from explaining her current circumstances to Linc. And deliriously relieved to not be out on the street with the pups. Also, she really was hungry, since she'd gotten distracted streaming a show on her iPad while folding laundry so she'd sort of forgotten about dinner. And then she'd heard a noise downstairs, so her hunger had been momentarily replaced by utter panic.

Finding a shadowy figure in the kitchen had just about sent her on a dead run out the back door. She'd have done just that if it had only been her, but she had the pups to think about. She was so grateful they had been silent, one of the first commands she taught all new dogs she fostered, because no one liked barky dogs and she never knew where she was going to end up next.

Linc sure was good-looking, she thought as she stirred the noodles in the boiling pot while she poured wine in the skillet that she'd almost used as a weapon to defend herself. It was a good thing Linc had sharp reflexes, because she'd been aiming for his head. Not that she could have hit him there, since he was very tall. He had a thick head of dark hair and some intense brown eyes. And one amazing ass that she was not looking at anymore, otherwise her shrimp were going to taste like Penelope's squeaky toys.

She drained the pasta, then poured the shrimp scampi over the top. She fixed up a basic Italian-style side salad with olives and tomatoes, along with an Italian vinaigrette dressing.

"Sorry about the paper plates," she said as she scooted a plate across the peninsula toward him. "I don't have dishes. Or a table and chairs. But there are barstools."

She handed him a plastic fork.

"Not a problem. This smells amazing."

"Thanks. I like to cook, and I went to the store today so it's all fresh."

He dug into the food, and since she was hungry, so did she, only occasionally slanting surreptitious glances toward him. Since the dogs got their cues from her and she'd accepted him, they had as well, though as with all strangers, they kept their distance, preferring to monitor Linc from across the room.

He finally looked up at her and smiled. "This is exceptional."

"You think so?"

"Absolutely. You can more than cook, Hazel. I've had plenty of excellent food in my lifetime, and this is . . . perfection."

"Really?" She'd rarely gotten compliments on her cooking from her ex-husband, who had always mindlessly shoveled food in his mouth and then left the table without a word. So to get praise like this was a boon to her sorely battered ego.

"I did forget to get bread. It's much better with bread, but it's too hot to make it in the oven right now."

He arched a perfect brow. "You make bread, too?"

"When it's a little cooler outside I can."

"Wow. Amazing."

When she finished the small plate she had made for herself, she leaned back on her barstool. "So, while you're doing your fixer-upper thing, what do you eat?"

He shrugged. "Sometimes I'll make a sandwich or whip up eggs for breakfast. Otherwise, I'll find a local chef who can curate some meals for me and I'll pay extra for that."

An idea immediately formed in her head. Then again, she didn't really know him. Like at all.

"How do you know Greg?"

"We've worked together a few times, doing some investment projects."

"So he'd vouch for you. You know, confirm you're not a serial killer."

He laughed. "Uh, yeah, I think so."

"Excuse me a second."

She disappeared and stepped outside, making yet another call to Ginger and Greg, who probably had second thoughts about their friendship with her. But Greg confirmed that Linc was a good guy and she had nothing to worry about, though Ginger asked why she wanted to know and if he'd done anything wrong. She assured her friend that he'd been a perfect gentleman and was even allowing her to stay for a few extra days. When Greg confirmed that was the Linc he knew, she felt immensely better.

When she got off the phone, she had a plan formulated. Linc would probably never go for it, but it might buy her some time to figure things out. She pulled up to her spot at the peninsula and said, "You must burn a ton of calories while you're doing your . . . your thing around here."

"You could say that."

"Wouldn't it be great to have an on-call chef to cook for you?"

He cocked his head to the side and studied her for a few seconds, then said, "Go ahead and tell me your idea."

She leaned forward. "Okay. Say the dogs and I stay here while you're renovating. I promise you we are very good at not getting in the way. And while you're working, I cook for you."

"You know I'm demolishing the kitchen, right?"

She shrugged. "There's a kitchenette in the guesthouse behind the pool. Has a mini stove and an oven. Plus there's the grill out back. Trust me when I tell you that I am very resourceful when it comes to cooking."

"And in exchange, you'd only want the ability to crash here."

"Not exactly. I still have to take care of the dogs and I have other expenses, so I'd expect a minimal salary."

"We can discuss that. But first you tell me how you ended up here, in an empty house, with five dogs and no furniture."

Damn. She was hoping she wouldn't have to reveal that part. "Fine. My ex-husband swindled me out of our house and all our money."

His eyes widened. "What? How did he manage that?"

"Let's just say I foolishly allowed him to handle our finances, and before I knew it, our bank accounts were empty, the house was double mortgaged, and there was nothing left. And then he filed for divorce and left the state."

His jaw dropped. "Wow. I'm sorry. That must have sucked."

"It did. We were a mess before that, but I guess I didn't pull the divorce trigger fast enough. And I have no one to blame but myself for letting things go south like that. I should have been paying closer attention. It wasn't like I didn't see the signs. He'd always been a shady shithead, I just didn't think he was that shady."

He stabbed a shrimp with his fork and pointed it at her. "People can hurt you more than you think."

"I guess so. Anyway, we lost the house to foreclosure, but by then he was long gone anyway and I was out of a place to live. I have a tiny bit of savings that I had in a separate account from money my grandmother left me after she died, so I rented a small house, but when the lease came up, the owners decided to sell, so I was out on the streets again. That's when Ginger and Greg decided to move and said I could stay here for an interim period. And now here I am."

"Huh. You sure got screwed, didn't you, Hazel?"

She shrugged. "I learned a valuable lesson about trust and always keeping my eyes wide open."

"That's a very good lesson to learn." He picked up the plates and dumped them in the trash, then started to take the skillet to the sink.

She slid off the barstool. "Oh no. Part of the cooking is the cleanup. I'm sure you have some unpacking to do."

"You sure?"

"Absolutely. Go on."

"Okay. Thanks again for dinner. It was amazing."

Her lips curved, and she couldn't help the warmth in her cheeks over his compliment. "You're welcome."

After he left, the dogs came over to sniff the area where they had eaten.

"There isn't a crumb in the vicinity, kids. Sorry. We ate it all."

She heard the door open and close a few times while she finished washing the dishes. Deciding to just let him do his thing, she took the dogs out back, enjoying the not-quite-cool breeze. But, hey, at least there was a breeze.

Linc came outside and sat in the chair next to hers. "Great backyard."

"Isn't it? The pool is amazing. The dogs love it. And before you ask, I always sweep out any dog hair in the pool and the filter basket."

"Noted. Though I wasn't going to ask."

"I also vacuum the floors every day. Or the robot does. And I pick up the poop out here every day so the neighbors don't complain."

"You're very conscientious."

"I try to be. Not everyone loves dogs." She studied him. "How do you feel about dogs?"

"I like them just fine. I had two Labs growing up."

She judged people harshly who didn't like animals, so she was relieved to hear that Linc wasn't one of those. "I love Labradors. I placed a beautiful chocolate Lab mix with the best family about six months back. They have two kids under ten who adore him. And he's just so happy now. They send me pictures all the time."

"Sounds like it was a good fit."

"It was."

Lilith came over and sniffed at Linc's tennis shoe, raised her head, gave him a growl, and sauntered away.

"That's Lilith. She's queen of the pack and she doesn't warm up to people easily. Especially men. I think some dude might have been mean to her before."

"She's so tiny. How could someone be mean to her?"

"Nothing surprises me about humans and how or why some of them mistreat their fur babies."

"Is that why you became a foster?"

"Yes. Someone has to love and care for them and make sure they end up with the right people."

He looked at her for the longest time, as if he was judging her. Or maybe that was her imagination. All she knew was that he had a beautiful face, and it had been a long time since a man had looked at her like . . . that. She eventually looked across the yard to see what the dogs were doing, except it was dark and she really couldn't see. Besides, if they were in trouble, there'd be yelping or growling, and she heard nothing.

"So, about your salary," he finally said.

"Oh, right." She'd thrown that out there, figuring he'd say no and she'd eventually capitulate, because just having a roof over her head and food to eat was enough for now. But if she was actually going to get paid? While not having to buy food or pay rent? She could start saving some money and eventually get back on her feet again. The knot in her stomach lessened for the first time in months.

This wasn't exactly the solution to her problems, but it was a start.

Linc leaned back and crossed his arms. "Let's start negotiating terms."

For the first time in . . . hell, further back than she could remember, Hazel felt the stirrings of something she'd long ago lost.

Empowerment.

CHAPTER THREE

*I*t had taken a full week for Linc to get organized, to get the layout and design in his head, and to have blueprints created for the new project. Then he'd had to order and buy all the supplies he was going to need.

That was all the drudge work. Now he was ready to dig in and get started.

True to her word, Hazel and the dogs had mostly stayed out of his way, though he'd assured her that she didn't have to leave a room whenever he was in one. The only thing she'd asked for were his food likes and dislikes. He had told her he didn't have any dislikes, and she'd smiled at that.

And, oh, man, did she have an incredible smile. It lit up her whole face and made her blue eyes shine like sapphires. It made him want to know a lot more about this mysterious woman who he was now kind of sort of living with. Though technically she was now living in the guesthouse and he was in the main house, which she'd insisted on so she could stay out of the way of his renovations, even though he'd insisted the only work he'd be doing on the extra bedrooms upstairs was paint. But maybe she wanted the distance, and he couldn't blame her for that. He was just some stranger, and a man at that, and many women would be uncomfortable sharing a house with some guy they didn't know at all.

He'd rented some basic furniture, because he sure as hell wasn't sleeping on the floor, and neither should she. She'd balked at first, and explained that her air mattress was perfectly fine.

He'd taken a look at the air mattress. It was thin and tiny and didn't look fine or comfortable. So when he'd placed his order with the furniture rental place, he'd ordered her a queen-size bed with a comfortable mattress, which would fit just fine in the bedroom in the guesthouse. Then he'd ordered some decent linens for the bed and some nice towels for her bathroom. When they were delivered she got out her phone, made some notes, then thanked him.

Why he was doing all that for her, he didn't know, especially since his initial reaction that first night was to throw her out on the street. Maybe it was the sadness and look of defeat on her face. And the fact he sure as hell could afford to give someone a break, and Hazel needed one.

Turned out, he'd been the lucky one, because he was eating great food now. So why not at least get her a decent bed and some good linens?

He'd also gotten a big-screen TV and put it in his bedroom. A guy needed his comforts during downtime.

He'd also checked out the cooking situation in the guesthouse. It wasn't ideal, but Hazel didn't seem to mind it. He liked the guesthouse for two reasons—one, it didn't need renovations, which was a plus. Two, it had its own bedroom and a kitchen, which did have a stove and a fridge. And they had the grill out on the patio, so he supposed it would do for Hazel, cooking-wise. He'd also asked her to make a list of cooking supplies she'd need. At first she balked, saying the cast-iron skillet and saucepan would be fine, since that's what she carried around with her. But he'd insisted, so she made a list, and he ordered everything on it plus a few extra items. Her eyes had widened when it had all showed up. She made some notes on her phone as she looked over the inventory.

"This is too much," she'd said, but he saw the delight in her eyes, and for some weird reason that had made him happy. And, hey, she was making him food, so that had made him happy.

She had started fixing meals the first day. Coffee and juice and a spinach and ham omelet for breakfast, followed by an amazing turkey, apple, and cheddar sandwich along with a salad for lunch, and then Southwest grilled chicken for dinner along with the most incredible green beans he'd ever tasted. Food would just appear while he was working, and she'd silently disappear.

During the day he'd see her occasionally, out at the pool with the dogs. He was slowly learning their names, though they were still a little leery of him so they mostly kept their distance. All of them, including Hazel. She was good at being invisible, even with her entourage of canines.

Today she'd brought him a grilled cheese sandwich for lunch that tasted nothing like any grilled cheese he'd ever had. It certainly wasn't plain cheese. And there was a pickle and some fruit salad, along with iced tea. He had just started to tape off the kitchen from the rest of the house, because once he started demo there'd be a lot of dust.

Now it was time to wreck the kitchen—always his favorite part.

The kitchen was a decent size, it just had older cabinets that had seen better days, countertops and a backsplash that needed upgrading, and the most hideous tile Linc had ever seen. He couldn't wait to make it all go away.

He hefted his sledgehammer and got to work.

*H*azel winced as the sounds of battering rams continued from the main house. That was some serious noise, and it had been going on for the past few hours. She hoped Linc had apologized in advance to the neighbors.

At least it was a corner lot, so maybe fewer people would be annoyed.

She had thought about going outside to take the dogs to the pool, but on second thought decided to wait until the sounds of a war zone ended.

If it ended. For all she knew, Linc might decide to do this into the night. She might have to dig into her backpack for her earplugs.

Instead, she got out her menu list for the day and started prepping dinner. If Linc was going to work late, he'd be hungry. And it was her job to see that he was fed.

While she was prepping ingredients, her phone buzzed. She glanced over, wrinkled her nose, and went back to working. Until her phone buzzed again. And then again. She washed and dried her hands and made the call.

"That took a while. Where are you?"

She rolled her eyes at the judgmental voice of her sister, Natalie. "I was preparing dinner for a . . . client."

"Oh, new job?"

"Sort of. What's up?"

"I haven't heard from you in two weeks. I hate when you disappear like that."

"I didn't disappear, Nat. You text me every day. I answer."

"It's not the same when we don't talk. I can tell from the tone of your voice something's wrong. And with you, something's always wrong."

Count to ten, Hazel. One . . . two . . . three . . . four . . .

"Nothing's wrong. Things are actually going well. I've got a job, a place to stay, good food to eat. It's all great."

"Hmm."

Hazel's big sister was notorious for her profound lack of belief in her. When she had gotten engaged to Andrew, neither her mother nor her sister approved of him and both warned her that he was going to break her heart.

Okay, so they'd been right about that part.

"Seriously, Nat. Everything's great. But I've gotta go so I can get this dinner out on time."

"But where—"

"We'll talk soon, okay? Love you, bye."

She clicked off before her sister kept her on the phone for an hour grilling her about . . . well, everything.

When her phone rang ten minutes later and she saw it was her mom, she ignored it, knowing that as soon as Nat had gotten off the phone with her, she'd called their mother to gossip about her. So instead, she put the stuff in the fridge and decided she'd risk the noise and took the dogs outside.

Fortunately, the uproar had ceased, at least for the time being, so she could relax and take Gordon for his swim, and the dogs could enjoy some outside time. After she removed Gordon from the pool, she climbed onto one of the rafts and just . . . floated. The sunshine and the pool felt amazing, and that tight coil of tension in her shoulders dissolved.

Until a giant tsunami of a wave washed over her, upending her into the water. She came up and dragged her hair out of her eyes to see Linc's grinning face in front of her.

"What the hell was that?" she asked.

"Cannonball, obviously. This water feels amazing." He pushed off and then he was under the water. Where he had gone, she had no idea, but he was under there for a while. Even Penelope got curious, peering over the side of the pool. Penelope was always concerned when people were in the water. Not that she'd rescue anyone, of course. But she was good at being concerned.

When he came up, shaking his head, Penelope took several cautious steps back and barked.

"Aww, I'm sorry, baby," he said, pulling himself out of the water. "Did I scare you?"

Penelope came over, sniffed him, then parked herself next to him and licked his arm.

He obviously had passed the Penelope test. Then again she'd always been the first one to make friends with strangers.

Okay, wow. She hadn't paid much attention to Linc over the

past week because he'd been in jeans and a T-shirt and she'd just been grateful to still have a roof over her head, so she'd kept her focus on feeding him and staying scarce so he wouldn't change his mind about her being at the house. But now? He wore board shorts and no shirt and there was tan and muscle and wet skin.

Linc was hot. She did not want to think about Linc being hot. She had a lot of questions about said hotness and tanness.

But she shouldn't engage with him.

"You're very—tan. Do you spend a lot of time outside?" she asked, immediately regretting opening her mouth.

Now he's going to know you were ogling his body. Good move, Hazel.

"I took some time off from my last project and did some fishing. Gotta unwind a little, you know?"

She would not know anything about unwinding. "Sure."

"And you obviously like the pool," he said.

"I do, but mostly because Gordon has arthritis and it's excellent therapy for him."

"I noticed you also bring a stroller for him when you take the dogs for a walk. That's very considerate of you."

She wasn't used to being complimented. "You notice a lot."

"Is that bad?"

"I guess not. I just assumed you were too busy wrecking the inside of the house to notice what I was doing."

"I see plenty. By the way, thanks for all the amazing food."

Her lips curved. "You've thanked me for every meal. It's what you're paying me for." Which she definitely appreciated. They'd negotiated what she thought to be an extremely generous salary, considering she was also getting to stay for free at the house and he was also paying for the food. Which meant she could bank the salary he was paying her. It would go a long way toward giving her money to put a deposit down on a rental whenever he was finished here and ready to put the house on the market.

"How long is this project supposed to last?"

He shrugged. "Six weeks to two months, give or take. And that's only if nothing major comes up or we don't have delays getting materials."

"Are there often delays?"

He laughed. "All the time. But I like to be hopeful."

Okay. She'd put some numbers together and figure out if the salary he was paying her would be enough for a down payment on a rental. If not, she could pick up some shifts at one of the restaurants she'd worked at before.

"How's that going, by the way?" she asked.

"The demo? Good. I've got the kitchen taken down and everything cleared away. You know you can come check it out if you'd like."

She had been curious, especially considering all the noise, but she'd tried not to bother him. "I would like to see it."

He hopped up and held his hand out for her. "Let's go."

"I'm all wet."

He laughed. "There's nothing in there right now, so you can't hurt anything. Though you might want to put some shoes on. I vacuumed the floors after I cleared the debris, but I'd hate for you to step on a nail or a piece of wood I might have missed."

She grabbed a towel and dried herself off, then slipped her

cover-up on over her suit, slid into her sandals, and followed him. She held her hand palm up when the dogs started to follow, so they all immediately stayed put, though none of them seemed happy about it.

She didn't blame them. After having free run of a big house, being cramped up in a one-bedroom guesthouse wasn't exactly roomy for either her or the dogs. But she was still so grateful to have a place to stay, she wasn't complaining.

She stepped inside, shocked at how different it all looked. The kitchen had been completely removed down to the floors, and all that was left now were walls. Actually, there was a wall missing, too. One that had separated the kitchen from the living area.

"Wow. You've done a lot. This couldn't have been easy doing it all yourself."

"It wasn't too bad. Plus some of the members of one of the local churches came by and picked up the appliances since they were still in working order, so all that was left was taking down the cabinets and counters, and pulling up the floors. Now that that's done, I can start rebuilding."

He made it sound easy when she imagined it was anything but.

"And you have it all planned out."

He nodded. "Yeah."

"Will the layout be the same?"

"No. I'm changing things up. Now that the wall is down between the kitchen and living room, I can expand the space."

"Really. That's a great idea. Are you putting in an island?"

"Of course."

"That'll be so much better than the peninsula that was here

before. What will you put on the island? A cooktop? Sink? Or will it be bare? And if so, where will everything else go?"

He grinned. "Would you like to see the blueprints?"

"I'd love to."

He grabbed a rolled-up stack. "Come on. We'll spread them out on the table on the patio."

She followed him outside where all the dogs surrounded them, sniffing them as if they'd just arrived from some secret location they'd never been, even though they'd just come from inside the house where the dogs had been so many times before. But dogs had to be sure.

Linc spread the blueprints out and leaned over the table, his triceps bulging as he did. Not that she noticed those kinds of things. Except how could she not? Instead, she studied the blueprints, checking out the layout for the new kitchen.

"Lots of counter space, which is so helpful. The island is huge, and I like that you're not putting a stove top or sink there, which will give someone a lot of room for meal prep and serving." Her eyes widened. "Double ovens? Be still my heart."

"I'm adding a good-sized pantry over here, too," he said, moving closer to her so he could point it out.

"Great idea. There was a definite lack of storage in the former kitchen, though you've added more cabinetry, too, including in the island. There can never be enough drawers and cabinets in my opinion. And with an extended island, the parties here will be killer."

"I can do that now that the wall is gone. The living room was already oversize anyway, so taking some space from there and adding it to the kitchen is no big deal."

She nodded. "And you already have a dining area over there, so you'll have this amazing open concept for entertaining. I like it."

"Thanks. Since you like to cook, anything you'd change, layout-wise?"

She gazed at the blueprints, imagining herself prepping food and cooking in this new and improved kitchen.

"You could add a spice cabinet, maybe . . . here." She pointed to the drawers under where the cooktop would be. "If you take a little space there and put in a pull-out spice cabinet, the new owners will love you."

"Show me what that would look like."

She went and grabbed her phone, typed in the search, and showed him her dream spice cabinet. She handed the phone to him. "It doesn't take up a lot of space, but it holds so many spices. Being right there by the stove, it saves so much time rather than fumbling through larger cabinets searching for spices. And instead of two cabinets here under the stove top, I'd suggest two deep pot drawers."

"I like these suggestions. I'll make the changes." He tilted his head and smiled at her. "Thanks."

Her heart did a little leap at the way he looked at her. "Hey, no problem. I have all kinds of ideas and would be happy to spend your money. All you have to do is ask."

He laughed. "Good to know."

She stood. "I should start dinner. I thought tonight we'd have pan-seared sea bass, along with colorful carrots and rice."

"Sounds amazing."

She started to walk away, then realized that Penelope was still hanging out next to Linc.

Huh. That was unusual.

"Come on, Penelope. Time to go."

The dog reluctantly followed, but she caught the knowing smile on Linc's face.

When they got inside the guesthouse, she closed the door. She leaned over and brushed her hand over Penelope's head. "You like him, don't you?"

Her only answer was that beautiful golden retriever smile.

Her dogs had always been a good judge of character. They had always helped her find the best homes for them. Dogs had an inner sense about who were good people and who weren't, and Penelope was one of the best at it.

It was heartening to know that Linc was one of the good ones.

CHAPTER FOUR

*L*inc had spent two days pulling up the flooring, which had been a giant pain in his ass. But now that project was done, and he could move forward.

If only he could find his hammer, which had suddenly gone missing. He looked through his tool bag but didn't find it there, and thought maybe he had left it outside. He was mostly storing his tools in the garage, but the only table he had was on the patio, and since he occasionally checked the blueprints there, maybe that's where he'd laid the hammer.

Certain that's where it was, he stepped out back to look. Huh. Not there. He scanned the yard and saw the dogs out there, hiding out in the shade under the trees.

He squinted to see Penelope happily chewing on . . . something. He didn't see Hazel out there anywhere, but the dogs were used to him wandering near them, and Penny—as he'd taken to calling her—was the friendliest, so he approached her. She was tucked beneath one of the palm trees.

"Hey, Penny," he said as he got closer. "Whatcha got there?"

It didn't take long for him to figure out she was gnawing on his hammer.

He got down on his hands and knees and crawled toward her, which then made Lilith come to investigate. He heard her warning growl—not the first time the Chihuahua had let him know she wasn't happy about his presence. Since she only weighed about six pounds, it wasn't like she was a threat, but he still liked to praise her.

"I hear you, Lilith. I promise not to hurt Penny." He came closer, and Penny seemed nonplussed about him being there, now more interested in him paying attention to her than she was the hammer. So he took the hammer, then sat next to Penny and rubbed his hand over her head and ears.

"Penny. Hammers aren't good for you. Got that?"

Penny just looked up at him with adoring eyes.

"What's going on?"

Hazel had come out and now leaned over with a concerned expression on her face.

"Penny borrowed my hammer for a little chew time."

"Oh." Hazel pulled up a spot on the grass. "I might have failed to mention that she has a tendency to steal things."

Linc looked down at Penny. "A bit of a klepto, are you?"

"She doesn't mean any harm. She just likes to collect items and hide them."

"Hey, it's no big deal. Other than I need my hammer."

Just then Gordon the pug came over and crawled into his lap, made himself comfortable, and went to sleep. Linc felt a rush of warmth and emotion that he wasn't expecting. He'd grown up with dogs but hadn't had one since he'd left home for college. He put his hand over Gordon's back and just let the peace of it wash over him.

"Gordon never lets any opportunity for a cuddle nap pass him by. Laps are his favorite thing. You've been warned."

Hazel's lips curved into a wry smile. Maybe part apology, part "you've been suckered, pal—deal with it." Either way, he'd been due for a break, and it wasn't too bad sitting under the shade of the enormous palm tree surrounded by dogs and a beautiful woman.

"You're good at getting to know their personalities," he said.

Hazel looked over the pack, who had surrounded them both. Gordon was in his lap, Penny next to him. Lilith had crawled onto Hazel's lap while Freddie the dachshund and Boo the pittie flanked her. "They make it easy since they're all so different. And they crave attention since they didn't come from ideal situations. Once you start giving them some love and affection, they'll show you who they are—quirks and all."

"And what are their quirks? I might as well know since I'm going to be around them."

"Okay. You've already discovered Penelope's thievery issues and the fact that if you sit at Gordon's level, he's going to use you as a nap bed. Boo likes to cuddle in bed with me every night with his favorite toy, despite my best efforts to crate train him. He has some separation anxiety issues. We're still working through that, but he was abandoned in an alley by his humans, so he has a fear of being alone."

"What assholes do that?"

"The assholiest of assholes, that's who." She smoothed her

hand over the stormy gray dog with the smooth coat, who had the friendliest and cutest smile Linc had ever seen.

"Okay, and what about Freddie?"

She turned her focus to the dachshund. "He's a chewer. He's especially fond of wood products. Guard your lumber."

"I'll keep that in mind. What about the leader of the pack?" He motioned to Lilith, who was staring at him as if she'd attack at any moment.

"Loud noises. Fears them terribly."

"No wonder she hates me."

She smiled. "She doesn't hate you. She's just slow to warm up to people, especially men."

"Wow. She's so tiny. How could someone hurt her?"

"People can be cruel, Linc. And it's not just men, either. Some people think animals don't have feelings or emotions, that they can't be hurt, that they're only for entertainment. I don't know. I can't begin to presume what goes on in the minds of people who don't love these beautiful creatures, who don't take care of them."

He could tell that it hurt her to talk about the abuses her babies had suffered. "I'm glad they have someone like you to look after them."

She glanced down at Lilith, then back up at him. "Thanks. I do what I can. I wish I could do more."

"You can only do what you can do. And that's more than a lot of people do."

He saw the blush stain her cheeks and wondered if she was unused to compliments. Someone who looked like her should be accustomed to being showered with them.

Obviously, someone had hurt her, too.

People really could be assholes. There was a sweetness and a vulnerability to Hazel that was unlike any woman he'd ever met before. It made him want to know everything about her.

But, he wasn't in the market for another girlfriend. That was just asking for trouble after what he'd been through. So he'd just be distant and friendly enough and treat her like an employee.

He gently placed Gordon on the grass, then stood and brushed off his jeans. "Okay, I should get back to work."

"Me, too."

He held out his hand for her, and when she slipped her hand in his, he hauled her upright. He felt a zap of something electric when they touched. From the look in her eyes, she had felt it, too.

He ignored it, pulling his hand from hers.

"Thanks," she said. "I'll see you for dinner, then."

"Sure." He turned and walked away, realizing he was already looking forward to it.

For the food, of course; not because he'd get to spend time with Hazel again.

CHAPTER FIVE

Well, sonofabitch."

Hazel grimaced, hating having been the bearer of bad news.

"I had noticed the guesthouse getting warmer throughout the afternoon, and I hadn't been baking at all so I knew it wasn't that."

She tried not to peer over Linc's shoulder as he checked out all the components of the guesthouse's air-conditioning system. Not that she knew anything at all about air-conditioning units, but she could tell from the irritated look on his face as he made his way from the electrical box to the main unit that he wasn't happy.

"Electrical is fine, but you're right that it's not cooling. Thermostat is climbing in here. You should grab your stuff and move over to the main house where it's cooler."

"Oh, we'll be fine in here."

"It's eighty-six outside with ninety-five percent humidity, Hazel. You're not fine in here. We'll move you to one of the guest rooms in the house until I can get this fixed."

She nibbled on her lower lip, hating to be a burden. "Okay. I can set up my air mattress—"

"Absolutely not. I'll move your bed."

She shook her head. "No. That's way too heavy, plus the mattress and all."

"The bed comes apart. And, fine. You can help me move the mattress if it'll make you feel better."

Not entirely better, but it was at least something she could do to help. "Okay. Thank you."

She had roughed it in hot weather before. She actually enjoyed camping and didn't mind sweating a little. But it was hot and humid, and being inside the guesthouse with temperatures climbing was going to be pretty uncomfortable. She figured she and the dogs would just sleep outside tonight by the pool. The pool area was covered, so she wouldn't have to worry about bugs, and there were nice, comfy lounges.

But if Linc insisted she and the dogs move inside to one of the bedrooms, who was she to argue?

She packed up their things, which included the dogs' beds and crates and all her stuff—which wasn't much—and carted it over to the main house. Except he hadn't told her which room to occupy. There were four bedrooms in the house including the master, and she figured he'd taken that room, so she chose one of the bedrooms down the hall that had an attached bathroom.

She'd left the dogs out back so she could start bringing linens and bed things into the house. She'd brought up the towels and blankets and sheets and had straightened everything up in the bathroom and was about to go check on the dogs when Linc appeared in the bedroom carrying part of the bed frame, those impressive muscles of his bulging with the effort and sweat pouring down the sides of his face.

Never once had she found a sweaty guy attractive—until now. She followed him outside and into the guesthouse and helped him carry the rest of the bed frame into the main house. Then they went back for the mattress. Penelope decided to follow them this time, and Lilith came, too. The rest of the dogs were in late-afternoon snooze mode and couldn't be bothered.

"It's okay," he said as he started to put the frame together. "You don't need to stay for this."

She gave him a look that told him she was anything but useless. He shrugged and they put the bed together, then laid the mattress on top. She grabbed the sheets and blanket, figuring he'd go back to work, but instead, he stayed and helped her make the bed, something that felt decidedly intimate, especially when he ran his hand over the flat sheet to smooth out any wrinkles. It made her shiver, imagining his hand sliding over her body like that. What would it feel like to have him touch her? Would his hand be calloused when he rubbed his palm across her nipple?

"Is that good?"

She looked up. "Is what good?"

"The bed."

She realized she'd been all in her fantasies and hadn't noticed they'd put the blanket on. "Oh, right. Yes, it's fine. Perfect, in fact."

"Uh-huh. I'm going to go do something about that AC."

"Yes, you do that. I'll rearrange dinner plans and prepare something on the grill."

Mentally rolling her eyes at herself, she followed him down the stairs, Penelope and Lilith on her heels. He headed toward the back of the guesthouse, while she went into the guesthouse and grabbed her notebook and pen, then opened the fridge, took a few seconds to glance at the contents, and headed outside.

She slid her bare legs into the shaded part of the pool and started to redo tonight's menu, hoping for some focus now that she wasn't in the same vicinity as Linc.

What had that been all about? That weird fantasy about Linc putting his hands on her? Because she so did not have any desire for him in the least.

Except she so did, and lying to herself about it wasn't going to make it go away. She already knew nothing was going to happen between them, so what was the harm in indulging in a little fantasy foreplay?

She paused as she made her menu, realizing again how ridiculous she was. She wasn't the only one making decisions here, and as far as she knew, Linc wasn't the least bit interested in her. So her fantasy about being stretched out on the bed and fondled by Linc was going to remain just that—a fantasy.

He was here to work on the house, not play with her. And that's how things were going to stay.

Besides, technically, she was his employee, and the two of them sleeping with each other would be a terrible idea. What if he immediately regretted it and fired her? Then she'd end up out on the streets, and she needed to focus on the pups and their welfare. Right now she had a great thing going on, and she needed to remember that.

Despite this being all in her head, it was important to keep it that way, and extinguish the fantasies while she was at it.

The paycheck was way more important to her future.

CHAPTER SIX

*L*inc was engrossed in plumbing fixtures when he heard the tapping on the concrete. Figuring it might be one of the dogs coming downstairs, he ignored it. Until he caught sight of Freddie grabbing hold of his ruler and taking off toward the steps.

"Dammit, Freddie." He straightened and headed up the stairs. He peeked in the open door to Hazel's room. She was sitting cross-legged on the floor, typing on her laptop.

"Hey," he said. "Sorry to bother you, but did Freddie run in here with my ruler?"

Her head snapped up. "Oh, I'm so sorry. I was engrossed in something and I didn't see him. Let me take a peek under the bed."

She laid the laptop down and then got on all fours, which positioned her very fine ass right at him. He tried not to look, but how could he help it?

She rested back on her heels to look up at him. "No, he's not under here."

"Huh. Okay."

Today she was dressed in cotton shorts and a tank top, and he

44

couldn't help but notice her long, tan legs and smooth shoulders. Her hair was wound up on top of her head, wispy little tendrils escaping that bun.

Why was she so damned beautiful? He didn't need that kind of distraction. He was trying very hard not to think of her as a desirable woman. Kind of difficult when her very amazing ass was right there. He decided to look out the window instead, waiting for her to get up, which, fortunately, she did. Because his attraction to her was his problem, not hers.

"Let me help you look for him. Freddie? Come here, Freddie." She left the room, so he followed.

"He usually comes right when I call him," she explained as they made their way down the hall. "Unless he's harboring a treasure—like your ruler—then he hides. Sorry about that."

Linc rolled his eyes and wandered into the two empty bedrooms. Closet doors were closed, so no dog hiding in there.

Which left his room. The dachshund had short little legs, so he knew he wouldn't find him on top of the bed. He bent down to check under the bed. And there was Freddie, happily chewing on his ruler.

"Dude. Seriously?"

Hazel joined him. "Oh, Freddie. This is not okay."

Hazel wriggled under the bed frame and gently grasped the dog, pulling him out and onto her lap. She extricated the now-mangled ruler and handed it to Linc, an apologetic look on her face. "I'll replace it."

"No need. I have others." He shook the ruler at Freddie. "Not a toy, Freddie."

Freddie barked happily at him, his tongue wagging in anticipation of Linc handing the ruler back to him.

"Ha. Not a chance, buddy. This thing is trash." He stood, then held his hand out for Hazel, who grasped it. He hauled her up.

"I'm really sorry," she said. "I thought all the dogs were in the room with me. I guess I lost track. Freddie's the sneaky one."

"It's fine. I'm going back to work now." He pivoted and went back downstairs, tossed the ruler in the trash can, then fished in his tool bag until he found another one. This time he intended to keep a close eye on it.

As he worked, he wondered if Freddie just needed a chew toy. He noticed some old toys spread around the house, but very few. When he took a water break outside he walked around the yard to do an inventory.

Yeah, not much, really. He was sure that Hazel didn't have a lot of excess funds for toys and chew things for the dogs. The care and feeding of them likely cost her enough.

He pulled out his phone and went to a pet toy site, searching for things that dogs could chew on and play with, adding them to the cart. Might as well add some treats, too. Who didn't like snacks? He sure did. He wondered what dog food she fed them. He went into the guesthouse to check, added a few bags and cans of that, then paused.

Why did he fucking care? These dogs weren't his responsibility. He started to cancel the whole thing, but then Lilith wandered in and sat, staring up at him.

"What's up, feisty?" he asked.

The tiny dog always had a judgmental look, as if she knew what was going on in his head. Which was just ridiculous. He crouched down and reached his hand out. Lilith inched over to give him a sniff, then shoved her head under his hand for a pet.

Okay, that was new. Typically, she avoided him. With a sigh, he rubbed his hand over her head and back, which she seemed to appreciate. Until one of the dogs barked outside. Lilith shot out the door like a rocket.

Shaking his head, he paid for express shipping and finished the order for the toys and food, then slipped his phone back in his pocket.

Hazel came outside, her entourage of dogs following. The dogs dispersed into the yard, and Hazel sat in the chair next to him on the porch. "There's a breeze. And it's cloudy. Have you looked at the weather forecast?"

He frowned. "No, I haven't. What's up?"

"Big storm blowing in. Supposed to hit sometime later afternoon or tonight."

"Great. Just great. I have someone coming to fix the AC in the guesthouse this afternoon. Hopefully, he can get that done before it starts to rain."

"I hope so. Then I can get out of the house and out of your way."

He was scrolling through his phone, searching for the weather app. "You're not in my way. It's not like you're sleeping in my bed or anything."

Realizing what he said, he looked over at her and found her staring at him, an unfathomable expression on her face.

"Uh, what I meant was . . . I was trying to say that . . . I didn't mean . . ."

Then she let out a big laugh, which released the tight knot that had formed in Linc's gut.

"It's nice to know I'm not the only one who shoves her foot in her mouth on occasion."

He was so relieved she hadn't been horrified by what he'd said. "Yeah, I mean, I don't know what I was saying, but it sure wasn't what I meant. You're welcome in my bed anytime."

His eyes widened. "Fuck. I'm going back to work before anything else stupid falls out of my mouth."

Her laughter rang in his ears all the way back to the house.

*H*azel had been in a really good mood all day, though she had no idea why. Okay, she knew why.

Because Linc had thrown bedroom suggestions at her, and even though he'd immediately corrected his wayward thoughts and fumbled over his words, the idea had to have been there in the first place, right?

Or maybe the bedroom idea is only in your head, Hazel.

She shrugged. Maybe that was true. But it had been a stroke, and she'd been beaten down emotionally since her divorce, so she could use all the strokes she could get. A fine-looking man like Linc making suggestive remarks like that? She would definitely not take offense.

The air conditioner repairman had showed up early, which had made Linc happy. Though when the guy had left about forty-five minutes later and Linc made his way back to the house with a stormy expression on his face, that couldn't be good.

"Is it fixed?" she asked as she followed him inside.

"Not even close. The amount of repairs it needs far outweighs its value. I'll have to replace it."

"Oh no. I'm so sorry."

"Not your fault. Just an expense I hadn't budgeted for. He's going to bring a new unit out and install it by the end of the week. And then the guesthouse will be back in business for cooking."

"Excellent. And the dogs and I will move back in there."

"The hell you will. I'm not moving that damned bed frame and mattress again. You and the dogs can stay upstairs."

That seemed rather definite. And he had enough to worry about, so she wouldn't inconvenience him. "Okay."

But she would be thrilled to be able to cook in the guesthouse again without the oppressive heat.

She took the dogs on a long walk, figuring if a storm hit later she wouldn't be able to walk them tonight. The humidity today was unbearable, so Gordon didn't make it very long before he plopped down on some nice cool grass at the corner and decided he was ready for a nap. She scooped him up and put him in the stroller, and they continued on. The other dogs didn't seem to mind the heat, though Hazel was a big, sweaty mess by the time they'd done a mile, so they made their way back toward the house. They were only a few homes from getting there when Sarah Ventura, Ginger's incredibly intrusive neighbor, came outside.

"Oh, Hazel, how lovely to see you."

"Hi, Sarah. How are you?"

"I'm great. You know, I saw Ginger and Greg had moved out a while back. Did you buy their house?"

"Uh, no. Someone else did. A . . . a friend of mine. He's renovating the place, so I'm staying there with the dogs for a while longer."

"How convenient for you." Sarah smoothed her blond hair back with her hand, though it was unnecessary since not a strand was ever out of place. How she managed that in Orlando's humidity was a feat that Hazel could not fathom. "I've noticed him coming and going. He's quite good-looking."

"Yes." She wasn't about to offer additional information, because that would only invite commentary from Sarah, which would mean extra boiling time in the heat.

"And, would you two be dating?" Sarah asked.

"No, we're just friends."

"Still, I mean, he's so hot, Hazel, and unless he's moved a wife or girlfriend in with him, I'd say why not go for it, right?"

"I will definitely take that under advisement. You know, the dogs need some water, and wow, is it hot today or what? I have got to go. It was great to see you, Sarah. Talk later." She pushed the stroller, and the dogs started moving. Grateful to be away from Sarah, she found her second wind and made the stretch back to the house in a hurry. She took the harnesses off all the dogs and lifted Gordon out of the stroller. The dogs all made a mad dash for their water bowl in the backyard, and Hazel headed straight for the guesthouse to grab some ice water, choosing a spot in the shade to dip her legs in the pool.

She sipped her water despite wanting to gulp it down. The clouds had thickened, which had done nothing to lessen the humidity. She was going to enjoy her shower later, but for now, a dip in the pool sounded ideal. Since she'd tossed her swimsuit on under her shorts and tank today, all she had to do was slip them off, which she did, and then she slid right into the cool water of the pool, which refreshed her immediately.

It wasn't long before Boo joined her in the pool, with the rest of the dogs deciding a nap under the shady palm trees was their preferred option. Boo swam a couple of laps, then got out to join the other dogs for naptime, leaving Hazel alone to float by herself. She closed her eyes and let the water lap over her.

But then she heard a low roaring sound in her ears. Figuring the dogs were barking at one another, she ignored it and continued with her float, tuning out the world. Until a hand grasped her arm and hauled her completely out of the water.

Shocked, she opened her eyes and saw Linc's angry face.

"Didn't you hear me?"

"Of course I didn't. My ears were under the water." But now she heard sirens, and the dogs were whimpering and surrounding her. The skies had turned from ominous to black. Plus, holy crap, that was some thunder.

"There's a tornado warning. Let's go."

She grabbed her clothes and she didn't even need to call the dogs because they were right on her heels as they ran inside. She was dripping wet, so the cold air chilled her as they made their way into the downstairs bathroom, the only room in the house with no windows. She grabbed a towel and dried her body, threw her sweaty clothes back on—yuck—and then bent down to check on the dogs.

Gordon had curled up on her discarded towel and gone back to sleep—the benefit of being old and hard of hearing. Freddie and Penelope were wrestling, completely oblivious to the impending storm. Boo nervously paced the length of the small room. Lilith was shaking and had peed in the corner of the bathroom.

"Oops. Sorry. Come here, baby girl." She scooped Lilith up and then grabbed some tissues to lay over Lilith's accident spot.

"It's a tile floor," Linc said. "It'll be fine."

Hazel was surprised he wasn't upset. Instead, he had his phone out and was watching the local weather people give updates about the storm.

Having lived here her entire life, this wasn't her first time in a bad storm. She'd weathered tornadoes and hurricanes before, knowing that you had no control whatsoever. All you could do was wait it out.

The wind howled, then hail and rain pelted loudly against the windows in the other rooms. Thunder boomed and Lilith trembled in her arms. Hazel stroked her while whispering words of comfort.

And then the power went out, turning the entire room black.

"Fucking great," Linc mumbled.

Hazel found a spot on the tile floor and leaned against the tub. Penelope and Freddie came over and lay beside her. Boo finally settled and curled up next to Freddie. And Lilith had stopped shaking.

As far as she knew, Gordon was still asleep on the towel in the corner.

At least the dogs were calm. Hazel inhaled some deep breaths and let them out.

"Are you okay?"

She nodded in answer to Linc's question, then realized he couldn't see her. "I'm fine, thanks for asking."

"Do storms bother you?" he asked.

"Not at all. I love the rain. I'd rather not have severe weather, but it comes with living in Florida."

He was searching on his phone again, the light bathing his face with an eerie glow.

"It looks like the storm is moving northwest. Should be past us shortly."

They both listened as the weatherperson spoke about the tornado chances weakening. Hazel let out a sigh of relief.

The loud fierceness of the storm did seem to be lessening.

And then the lights came back on. Freddie barked at them, which made Hazel smile.

"It's all going to be okay," she said, reaching out to smooth her hand over all the dogs. Except Gordon, who was across the room, still sound asleep.

"I'm going to go check things out," Linc said. "You wait here."

She rolled her eyes. "Not a chance. I'm going with you."

"You aren't even wearing shoes."

"Because you plucked me out of the water like a fish and didn't let me put my shoes on."

He bent his head toward hers, flashing angry dark brown eyes at her. "You're not going out there."

He turned and walked out the door, closing it behind him.

What. The. Hell. As if he had any control over her. Who did he think he was, anyway? Her ex did that to her, thinking he could tell her what she could and couldn't do. Just remembering it made her blood boil.

Not again. Not ever again. Those days were over.

She pulled the door open and immediately checked the floor for broken glass, which she knew wasn't there because she'd been in more severe storms than this before. Shutting the dogs in the bathroom for their safety, she dashed up the stairs, slid into her tennis shoes, then headed outside.

It was still dark and cloudy, but the rain had let up some. As far as she could see, there was no major damage other than a few palm fronds that had shaken loose in the wind, and a lot of crap that had gotten into the pool since the gate had blown open. So, mostly easy fixes.

Linc came out of the guesthouse and glared at her.

"I see you ignored me."

"You're not the boss of me. Except as far as you paying me to cook for you. Otherwise, you can kiss my ass. I grew up here and know how to take care of myself in a storm."

He stared at her for a beat, then nodded. "Fair enough."

He walked back inside, and Hazel stayed where she was, trying to calm her rapidly beating heart. She couldn't believe she'd said those things to Linc. But she had and he hadn't fired her or yelled at her. And she'd stood up for herself because she'd been right.

She felt somewhat victorious, all things considered. If that had been an argument with her ex, there would have been yelling and finger-pointing and him calling her an unreasonable bitch and putting all the blame on her. And she'd have stood there bone silent until he'd finished with her and walked away, leaving her feeling small and defeated.

She'd always hated that. After the divorce, she'd told herself over and over again she'd never let another man do that to her.

Huh. Maybe all those self-talks and affirmations had worked. Maybe it had also helped to argue with a guy who wasn't a complete and utter asshole.

Either way, it felt good.

CHAPTER SEVEN

*L*inc had to spend the rest of the day inspecting the house for damage and cleaning up what the storm had left behind. Hazel helped, sweeping the back patio and picking up palm fronds and whatever else had made its way into the pool while he took care of the front. Some of the flowers and bushes had taken a beating, but he'd fix that with pruning and maybe replanting if necessary.

Of course the humidity after the storm hadn't lessened. In fact, it had gotten worse, so his T-shirt stuck to his chest, and every part of him was sweaty.

He climbed up onto the roof to check for damage but didn't see any, which was good. All in all, he'd dodged a bullet. Just some downed tree limbs and a bit of a mess, but otherwise, everything was still standing.

He made his way into the backyard so he could check things out and discovered Hazel standing at the grill.

"Something smells amazing," he said.

"I don't know about you, but I'm hungry, and I already had this meal prepped, so I hope you're ready to eat."

"Starving."

"Good. It's nearly ready."

"Then I'll go wash up and set the table."

"Okay."

He went inside, noticing that Penny followed him, something he was getting used to. After washing his hands upstairs in his bathroom, he took a look in the mirror. His face was dirt streaked and sweaty, and God, he really needed a shower. But that would have to wait, so he grabbed a washcloth and pulled off his sweat-soaked T-shirt, then scrubbed his face and neck and tried to wash off some of the sweat under his arms. He could at least apply deodorant so he wouldn't smell up the dinner table. He put on a clean T-shirt and, feeling at least marginally presentable, headed downstairs.

He went into the living room, where Hazel had a small table that she used to store the plates and utensils. He grabbed two plates along with knives, forks, and napkins and set them up. And just in time, since she came inside with the food and placed it on the table.

"Wow," he said, eyeing the feast before him.

"It's the best I can do since it's too steamy to cook in the guesthouse right now, but tonight we're having grilled salmon along with sugar snap peas with pine nuts, and lemon roasted potatoes."

"You did all this on the grill?"

"Well, yeah. I had to juggle the pots and pans around a little, but it worked. I just cooked the salmon last so it'd be nice and hot."

He held a chair out for her and she sat.

"This is incredible," he said as he dug into everything. "I still can't believe you made this on the grill."

"Thanks. I'm glad you like it."

He also noticed she'd made extra of everything, which made him happy because he was extra hungry.

He paused before taking the second slice of salmon. She smiled at him.

"I made that for you," she said. "You should definitely eat it."

She didn't have to tell him twice. "Good. I'm hungry."

"You burn a lot of calories with the amount of work you do. And this is a fairly low-calorie meal."

She never made cracks about the amount of food he ate, which also made him happy.

"My ex-girlfriend used to count the calories of the food I ate."

She made a little snorting sound. "Your ex-girlfriend and my ex-husband would make a good pair."

"He did the same thing?"

"All the time. He preferred me thin."

He gave her the once-over. "You look damned good to me."

A blush stained her cheeks, but she smiled. "And you look good to me. So I'd say we're eating just fine."

He lifted his glass of water toward her. "I'll drink to that."

She clinked her glass with his. "Honestly, I try to fix healthy food for myself. So I'll fix it for you as well. But indulging in a treat now and then isn't harmful."

"That's what I say. But Stefanie—that's my ex—she was a personal trainer. And was religious about eating, to the point where she'd scream at me if I ate a piece of chocolate, as if I were personally attacking her."

She stabbed a potato and slid it into her mouth, nodding as

she chewed. "A little chocolate never hurt anyone. My ex wouldn't let me eat carbs. He said they'd make my thighs huge and then he wouldn't want to fuck me."

"Your ex sounds like a grade A asshole."

"Yes, he was. It just took me longer than it should have to see the light."

He took a long swallow of water. "I think it's normal to want to believe we've made the right choice in a partner. And maybe we don't want to admit we were wrong."

"You're probably right. I was living in oblivion for way too long. Long enough for him to run off with all our money. Wasn't I clueless."

He shrugged. "I don't know. Maybe you just didn't want to see it."

"You're being very nice. It's okay to say I was a dumbass for not seeing what was right in front of me for so long."

He shrugged. "Sometimes the most valuable lessons learned are the most painful ones. I'd say you've had yours, and you'll never make the same mistake again."

"Thanks for saying that. My mother and my sister have always told me I'm too trusting. They warned me Andrew was all wrong for me, though they could never pinpoint why. But then after he jetted off for parts unknown with all the money, they said they knew it all along. Which they didn't. But that didn't stop them from saying, 'I told you so.'"

"Family." He shoved his plate to the side. "They always have an opinion, and it's usually wrong."

"Tell me about yours."

"My opinion?"

She laughed. "No, your family."

"Oh. My dad died five years ago. As I mentioned earlier, my mom is a high school history teacher. I have two brothers, Warren and Eugene, also named after historical figures."

"I'm sorry about your dad."

"Thanks. It was sudden, and a shock to all of us. But Mom is the epitome of strength and resilience. She's the glue that holds the family together."

"I'm sure it helps that she had you and your brothers to support her through it."

"We did our best, but she's strong enough not to need any of us."

"She sounds like an amazing woman."

"She is." He paused, then asked, "What about your family?"

"My dad died my second year in college. My mom remarried a few years later. My stepdad is a great guy. Mom is a loan officer. My older sister, Natalie, is married to a radiologist and they have two kids. Natalie used to be an interior designer, though not so much these days. Now she's into perfecting her family life and getting into my business as often as she can."

"Sorry about your dad. Something we have in common that really sucks."

"It does. I feel his absence all the time."

"Same. I mean, Mom is awesome and all, but not having a dad leaves that gap, ya know?"

She nodded. "I do. My dad was a calming presence, especially with my mom, who has a tendency to be a little scattered. And she's a lot like my sister, wanting to get into my personal life. Dad had always run interference on that, reminding them both to mind their own business. After he was gone they made it their personal mission to"—she held up her fingers to make air quotes—"take care of me."

Linc grimaced. "That couldn't have been fun."

"It wasn't. At the beginning it was okay because I was missing my dad and he was my comfort, so I felt surrounded by their love and concern. But then it never stopped."

"They still do it?"

"All the time. Granted, I haven't made the best decisions, so I understand why they feel like they have to constantly check up on me. But I am an adult and I'm trying to make my own way, even if sometimes it's the wrong way. I don't need them right on my heels telling me how I'm screwing up my life."

He reached across the table and grasped her hand. "You have a plan for your life, right?"

"Yes."

"Then you're doing fine. Don't let anyone tell you otherwise."

She wasn't used to someone pumping her up, or telling her she was doing well. Plus, his hand on hers? Some zingy electricity thing going on that made her feel all kinds of things.

"Thanks. I appreciate your confidence in me."

"Hey, I know how it feels to have people not believe in you."

"Oh? You have the same kind of family?"

"They thought it was crazy that I left my cushy investment broker job to flip houses. They thought I was gonna fail and go broke. When the fact of the matter is, I'm—"

He paused.

"You're what?"

He smiled. "I'm having the time of my life, and I'm not broke."

"That's great. And you should work at something you enjoy. Life's too short to be stuck in some stuffy office if you hated it. Are you having fun doing this?"

"I am. And I don't flip every house I buy. I invest in some, I have rental properties, and I do commercial investments as well."

She cocked her head to the side, studying him. She learned something new about him every day. "Aren't you just so busy."

"I like being busy. And keeping my body occupied as well as my mind."

"Then I'd say you're living the dream, Linc. We should all be so lucky."

He took a long swallow of his water. "Aren't you doing the same?"

"Not exactly yet. But I have plans to get there."

He studied her for a few seconds, then asked, "What's your dream, Hazel?"

"To run my own rescue organization. To be able to take in as many unwanted and abandoned animals as I possibly can and find homes for them. Which I know isn't going to make me a lot of money, but it'll make me happy."

He nodded. "Admirable. And expensive."

"Yes. It'll take me some time, but I'll get there. And I have other ideas for how to make money. But I have to start somewhere, and finding a place for me and the dogs to live is the first step. We'll get there."

"I like your confidence. You have to believe in yourself and in your dream to make it happen."

She stood and started gathering the dishes to take out to the guesthouse to wash. "Thanks. And I do."

Not once had Linc laughed at her or told her that her dream was impossible.

She liked him more and more every day. Maybe it was because they both came from families who didn't believe in their dreams. She'd watched the play of emotions on his face when he'd talked about his family. He'd treated it with a shrug, but she saw the hurt, knew what that felt like. They might be different in a lot of ways, but in this, they were very much alike.

And that hand-touching? They had some chemistry. Because when he'd touched her, she'd seen the reaction in his eyes, in the way his lips parted, in how he'd absently rubbed his thumb over the top of her hand.

That zingy thing between them? It might be fun to explore.

When she was ready.

And she wasn't ready just yet.

CHAPTER EIGHT

*L*inc was elbows deep in wiring when his phone buzzed. He pulled it out of his pocket, rolling his eyes when he saw Warren's name pop up. He clicked and pressed speaker, laying the phone on the floor while he worked.

"What's up, Warren?"

"Just checking to see if you've worked your way into bankruptcy yet."

"Funny. And, no. But I am busy."

"I don't know why you insist on putting in all that sweat and labor when you make enough money to hire people to do that. Hell, man, you're a multimillionaire. You don't even have to be there. You could be at the lake right now, on the boat."

He looked around to see if Hazel was within earshot of his brother's remark about his financial status. He didn't throw money around and didn't like people to know about his wealth. It often changed someone's perception of who he was, and frequently it wasn't changed in the right direction. He liked Hazel, and he didn't want her to think differently of him because he had money.

"I like working with my hands. Sitting at a desk all day is boring."

"You've always been like that. That's why you were always in trouble in school."

"Fuck off."

Warren laughed. "I see you're doing fine. I just called to remind you the anniversary is coming up."

Linc sighed. The anniversary of their father's death was never an easy one. And even though it had been five years, his parents had loved each other deeply.

"How's Mom doing?"

"That's why I'm calling. She usually gets quiet and morose this time of year, but actually, she seems fine. She mentioned something about going on a cruise with her friends during that time."

"Maybe it's good that she's moving forward," Linc said. "She's always wanted to go to the cemetery and then have all of us go out to eat and reminisce about Dad."

"I agree," Warren said. "I see this as a positive step."

"What does Eugene think?"

"Hell if I know. I can barely get him to answer his phone. He prefers to only text, and then it's in some bro-language I can barely understand, littered with bullshit emojis."

Linc snorted out a laugh. "That's cuz you're old. Bro."

"Kiss my ass. I'm due to argue a case in court in an hour and I've got to prep. Talk later. Love you."

"Love you, too."

Linc clicked off, then stared down at his phone and smiled, feeling oddly warm and happy. Ever since their dad had died, the three boys had grown closer, not only with their mother, but with one another. The "I love you" thing had never been hard to say, since Dad had always been freely affectionate, and both of his parents had smothered them with unconditional love for as long as Linc could remember, sprinkled in with the discipline that the three boys had rightly deserved.

And they always made sure the love they had for one another was spoken. It was important, because tomorrow wasn't guaranteed.

The back door opened and Hazel slid in, her clothes—all of her—totally drenched.

"Did you get really hot out there and decide you had to take a dip right now, fully clothed?"

She held up a finger, clearly irritated, then pointed outside where Penny stood at the door, her tail moving wildly. Without another word, she marched up the stairs.

Linc looked over at the door. He grabbed his bottle of water, then stepped outside and took a seat in one of the chairs on the patio. Penny came over and laid her head on his knee, so he gave her some love.

"You in trouble, girl?" he asked, smoothing his hand over her soft fur. "What did you do?"

Penny didn't divulge an answer, just put her paw on his leg to be sure he continued to pet her.

About ten minutes later the door slid open and Hazel stepped out, having changed into dry clothes, though her hair was still damp.

"Oh, sure, Penelope. Play all sweet and innocent. You know what you did."

Penny immediately ran over and parked her butt in front of Hazel, her tail wildly moving back and forth.

Linc leaned back in the chair. "What happened?"

"I was walking past the pool and Penny threw me in."

He arched a brow. "She threw you in."

"Well, obviously, she didn't throw me. More like barreled into me like a linebacker. Next thing I knew I was in the water, with my clothes on, and there was Penelope looking down at me all innocent. But it was totally deliberate."

Penny looked utterly clueless and totally happy. "I don't think she feels guilty."

Hazel sighed and reached down to pat the dog on the head. "Of course she doesn't."

"Hey, you had a dip. That had to be refreshing."

She slanted a look at him. "Sure. Nothing like tumbling headfirst into the pool with all your clothes on when you're not expecting it. You should try it sometime."

"I'll pass. It'd take a week for these work boots to dry out."

"Then I'd advise you to keep your eye on Penelope. She can be very enthusiastic when she's in the mood to play."

"Oh, you want to play, Penny? Do you?" He had a minute to spare, so he got up and threw the ball around the yard. Boo and Freddie got involved, too, and Lilith barked at them like a coach, letting them know they were doing it wrong. Gordon was content to monitor the activities from his favorite spot under the palm tree.

After about fifteen minutes, Linc had worked up a sweat and the dogs' tongues were hanging out, so he gave it up and headed over to grab his drink. The dogs did the same, going over to lap up water from their bowl.

The doorbell rang.

"I'll grab that," Hazel said. "You take a break from your . . . play."

He laughed. "Okay."

She was gone for a bit, and he wondered who had been at the door, so he went inside. Hazel was in the living room pushing boxes from the entryway into the room.

"You got quite the delivery," she said.

He looked at the return address on the boxes. "Oh, those are actually for you."

She frowned. "For me?"

"Yeah. You can open them." He pulled the knife out of his pocket and sliced them open.

She kneeled and opened the first box, her eyes widening when she saw all the dog toys, then looked up at him.

"Keep going."

The second and third boxes contained dog food.

"I don't understand. Why would you do this?"

He shrugged. "Their current toys are crap, and I'm sure food is expensive. Thought I'd help out."

She shifted, sitting on the floor. "This is a lot, Linc. I wish you hadn't . . . You didn't have to . . . I don't know . . . Wow." She dragged her fingers through her still-damp hair, then looked up at him. "I don't know what to say other than thank you." And then she got out her phone and made notes.

He kept wondering what kinds of notes she made.

"You're welcome." He'd seen the tears sparkle in her eyes. "Anyway, I should get back to work. Hope the dogs like their toys."

"Wait." She walked over, threw her arms around him, and hugged him tightly.

Since he didn't want to seem as if her hug wasn't reciprocated, he wound his arms around her. They stood there like that for a full minute or so, and he had to admit he didn't mind having his arms around Hazel. Her body felt good, the kind of body he'd like to explore further, except he knew this was a "thank you" hug, not a "hey, grope me" kind of hug.

She pulled back. "Thank you. This means a lot to me. And to the pups."

His throat was thick with emotion, so all he could do was nod. She finally walked away, so he blew out a breath as he made his way back into the kitchen, realizing if he wasn't careful, Hazel—and her dogs—could worm their way into his heart.

And that just couldn't happen.

*H*azel unwrapped half the toys that were in the box—because good heavens, Linc had purchased so many—and put the rest at the top of her closet for later. She took the new toys outside, and it was suddenly like Christmas for the pups. Boo immediately claimed the stuffed bunny as his own, while Penelope and Freddie ran off to opposite shady corners of the yard to chomp down on their new bones. Lilith was currently killing a squeaky toy with utter glee. Gordon found a soft toy and marched over to the door for Hazel to let him in. She figured he'd had enough of the humidity and would lie by the door on his new toy. But then she saw him make his way to the stairs and stand there. Linc must have seen him as well because he walked over, scooped up him and his toy, and carried them upstairs.

Her heart swelled with gooey emotion. She shook it off, because there was no way she was going to become attached to Linc. He was too fine-looking, and she'd already made the mistake once of marrying a good-looking man who seemed to be perfect on paper, and look what happened there.

No, she had a life plan, and said life plan did not include getting all messy over some guy just because he'd been nice to her dogs. They just so happened to be cohabitating at the moment and that was all.

Her phone buzzed and she took it out of her pocket. It was a text from the foster agency. She read it, her stomach dropping as she read the message twice, then fell into the chair on the porch.

"Oh." She knew this day could come, that it was what she wanted, what everyone at the agency wanted. But still, the thought of it hurt so much fresh tears sprang into her eyes.

The door opened and Linc came out, smiled at her, then immediately frowned.

"What's wrong?"

She swiped at the tears, then smiled. "Oh. Nothing. Good news, really. Someone is interested in meeting Boo for a potential adoption."

"That's awesome, right?"

"Of course it is."

He took a seat next to her. "You don't seem happy about it."

"I'm totally happy. The whole reason I foster dogs is to make sure they're safe and well taken care of until a forever home is found for them. This couple saw his profile on the foster group and they want an introduction and possibly a one-week trial of having him live with them."

"Wow. Big steps."

"Yeah."

"When's that going to happen?"

"Tomorrow. I have to take Boo to meet them. And if all goes well, he'll go home with them for the trial period."

He reached across the table to take her hand. "You don't want him to go."

She jerked her hand away. "Of course I do. It's my job to prepare these dogs for their happily ever after. Why wouldn't I want him to go?"

"Because you love him and you think of him as your dog?"

"Oh, and you know this how? Because you've spent all this time with me? Because you know me? Well, let me tell you, Lincoln Kennedy. You don't know anything about me. I will take Boo to meet his potential new people tomorrow and I'll be damned happy about it."

She walked away, feeling righteous in her anger.

How dare he presume to know how she felt or what her motivations were. She headed outside and found Boo happily gnawing on his bone, so she pulled up a spot next to him and ran her fingers over his smooth, silky fur.

"Guess what, my Boo baby? There are some people who want to meet you and maybe take you home, and we're going there tomorrow. Which means you might just be the luckiest pup in the whole world. Wouldn't it be great to have forever parents who are gonna love you and take care of you for the rest of your life?"

Boo ignored her because bone, of course. But she could tell he was happy about it. Because, dammit, she was happy about it. Or she was going to be.

No matter what Linc thought. After all, he didn't know anything about her or how she felt.

She wiped away the tears that she couldn't hold back.

CHAPTER NINE

Despite having a full day of work that he needed to do, Linc couldn't help but think about Hazel the entire day.

She'd gotten up early and made breakfast, fed and walked the dogs, and after that she'd gone upstairs to shower. A little while later she asked Linc if he wouldn't mind keeping an eye on the other dogs today while she took Boo to meet his potential new family. He'd told her he'd take care of them. She thanked him, then she'd harnessed Boo and left. She'd seemed subdued this morning, and the rest of the dogs had definitely picked up on her mood. They'd been especially confused by her leaving with Boo, but he'd distracted them all with toys, and they'd seemed fine, so he'd gone back to doing his thing, occasionally stopping to check on the pups.

Gordon liked being inside most of the time, especially on hot days like today. Linc was doing some electrical work that wouldn't generate a bunch of dust, so he'd piled up some blankets in the corner of the dining room, and Gordon had made a little pallet there. Then Lilith started pacing in front of the back door, so he opened it and she came in and curled up with Gordon. Before long,

Penny and Freddie were whining at the door, so he had to stop what he was doing again to let them inside. They ended up lying next to the pile of blankets, close to Gordon and Lilith.

Maybe they all knew something was off since Boo wasn't with them. Dogs were pack animals, after all, and when one of the pack was missing, they weren't a complete unit. But since they all finally settled in the corner for a nap, he could go back to work.

He had the wiring done in the ceiling for the new LED can lights. He'd thought about maybe a chandelier in the dining area, but it being right off the main door leading outside, it seemed too fussy, so he decided he'd wire that for cans as well. If the buyer wanted a chandelier there, it would be an easy fix.

By the time he broke for lunch, the dogs were ready to go out as well, so he opened the door and they all piled outside, while Linc made his way to the guesthouse.

The new AC unit had been installed, which meant the guesthouse was now livable again—or at least you weren't going to die when you walked in there.

Before she left this morning, Hazel had told him she'd fixed him a sandwich for lunch and tucked it in the fridge. The one thing he liked about her—okay, there were a lot of things he liked about her, but this was on the list—was that despite having her own worries, she still did her job. He wished some of the people who had worked for him in the past had done that as well.

Which was partly the reason he enjoyed working on houses by himself. He knew what he was doing, he did the job well, and he didn't have to rely on anyone else. Sure, on occasion, he'd have to get an expert to come in or he'd need to hire a few assistants to help with a job. But otherwise, if he could do it himself he would.

He grabbed the bag Hazel had packed for him, pulled a soda out of the fridge, and took it outside to eat on the back porch. The humidity had lifted a little, not a lot, and the wind had picked up, making it tolerable to be outside. The dogs all came over and lay at his feet while he ate, no doubt hoping for some crumbs.

"Not a chance, kids," he said. "I'm hungry."

He checked emails while he ate. There was one from his investment broker about a house up for sale in Phoenix. He scrolled through and looked at the pictures. It was a decent-sized house, definitely needed some upgrades, but it was only twelve years old, so plumbing, electrical, and HVAC should be okay, and he wouldn't have to put on a new roof. It was a lot like this house. Some cosmetic changes, and in a good area. The only problem was that he wouldn't be able to get started on that one until he finished this one, and that would mean a longer turnaround and less profit.

He replied to the email with a "not right now." But if the house was still available when he finished this one, he'd definitely consider it. Spending late fall in Phoenix wouldn't be a terrible idea. The thing he liked best about doing what he did was the ability to travel, to spend time in new locations with every house he worked on. And he could still monitor his investments no matter where he was working and living at the time.

He'd enjoyed this nomadic lifestyle for a few years now. Maybe someday he'd find a place he liked enough to settle down and stay there, but right now he was happy doing this.

He went back to work and had the light switch in the dining room finished when Hazel walked in. The dogs were outside, so she waved to him and went out there. He shoved his screwdriver in his pocket and followed her.

The dogs had all rushed to greet her and, more specifically, smell her. She bent down to say hello and pet them.

"I know," she said. "I didn't bring Boo back with me. But he's doing just great, so don't you worry about him."

"How did it go?" he asked after she took a seat next to him.

"It was awesome. The couple looking to adopt Boo absolutely loved him. And the feeling was mutual. He adored them. They have a two-year-old Labrador that they'd brought with them for a meet and greet with Boo, and the dogs hit it off like they'd been besties forever. They lost their senior pittie six months ago, and they've been searching for another dog. When they saw Boo online, they knew he was the one."

"So, now what?"

"Boo will spend a week with them as a test run, but it's mostly a formality. I could feel their connection with him right away. It's a done deal."

"That's good, isn't it?"

She lifted her gaze to his and gave him what he considered the worst fake smile he'd ever seen. "It's fantastic. I couldn't be happier that Boo has found his forever home."

He could tell she was down and upset. "I'm sorry. I know you love him."

"I love all of them. And, yeah, it's hard, but letting them go is part of the job. Otherwise they'd never end up in their happy places. Boo was so happy today. Once he met Savannah and Leo, he never once ran over to me for comfort. It was like I had ceased to exist."

He was sure that had to have hurt. "You know it's because you gave him confidence and so much love that he was capable of feeling that free to love other people."

Her smile this time was genuine. "Oh, I know. And thank you for saying that. It means a lot."

"Hey, it's true."

She stood and called the pups. "I'm going upstairs for a while. Thanks so much for watching the dogs."

"We had a great time."

He watched her walk inside, the dogs happily following her.

She was upset. Sad. Her heart had been broken. She probably did want that alone time. He knew if it had been him, that's what he'd want.

He walked upstairs, intending to wash up, but then he heard her crying.

Well, damn. He went to her door and knocked softly. "Hazel, can I come in?"

It was a few seconds before she answered with, "Okay."

He opened the door. She was on her bed, sitting with the pillows propped up behind her. Her legs were crossed, and the dogs were on the bed with her. Her eyes were red rimmed and swollen, and tears ran down her face.

"Is it okay if I sit here with you?"

"You don't have to do that. I just need to cry it out and then I'll be fine."

He untied his boots and kicked them off, then climbed onto the bed next to her, much to Lilith's irritation, which she addressed with a low growl. Hazel scooped her up and put the dog on her other side.

"You might be fine tomorrow, or next week, or next month, but I get how much you love your dogs, and it's okay to not be fine today."

She choked out a sob. "I really am happy he's found his forever family. You have to understand that."

"I do."

"He's just the best boy and I'm going to miss him so much."

"I know you will." He put his arm around her, and she laid her head on his shoulder and cried while he comforted her the best way he knew how—just holding her.

Eventually, Gordon climbed onto his lap and curled up into a ball, immediately going to sleep. Penny stretched out alongside his legs, and Freddie lay next to Hazel. This all felt . . .

Comfortable.

Weirdly comfortable. Even with Hazel crying, though eventually she stopped and sighed and blew her nose, but still lay there with her head resting against him. And until she decided she wanted to move away, he was going to stay just like this.

Because sometimes you needed someone to offer comfort while you felt miserable and shitty. And this was one of those times.

So he was going to be there for Hazel for as long as it took.

CHAPTER TEN

*H*azel had barely gotten any sleep last night. How could she, when Boo had always managed to wriggle his way into the bed and press his chunky little body next to her?

She'd warned Savannah and Leo about his propensity for sleeping in the bed. They had just happily smiled and said it was no problem at all. She'd told them he was a toy gatherer and carried one around with him all the time. In fact, he'd brought along the bunny that Linc had given him.

Leo and Savannah said he was adorable.

Of course they'd said that, because it was true. She'd truthfully lined out all of Boo's bad habits, including the occasional backyard digging. They said he was a pup and they'd certainly work with him.

Dammit, they had loved him. How could they not love him? He was sweet and cuddly and had the best smile.

The problem was, Hazel had loved him, too, and giving him up had taken a piece of her heart. But she knew going into this job that every time she had to give up one of her babies, it was going to be painful. And every time she'd happily smiled and given that last hug to one of her foster dogs, it had hurt. It had also made her heart soar with happiness. And wasn't that a conundrum.

She'd get over this. She had before and she'd do it again. It was her job, and she loved it, even when it hurt.

She got dressed and went downstairs to make breakfast. She was surprised not to see Linc already in the kitchen working, since he was usually up well before her. She let the dogs outside, then went to the guesthouse to make coffee.

Linc was there sipping his coffee and brewing another cup for her. When it finished, he handed it to her.

"Thanks," she said, going to the fridge to grab the cream. She poured a small amount into her cup, then took a few life-affirming sips. "Did you sleep in this morning?"

He shook his head. "No, I just had some calls to make. What are your plans for today?"

"Plans?"

"Yeah. It's Saturday, Hazel. It's the weekend."

"It is?" She'd kind of lost track.

"Yeah. I thought it would be fun to drive to the beach with the dogs. You know, relax and have some fun."

She couldn't quite comprehend the idea of taking the day off and going somewhere with Linc and the dogs. "Why would you want to do that?"

He shrugged. "You had a rough day yesterday, and the beach is fun. Besides, I could use a break, too. What do you say?"

Her mind was a jumble of thoughts, and a lot of emotion only added to the mix, so she didn't answer him.

"Say yes, Hazel. We'll all have a good time."

Would they? Would she? More importantly, would Linc? She didn't think he was fully aware of what a road trip with her—and more importantly, the dogs—would truly entail.

"You know, it's not easy maneuvering five—I mean four dogs."

"I think we can handle it. We'll take my truck."

She winced. "My car is already dog proofed. How about we do that instead?"

"Sure," he said with a shrug. "If that makes you more comfortable, we'll take your car. And I'll drive."

She cocked her head to the side. "No you won't. It's my car."

"But I'm the guy."

She snorted out a laugh and walked past him, cup in hand. "Now I know you're joking. I'm going to feed the dogs, then start breakfast."

After feeding the dogs, she made a quick scrambled egg and bacon wrap for them for breakfast, then they both went upstairs to get ready for their trip. Hazel didn't truly understand why Linc would take a whole day off just to spend it with her. She was fine.

Okay, she wasn't exactly fine. She missed Boo. But that was just something she was going to have to get used to. It wasn't the first time she'd fostered a dog who ended up leaving, and it wouldn't be the last. Eventually, she'd get better at letting go.

Hopefully.

She should probably stop thinking of these dogs as hers. But how could she not fall in love with them and bond with them since they so clearly needed her? How was she supposed to maintain an emotional distance when they relied on her for everything, including love?

She couldn't. So she'd just have to suck it up and take the heartache whenever they left.

Heartbreak should be something she was used to by now.

She stood in front of the mirror and brushed her hair, then wound it up in a bun on top of her head while she glared at herself.

"You sure are feeling sorry for yourself today, aren't you?"

Why, yes, yes, she was.

Maybe she did need a nice day out at the beach. It would help clear her head—and her mood.

She packed her backpack with essentials for the day, then headed downstairs and went into the garage to grab all the dog leashes and harnesses. She got those ready and tossed her backpack in the trunk.

Linc came downstairs wearing shorts and a sleeveless shirt, looking tan and delicious and, wow, did he ever smell good. She had the sudden urge to follow him around and just breathe him in. Or maybe lick his neck. Maybe hump him a few times.

She stopped and inhaled and exhaled.

Fine, so maybe she needed to take a weekend off sometime and have awesome sex, because she was so easily distracted by good pheromones right now. And Linc? His were outstanding and definitely calling to her. Spending time in the car with him should be delightfully distracting.

Maybe she should let him drive. Then she could take her time looking at him. And breathing him in.

Deciding to focus her attention on the dogs, she called them inside and put on their harnesses, took them on a walk to wear off some of their excited energy, then, after they all got a post-walk drink, loaded them up in the back seat of the car.

"How do they do in the car?" Linc asked as he peeked his head into the back seat while Hazel was getting them all tethered to the seat belts.

"Mostly fine. Gordon has his blanket and will go to sleep. Penny and Freddie will look out the windows, and Lilith will want to be on my lap because she still gets a little nervous in the car, but she'll be fine after about five miles."

"You've got this all down to a science, don't you?"

She nodded. "Pretty much."

"Then let's go."

"Okay." She scooped Lilith up in her arms, then handed Linc the keys. "You drive."

He arched a brow. "You sure?"

"Yes. It'll be easier for me to keep my eye on the pups."

"You got it." He clutched the keys in his hands, immediately making an *oof* noise as he slid in. "I could have sworn you had long legs."

She got into the passenger side, rolling her eyes while he grunted and made adjustments to the driver's seat.

"Oh, come on," she said. "It's not that bad."

"You wouldn't say that if your balls had just gotten crammed up your ass."

She laughed. "Well, when you put it that way, it does sound that bad. Sorry about your testicles. I hope you've stretched out enough now. Though when you put your seat far back like that—"

Before she could warn him, Penny licked the side of his head.

He swiped away the slobber. "Aww, come on, Penny. That's gross."

Hazel turned around and smiled. This trip was going to be so much fun.

*F*ortunately, it only took a little over an hour to get to the beach. But really, the dogs were fairly chill. Freddie was excited at first, and Linc could see why they were strapped in, because between Freddie and Penny, if they'd had the full run of the vehicle they might have been jumping into the front seat. But they finally settled after about twenty minutes and spent most of their time looking out the window. Freddie occasionally barked at a car next to him, which then got Penny's dander up so she had to bark at whatever she saw out her window.

Quite the competition between those two. And Gordon? He slept through it all.

Lilith started out kind of shaky, trembling and trying to climb into Hazel's armpit, but after a few miles she settled down on Hazel's lap, content to just be chill and pretend she'd never been nervous in the first place. He admired her ability to fake it. All in all, a fairly peaceful drive.

Since it was the fall, finding a parking space wasn't hard at all, and they were able to park close to the beach. Once he and Hazel attached leashes to all the dogs, they got them out of the car and headed straight for the beach, the dogs excitedly lunging ahead.

"I think they really want to be in the water," he said.

She nodded. "They love to play in the ocean. The good news is they'll exhaust themselves and sleep the whole way home. The bad news is they'll exhaust us, too."

He laughed as Penny and Freddie jerked on their leashes, dragging him along. "Just think of it as fresh air and exercise."

It wasn't overly crowded—or actually, crowded at all. There were several people, some with dogs, some without, but no one even blinked when they arrived and the dogs excitedly started barking at the water.

Hazel kicked off her shoes, then took the leash off Gordon and Lilith. Gordon wandered slowly toward the water's edge, sniffed, then plopped down in the wet sand just out of reach of the approaching waves. Lilith pranced around in the water, getting her feet wet but mindful of the waves. Linc held on to Penny's and Freddie's leashes, waiting for Hazel's cue.

"You can let them off leash," she said. "They know what to do."

He unhooked them, and the dogs ran happily toward the water. Of course Penny, being taller with longer legs, got there first, but Freddie ran as fast as his short legs could get him there, his floppy little ears flying in the ocean breeze. Penny ran straight into the water, and Linc could swear she was smiling as she did a dive underneath the waves. Freddie, not quite as brave, barked at the water, danced around in circles, then let the waves lap over his feet before scurrying back to the sand and repeating the process again. Lilith stayed firmly on the sand and guarded her siblings.

Linc walked over to Hazel. "You're right. They're all having a good time. Even Gordon." He motioned with his head to where Gordon had gotten up, stretched, and padded toward the water's edge, got close enough to have a wave wet him down, then calmly extricated himself and lay down next to Lilith.

Hazel smiled. "For Gordon, that was an enormous under-taking."

They watched the dogs frolic—or sleep. Hazel kicked off her flip-flops and dug her toes into the sand, trying to relax.

She should be able to relax. This was an ideal location, the sun was shining, the ocean breeze sprayed her with cool, salty mist, and she had a sexy-as-hell man sitting next to her. The dogs were content, so why did every part of her body feel as tight as Spanx in August?

Maybe she was overanalyzing and worrying about nothing. That was standard for her. She could try relaxing and letting her mind just . . . go. Clearing her mind and thinking about nothing just wasn't something she did, though. Not when she had her future to think about, and where the money would come from. It was a constant worry in her head, and it wasn't going away.

Linc got up and went to the water's edge, distracting her. He played with the dogs, who went crazy, barking and lunging at him as he splashed water at them. Even Gordon got in on the act—playfully bending into his downward dog pose and giving Linc tiny barks. Meanwhile, Lilith ran circles around Linc, and Hazel was sure she'd never seen the Chihuahua happier as she pranced and growled at him. And when he scooped her up in his arms and ran his hand over her head, her little tail whipped back and forth and she licked Linc's face.

Wow. Her girl had come a long way. To see the level of trust that Lilith had developed with Linc was a big deal. Maybe it was because Linc knew he would never hurt her, so Lilith somehow also knew that. Hazel didn't begin to understand the inner workings of a dog's mind. She knew they had emotions, including hurts, so she simply accepted their feelings and worked with what they felt at any given moment.

Like right now. Right now, her dogs were all happy. Linc had been right—they all had needed this day.

Especially her. She'd been sad about losing Boo, but she knew he was going to be so happy at his new home. And at the moment, how could she feel down when dogs were barking, sand was flying, and Linc had that incredibly deep laugh that he used with abundance as he rolled around in the surf with the pups?

It had been so long since she'd felt that kind of unrestrained joy. It was time for her to recapture these moments and grab a bit of the happiness that had eluded her over the past few years. Even if it was temporary.

She got up and joined them, immersing herself in the maelstrom of flinging water and barking dogs. They'd spent at least half an hour running amok with the pups until she'd laughed so hard she couldn't breathe. When even the dogs had begun to slow down, they leashed them and went in search of something to drink, finding an outdoor restaurant and drink spot about a half mile down the beach. Linc bought some bottles of water for the dogs and a couple of beers for them. She poured water into the dogs' bowls, and they all drank greedily, then passed out at their feet while Hazel and Linc took seats and sipped their beers.

"That was fun," Linc said after taking a couple of long swallows.

"It was. Also exhausting."

"Yeah." He reached out and swept his hand across the top of her head. "You have sand in your hair."

She shrugged, not feeling at all embarrassed at being seen as less than perfect, since he'd already seen her at her worst. "And your hair's standing straight up. It looks like you got struck by lightning."

He laughed and shoved his hand through his hair. "Then I'd say we're a pretty good match."

Her stomach did a tumble at his comment, but she knew it was a throwaway joke and not a come-on. "Yes, we definitely are."

"You hungry?" he asked.

"A little."

"Let's grab something to eat. I'll get us a menu."

Fortunately, the little shop they had stopped in had food, so they ordered some tacos, which were delicious. She hadn't realized how hungry she was until she bit into the taco, then ended up devouring the entire thing and wished she had ordered more than one. But she'd also noticed Linc had only had one as well.

"Aren't you hungry?" she asked as she wiped her mouth with a napkin.

"Yeah, but I thought we might go out for dinner tonight, if you're game."

"You want to go out for dinner? With me?"

"Yeah, with you. I told you we were taking the day off, so why not make it the entire day and have some fun? You're always cooking, and you should have someone else cook for you for a change."

"Oh, well that's not necessary."

He cocked his head to the side. "Hazel. I want to take you to dinner."

"Uh, I don't really have 'going out to dinner' clothes with me. Since the dogs and I are on the move a lot, I only keep the minimum with me. Most of my stuff is stored with a friend."

"Okay, so we'll go shopping. How's that?"

She winced at the thought of spending money but gave him a weak smile. "Sure."

They headed back to the house. Once there, Hazel unleashed the dogs and put them out back. Typically, they'd run around, but they all crawled under the shady palms and passed out. Obviously, all the fresh ocean air and frolic had done them in, and all they wanted to do was sleep. Which would be great when she went out tonight, because she doubted they'd even miss her.

The dogs roused themselves long enough for her to feed them, then they wandered the yard while she went upstairs to get ready.

She took a shower and dried her hair, then dug into her kit for makeup, which she rarely wore. She settled for a bit of mascara, some brow touch-up, and lip stain, hoping that was good enough.

Maybe she should have asked Linc where they were going. She hoped it wasn't anywhere too fancy. She didn't have the budget for an upscale dress and shoes. Right now all she owned were a couple of sundresses, and even those were old, and as for shoes, she only had flip-flops and tennis shoes.

Her life wasn't glamorous enough to need anything more than that.

She chose one of the sundresses and her nicest pair of flip-flops—the ones that had a touch of bling, which wasn't saying much, but it was all she had.

When she came downstairs, Linc was holding Lilith, whispering to her as he petted her softly. Lilith leaned her tiny body against him like he was the best person she'd ever known. Her little eyes were partially closed, and Hazel could see—and feel—the bond that had formed between the two of them.

Her pulse rate kicked up when she got a good look at him.

"You shaved." Her fingers curled into her palm to keep from reaching up to swipe her hand over his smooth jaw.

"Figured I should since we're going out."

She wondered how that smooth jaw would feel rubbing against her inner thighs.

Down, girl.

He wore dark slacks and a black button-down shirt, not seeming to care at all that Lilith was going to leave hairs on the shirt. Then again, all the dogs currently surrounded him, and Hazel knew from experience that their fur was like a magnet to clothes—especially dark clothes.

Still, Linc bent and petted all of them, and picked Gordon up to give him extra cuddles.

She couldn't help but sigh. She was a sucker for a guy who loved dogs.

He set Gordon down and smiled at her. "You look really pretty."

"I'm sure I'm not dressed appropriately, but like I mentioned, I don't exactly have 'going out' clothes. I was kind of hoping we could stop along the way and I could pick up something more appropriate."

"If you'd like, but you look nice."

"Thanks. But I'd feel better in something more suitable to— where are we going?"

"I thought it would be fun to eat a little upscale tonight."

Oh, crap. Upscale meant a nice dress and heels. "Uh, sure. That sounds great."

She settled the dogs with their toys and blankets and water bowls, though it appeared as if their day by the water had done its job, and they all curled up together in a ball of floof, surprising her as she and Linc walked out the door.

"They weren't even nervous that I was leaving," she said as he shut the front door behind him.

"That's a good thing, right? Raising confident and secure dogs?"

"Of course." She sometimes forgot that she didn't want the pups dependent on her. "They're doing great, aren't they?"

"Yeah, they are."

He opened his truck and she climbed in, surprised to see it so clean in there.

"No work tools or anything," she said.

"I cleaned it out earlier." He gave her a knowing smile.

"I see."

They drove to the mall—the trendy, fancy, high-dollar one. Shit.

"Linc."

"Yeah?"

"I can't afford this mall." She wanted to wither up and die right here in the car. And, maybe, if she was lucky, she'd subsequently disappear in a cloud of mortified ash.

"Oh. Sure. You know, I could buy—"

"No. Absolutely not."

He gave a quick nod. "Got it. Where would you like to go?"

She gave him directions to a discount store, and fortunately, he didn't say another word until they got there.

He got out with her.

"You don't need to come in with me," she said, not wanting him to see her flail around to find something she could afford.

"But I want to."

"Okay."

They went inside and she headed to the dresses, hoping he wasn't embarrassed to be seen in here with her.

Apparently, he wasn't, because he started going through the racks, zeroing right in on the correct size, too. She didn't know whether to be supremely impressed or irritated that he knew so much about women.

He pulled one off the rack. "This would look great on you."

He had a good eye, that was for sure. It was a blue-and-white short-sleeved dress that would hit her at the knees. She wanted to immediately grab the price tag, but she could do that in the dressing room. "I'll try it on, but I want to pick out a couple other dresses, too."

"Okay."

She found two other dresses she thought were reasonably priced, then headed back to the dressing area. The first thing she did was check the price tag on the one Linc had chosen, holding her breath as she read the tag. She exhaled when she saw it was on sale, and though at the top of her price range, at least it was in the ballpark.

She undressed and tried on the two she had chosen. They were serviceable, but she didn't love them, so she slipped on the dress Linc had picked out, feeling it slide over her body like silk. When she turned and looked at herself in the mirror, she smiled.

Oh, yeah. This one was nice. Really nice. It hugged her curves, and the scoop neck showed off just a tiny bit of cleavage. Sexy without being overt, but perfect for a nice dinner out, and it wouldn't break the bank.

She left the dress on and came out of the dressing area. She could swear she saw Linc's gaze sparkle with interest, but that was probably just her imagination.

"You look amazing in that."

"Thanks. I think this is the one. I just need shoes now."

"Okay, let's shop."

She was happy that he didn't put up a fuss about her doing this on her terms.

The shoes were the easy part. Sandals, but with a low heel, and also on sale. She slipped them on, and they looked amazing with the dress.

Linc came up behind her as she looked in the mirror. "Now you're ready for dinner."

She couldn't help but grin. "Yes, I am."

She went up to the counter and paid for the items, then had the cashier remove the tag from the dress since she was wearing it out the door. Once in the car, she slipped on the shoes.

She felt a lot better now.

CHAPTER ELEVEN

*T*his was some kind of fairy princess night for Hazel. First, she was going out to dinner. And not just your average dinner, but dinner at a highly rated steak and seafood restaurant. She'd always wanted to eat at Victoria & Albert's but of course could never afford it. And now, here they were, being seated in a private room that they would apparently have all to themselves, rather than in the main dining room. It was all lush and decadent and she was so excited she felt like she might burst.

Linc held out the chair for her and she slid in, certain there must be birds singing over the top of her head. Or maybe it was just this magical night.

Their server presented the wine list along with the menu.

"Any particular favorite on the wine?" Linc asked as he opened the book to page through it.

Normally, she would have let him choose, but this was her new life—the one where she promised to find her voice. "I'm fond of pinot noir."

He looked up at her and nodded. "Me, too. Would you like to choose?" He slid the wine list over to her.

She perused it, her eyes nearly bugging out at the prices per bottle. "Holy crap, Linc."

"Stop looking at the prices and just choose one that looks good to you. I can—I have money saved up for special nights and this is one. I want you to relax and enjoy this."

She blew out a breath and let her pulse rate settle, then looked over the wine list until she found one that sounded good to her. She pointed it out to Linc.

"This one," she said.

"You chose a California wine because it's cheaper, right?"

She shrugged. "Maybe."

"You wouldn't want to, say, go with something French?"

"I've never had one."

"Would you want to try?" He flipped through the pages and slid the book back to her. She looked, unable to avoid seeing the prices.

Good Lord. "Linc, I—can't choose. You do it." She shoved the book back at him.

He smiled at her. "Trust me?"

"Sure."

When the server returned, she wanted to cover her ears while Linc ordered a bottle of the French pinot noir that she was sure cost over five hundred dollars.

Who did that? Not her, that was for sure. Her indulgences in wine typically came in a box from the grocery store. Not that she didn't enjoy fine wine. She'd had her share of the good stuff, but that had been a long while ago. And never anything as expensive as what Linc had just ordered.

"You know, a less expensive bottle would have been fine."

He shrugged. "Yeah, but you've been working hard, and isn't it fun to indulge every now and then?"

"I wouldn't know."

"Well, tonight you will. And you deserve it."

"Do I?"

"Hell yeah, you do. You work hard. You take care of dogs who otherwise wouldn't have someone to look out for them. You got a raw deal from your ex, and you've been down and out for a while, right?"

"Yes."

"Okay, then. You deserve to be pampered a little. So remind yourself that you're worth it."

"You have a point. But I'd rather be paying for all of this myself."

"Someday, you will. Until then, allow me, at least tonight? And then we can go back to sandwiches for lunch and food cooked in the tiny stove in the guesthouse."

She crooked a smile. "I don't recall you complaining about the food I cook."

"I wasn't. The food you've made for me could rival anything the chefs prepare here."

"I don't know about that, but thanks for the compliment."

"I believe I rave about your meals every time you serve them up."

"You do."

"Which doesn't mean you don't deserve a night out and having someone pamper you, does it?"

He had a point. "I guess not."

"Okay, then. So admit you deserve this."

Linc certainly had a way of winning an argument. Not that they were having one, but she appreciated that he realized what she'd been through.

And when the server brought the bottle of wine and poured her a glass, she took a sip and had to admit that there was a world of difference between box wine and this amazingly smooth pinot noir.

"Well, this is the best pinot I've ever had," she said, rolling the deep red liquid around in the glass.

"It is pretty good," Linc said. "I'm glad you like it."

"Like it? I want to pour it all over myself."

He arched a brow. "That's an idea. Can I lick it off?"

And that was an idea that was now milling about in her very vivid imagination. "It's definitely open for discussion."

His lips curved, and her nipples tightened against her bra.

Oh, the things she wanted to do with this man. She studied him over the rim of her wineglass, noting the way his fingers curved over the stem of his glass, watching him as he took a drink of wine, the way his tongue licked over his lips, all the while imagining those same fingers curving around her neck as those amazing lips pressed to hers, his tongue sliding inside her mouth to tangle with hers.

And suddenly, the formerly cool atmosphere of the restaurant grew decidedly warmer. She was grateful the dress was cool against her body, though right now naked would be better. Then she could straddle Linc and act out all of her fantasies.

Ha. If only they were alone. Which they would be later.

Wow, this wine was really hitting the mark, wasn't it? She had a nice buzz going and her inhibitions were loosening.

Who was she kidding? She had zero inhibitions where Linc was concerned. She wanted him.

"Thank you for bringing me here. And for shopping with me for the dress."

"The dress is very nice. The woman who's wearing it is better."

He slanted a heated look at her that made all her parts swell with need and desire. She blew out a breath and this time took a sip of her water.

Okay, time to calm down, Hazel.

She still had to get through dinner before she could let her desires run wild. If she even should. After all, he was her employer. Technically.

"Do you have any concerns about this?" she asked. "You and me, this teasing, bantering foreplay we're doing?"

"Me? None at all."

"Well, I do work for you."

He set his wineglass down. "That's more of a technicality. You're not my employee. Not in the traditional sense of the word. You make food for me, food of your own choosing. I don't tell you what to make or set your hours. I don't control what you do or don't do. You have freedom to do or not do whatever you want. I would never presume—"

She waved her hand. "I get it. I just didn't want you to get the wrong impression about me."

"Same. And if you have any concerns in that regard, Hazel, this stops now."

Okay, that seemed rather definite. "No, I'm having a really good time with you, Linc. I just didn't want you to think I had any ulterior motives other than enjoying being with you."

"Good. Then we're on the same page." He picked up his wineglass to take a drink and that was settled.

She felt better now that they had discussed it, that they both knew that this thing wasn't a big thing. It was just a thing. Which didn't make sense at all, at least not at the moment, but then again, she'd had some wine. Some very excellent wine.

Dinner was an amazing tasting menu featuring a vast array of seafood and beef, each course elegantly presented in ways that made Hazel wish she'd brought a notebook, because the menu sparked ideas. From langoustine and passion fruit to turbot to wild boar and a melt-in-her-mouth Kobe beef, it was a taste explosion. Not to mention the cheeses and then the chocolate mousse. And through it all, she and Linc discussed and argued favorite flavors and textures while sipping more of the most excellent wine.

It was a dizzying experience. She couldn't remember ever having a better time. And what had captured her most was the attention that Linc paid to her. Not once had he pulled out his phone or glanced away to stare at a woman walking by—one of her ex's favorite pastimes.

Instead, he asked her questions about her interests. They talked books and movies and things they each enjoyed doing when they had free time.

"I never asked you where you were from," she said as she

sipped on her cappuccino. "I mean, I know you travel around and do the whole house renovation thing, but I assume you plant your flag somewhere."

"My family lives outside San Francisco, and that's where my office is."

"Oh. Fancy. And on the other side of the country. It's like night and day difference from hot and muggy Orlando."

"That's true. But I like seeing different places, meeting people who live different lives than where I come from."

She'd always considered travel a luxury, and something she'd rarely been able to afford. "Where have you renovated homes?"

He leaned back in his chair, thinking for a minute before answering. "This year I've done Boston, Phoenix, Detroit, and Las Vegas. And now here."

"That's definitely a whirlwind. What's your next project after you finish this one?" Which she hoped wasn't over too quickly, since she was getting used to having him around.

"I haven't decided yet. What's next for you? I know you said you wanted the rescue organization. What else? How will you make that dream come true?"

Wasn't that a loaded question. "Oh. Honestly? I don't know. Thanks to you writing me a paycheck every week, I'm able to put some money aside so I'll at least have a roof over my head. That's a start. From there, I'll figure something out."

"But surely you have an idea of how you'll get from point A to point B."

"Of course. I'll work at a restaurant—or find other jobs until I'm financially capable of putting my dream plan into action."

He swept his thumb over the rim of his coffee cup. "And if you could, what would it look like?"

She inhaled and let out a breath. "The aforementioned place to live, of course. One with enough room for the dogs to run, with space to allow me to take care of even more. But that's a big dream for someday, you know, when I'm all kinds of wealthy."

He shrugged. "Nothing wrong with big dreams, Hazel. We all have them."

"I definitely do."

He gave her a direct look. "Wanna share?"

"Maybe someday."

"Why someday? Why not now?"

She shrugged. "I don't know."

"Afraid to put your dreams out in the world because they might not come true?"

He'd hit the mark on that one. "You know something about that?"

"I might. But it's okay to talk about them. Talking about them gives them life."

He had a point. "I like cooking. I think you know that. So there's a hint of a dream of someday maybe doing something with food."

He took a sip of coffee. "That's . . . vague. Do you mean working as head chef at a Michelin-starred restaurant, or owning your own place?"

She fiddled with her napkin, then looked up at him. "I don't know. I just like to cook. I haven't delved into dreams beyond that."

"But the idea of something cooking-related appeals, doesn't it? Being head chef, owning a restaurant, something along those lines?"

It was odd that he seemed to know her inner thoughts, could seem to read her body language in a way that didn't make her uncomfortable, but instead . . . warmed her.

"Yes. One is better."

"Tell me."

"I want to own a restaurant. But I also want to run a rescue. I can't do both."

"Why not?"

"Linc." She tilted her head to the side. "Both are full-time jobs."

"You have drive and ambition. You can do anything you set your mind to do, Hazel. Don't give up on yourself, on your dreams. You can do this. You deserve it, Hazel. You deserve to have everything and anything you want."

She could only gape at him. No one had ever believed in her or her potential like this. It made her want to believe, too. And that felt good.

Their server arrived with the check, and Linc whipped out his credit card. She was afraid to try and peek at the total, which she was sure was astronomical.

After Linc paid, they got up and left the restaurant. He helped her up into his truck, and they headed back toward the house.

On the drive back he kept giving her quick glances, and when she met his gaze he'd smile. Not a polite smile, but a hot, direct look.

"Feel good?" he asked.

She smiled, and the look she directed at him wasn't a polite one, either. Instead, she telegraphed her feelings quite directly.

"I feel very good."

His lips curved, and she couldn't help but stare at his mouth.

"Yeah, me, too." His fingers gripped the steering wheel, and she wondered what he was thinking about, while at the same time wishing he was grabbing her right now, all that power and muscle barely restrained as he touched her.

Damn. She didn't know what to do with that.

Hazel had never been the kind of woman men noticed. Or chased. She'd always wanted to be pursued. That had never happened. She and her ex had dated long term, and they got along fine, so it was assumed they'd get married. Then they had. But it had been more of a comfortable arrangement rather than an all-consuming passion.

She wanted all-consuming passion, to feel zaps of sexual energy whenever a man touched her, to know that he wanted her beyond all reason.

Maybe those longings weren't realistic, but dammit, she had them.

She deserved to fulfill them.

You deserve it.

Linc's earlier words rang in her ears.

You deserve it.

Hell yes, she deserved it.

And he definitely made her tingle—merely by those hot looks he was sending her way.

So she supposed the question of the night was . . .

Was she brave enough to go for it?

CHAPTER TWELVE

Do you think the dogs would be okay if we stayed out for a while longer?" Linc asked as he drove them away from the restaurant.

"They're fine. Why?"

"I'd like to take you somewhere else."

"Really? I'm curious."

Linc couldn't remember ever enjoying a night out more than he had tonight. He wasn't ready for it to end. Besides, Hazel looked amazing, and he wanted her to live it up a little bit longer. He got the idea she didn't get to go out and party very often, at least lately, though he didn't know what her social life had been when she was married.

"Did you and your ex go out much?"

"Not really. He wasn't much for hanging out with people. He liked staying home and preferred I do the same."

"But you had friends to go do things with, right?"

She shifted in her seat, and he caught a glimpse of her tanned and toned legs. "For a while. But Andrew slowly whittled them down until I only had one or two close friends left. Ginger was one of them. Now she's moved out of state."

"That's too bad. It's important to have friends."

"How about you? Do you still have good friends or is it hard to maintain those friendships since you're always traveling?"

He let out a laugh. "Guys don't need to be in touch all the time. We can be separated for a year or more, then get together and grab a beer and catch up like no time has passed."

She stayed silent.

"Why?" he asked. "Is it different for women?"

"It doesn't have to be."

"But it was for you."

"I guess. It shouldn't be."

"No, it shouldn't. Not if you make the right friends. If a year goes by and you meet up with your friends for drinks, you should be able to pick up right where you left off. Or at least catch up, knowing that your friends will always welcome you back into their circle no matter where you've wandered or for how long."

"You obviously have a good group of friends."

He smiled. "I do." Then he looked over at her. "And you?"

"I suppose I do have that. There's Ginger, and I know I can call her anytime, show up on her doorstep no matter where she lives. And I have Sandy—she runs the foster organization. We're not lifelong friends or anything, but she's been there for me during some rough times. And we get each other. We're both divorced and we both love animals."

"Those are good friends, aren't they?"

"Yes."

"Sometimes that's all you need. There's no minimum—or maximum—number on friends. Just ones you trust."

He was right about that.

He pulled up to the nightclub, one he'd read about and wanted to check out. The parking lot was full, so that was a good sign, and the music was jamming, so he figured this was a good place to get into, have a few drinks, and maybe hit the dance floor and show off his gorgeous date.

His date.

He hadn't really thought about Hazel in that way. He'd just wanted to take her out and show her a good time.

Yeah, right. Who was he kidding? He liked her. He really liked her, and the attraction between them was incendiary. No reason not to explore that and see where it went, as long as both of them stayed aware that this was a temporary situation. Because as soon as he finished renovations on this house, he'd be gone, and they'd be done.

Better make sure she understands that.

Yeah, he needed to be clear about that, because the last thing she needed was to be hurt again.

"This looks fun," she said as they walked inside.

He took her hand and led her past the groups of people standing around.

"They all look really young," she said, leaning against him so she could be heard over the loud music. "I'm not sure this is where we should be."

He laughed. "I don't think there's an age limit, Hazel. We're fine." He put his hand on her back and directed her toward the stairs.

They walked up toward the VIP area. Hazel's eyes widened.

"We definitely shouldn't be up here."

"Sure we should." He gave his name to the guy standing there, who looked on his list and nodded. "Section Four is yours."

After he directed them where to go, Linc smiled. "Thanks."

The sections were marked so they were easy to find. It was a nice area, not oversize but not too tight, either. They slid into the booth, which had a nice view of the dance floor and bar area below.

A tall, leggy brunette came right over. "My name is Bonita. What can I get for you?"

"Hi, Bonita. Tito's on the rocks with lime for me." Linc looked over at Hazel.

"Oh," she said. "Umm, I'll have a margarita."

"What kind, honey?" Bonita asked.

Hazel lifted her hands. "I don't know. Surprise me with something fun and spicy."

Bonita grinned. "Sure."

After she left, Hazel shifted to face him. "You made a reservation so we could be up here."

"I'm not much for standing around in crowds."

"This is very nice."

"It'll do."

Bonita came back a few minutes later and set their drinks down.

"This is a pineapple jalapeño margarita," she said. "I hope you like it."

Hazel took a sip, then another, then grinned up at Bonita. "I love it."

Bonita smiled and nodded and made her exit.

"So you like spicy, huh?" Linc asked as he sipped his drink.

"In some things, yes. This drink is especially good. You want a taste?"

He wanted a taste all right, just not of the drink. "I'm good with this."

"You don't know what you're missing. It's tart and sweet, and then, pow—the spice sneaks up on you."

"So kind of like you, huh?"

"Me?" She put her hand to her chest. "I'm not spicy."

He laughed. "Yeah, you are. You're also sweet. And a little tart."

She laid her glass down and swiped a finger across his hand. "And how would you know? You haven't even tasted me."

His balls quivered at the thought of having his mouth on her—anywhere on her. "Is that an invitation?"

Her voice went low, but he still heard her clearly over the music. "Yes."

He didn't need more encouragement than that one word, and the heated look in her eyes. He leaned close, cupped the side of her neck to pull her close, then touched his lips to hers.

Yeah, just as he thought—fiery, hot, and spicy. She opened for him and he slid his tongue inside. Tasting her was like an explosion of desire, as if he'd banked it for far too long and that need for her was finally freed. Only here they were, in a public place, and they weren't the only VIP booth up here.

This was a tease, and the rest of the feast was going to have to wait for later, unfortunately. But for now, he liked having his mouth on hers, feeling the way she had grasped his forearm to hold on, as if the kiss had made her feel as off-kilter as he felt, too.

And when a woman in a nearby booth let out a loud laugh, Hazel pulled away, making him instantly regret bringing her someplace so public. Hard to be intimate in an environment like this. Then again, that had been the whole idea, hadn't it? To get out, let loose and have fun? He could think of a lot of fun things he wanted to do with Hazel, and none of them could be done in public.

"How about we get out on the dance floor?" he asked.

"Oh, I haven't danced in . . . well, long enough for me not to be able to remember."

He stood and held his hand out for her. "Like riding a bike, Hazel."

She stood and hesitantly slid her hand in his. "For the record, I'm not very good at that, either."

He laughed and led her downstairs and onto the dance floor.

*D*ancing with Linc on this lit-up dance floor where bodies were jamming and swaying was going to place in Hazel's top-ten list of fun things she'd done.

At first she'd been reluctant about being here, feeling out of place, like she didn't belong. Everyone looked so young and twentysomething, and she was neither. But Linc seemed to be at ease, and despite her reservations, no one seemed to be paying any attention to them. The music was amazing, and how could she not want to dance, especially with such a hot partner? A partner who just a few minutes ago had kissed her.

Oh, what a kiss it had been. She still felt the flutters in her stomach remembering the way his mouth had moved over hers, taking possession, offering things she definitely wanted. It was too bad they were in this crowded place where they couldn't explore each other. Still, she couldn't help but dive in and enjoy the moments, like dancing. She felt freer than she had in years. They'd danced through three songs before she was out of breath and epically dry mouthed.

They went back upstairs, and she took a couple of long swallows of her drink. Bonita came by, and Hazel asked her for some sparkling water along with a refill of her margarita. Linc got another drink, too.

"You can move," Linc said. "I liked watching you dance out there."

She felt her cheeks grow warm. "Thank you. It didn't hurt that I had you to follow."

He reached out his hand to lay it over hers, and there went all her nerve endings pinging all over the place.

"What do you like to do for fun?" he asked.

She blinked. "Fun? Uh, hanging out with the dogs. Cooking. I like the pool in the backyard. It's great for doing laps and relaxing." Listening to her list out her activities, she realized Linc probably thought she was the most boring person on the planet. He was going to drive them back to the house and never take her out again.

"So you're pretty chill, then," he said. "I like that."

She waited while Bonita returned with the drinks and laid them on the table. She took a couple of sips of the water, letting the coolness of it refresh her dance-dry throat before looking at Linc.

"You think I'm chill? I thought maybe you'd think I was dull."

He frowned. "Why would I think that?"

She shrugged. "I don't know. Maybe because I don't crave adventure and I don't need constant entertainment or have a burning desire to travel the world. I'm pretty content with simple things."

"Nothing wrong with simple. In fact, a simple life leads to contentment."

She sent him a querying look. "Is that some proverb?"

He laughed. "No, I just made it up."

So he was amazing-looking, great with his hands, nice, and he was smart, too?

This guy couldn't be for real. And she'd had way too much fun with him tonight. More importantly, she'd relaxed and had felt more like her old self, something she hadn't done in far too long. And she liked the person she was around him. Which had nothing to do with the impressive dinner or this very cool club, and everything to do with Linc.

"I'm ready to leave if you are," she said.

He looked surprised, then nodded. "Oh, yeah, sure."

He signaled for Bonita and paid the check, then they headed out. She was quiet on the way back to the house, her head filled with all kinds of thoughts, mostly about Linc.

When they got to the house, the dogs were excited to see her—and Linc.

Linc bent to pet them all, seemingly unconcerned about getting dog hair on his nice clothes.

"Hey, kids," he said to the dogs. "Did you do okay while you were alone?"

The pups ate up all the attention. It surprised Hazel how attached they'd become to him. Then again, he had a magnetism about him, so it shouldn't surprise her the dogs would gravitate to that. She certainly had.

"Come on, babies." She let the dogs outside, then shut the door and turned to face Linc. "I had a really good time tonight."

"Me, too."

Boldness wasn't really her thing, but tonight she felt emboldened. Maybe it was the wine. Or the spicy margaritas. Or the new dress. She had no idea. For whatever reason, she felt exceptionally good.

She moved in closer to him, tilting her head back to peruse his ruggedly handsome face, realizing she wanted to study all those planes and angles for hours, then map them with her fingertips. The way he looked down at her—all that pent-up desire easily readable in his eyes—made her wonder if his heart was pounding as hard as hers was right now. She laid her hands on his chest, felt the rapid beat of his heart, and smiled up at him.

Then she rose up on her toes and wrapped her hand around the nape of his neck, pulling his head to hers.

Before she took her next breath he had tugged her close and his mouth was on hers and everything she wanted was right there. His chest against hers, their mouths plundering each other with a needy passion, tongues intertwined in a mad dance. She was dizzy with desire, with the feel of all that muscle pressing against her, the taste of him so maddening she whimpered against his mouth, causing him to growl in response.

She'd never felt so fully consumed before, so utterly wanted as she felt right this moment.

She pulled back. "How about we take this upstairs?"

He arched a perfect brow. "Are you sure?"

"Yes. Absolutely certain it's what I want. If it's what you want."

"Hell yeah, it's what I want." He took her mouth in a hard kiss that turned her brain to mush. Then he lifted her, scooping her up in his arms as he carried her up the stairs, and she finally understood all those romance books she'd spent her entire life reading.

This was what swooning felt like. She held on while he took the steps what seemed like two at a time, their mouths still fused together in the swirling heat of passionate need.

How could Linc see where he was going? More importantly, did she even care?

No, she absolutely did not, because he had a tight hold of her and she knew he'd get her there. She could bet he'd get her there in many ways.

He pushed open the door to his bedroom and put her down.

"We need to get you out of your pretty new dress."

She slanted a half smile at him, then turned around to give him access to the zipper. As he drew it down, his fingers brushed the bare skin of her back, making her shiver all over.

"You okay?" he asked.

"Definitely okay." If his slightest touch elicited that reaction, she couldn't imagine what would happen when . . . well, she actually could imagine. She'd imagined it a lot lately. She just wasn't certain she'd live through it.

The dress pooled at her feet. She bent over to pick it up and heard Linc groan. When she turned around, his lips curved.

"You have a great ass, Hazel. And that fancy lacy underwear? Damn."

Her insides fluttered when he complimented what she thought was average underwear. And, okay, it was the finest she had. Maybe she'd had some insight that things were leading here. Either way, she was grateful she'd worn the good stuff. "Thank you." She felt pretty. And desirable. Two things she hadn't had in her vocabulary in far too long. She wasn't going to question it or put conditions on it. Tonight, she was going with it.

He took the dress from her and hung it up in the closet, then led her to his bed, sitting her on the edge of the mattress. He bent down and removed her shoes, smoothing his hands along the undersides of her legs, eliciting chill bumps on her skin.

"Amazing legs, too." He pressed a kiss to her knee, then paid attention to every nook and curve of her legs before standing and removing his shirt while simultaneously kicking off his shoes. Next came his pants, leaving him in only his boxer briefs.

Now they were getting somewhere. And, whoa, Linc had quite a body. She couldn't wait to get her hands and mouth all over him. In fact, she started to get up to do just that, but he leaned over her, giving her shoulder a gentle shove to lay her down on the bed. He swept his fingertip across the curve of one breast, then the other, making her breath catch.

He captured that breath with his lips covering hers. She

reached up, needing to feel that contact of his warm skin touching hers as his tongue slid into her mouth, eliciting shivers, making every part of her hyperaware of every part of him—especially that hard part of him pressing against her thigh.

And his hands. They were everywhere, sliding along her rib cage, cupping her butt, exploring every inch of her skin and making her writhe against him because she needed him to touch more of her. She wanted his hands everywhere, and when he teased his fingertips across the top of her bra, the sensation shot straight south to her core. In response, she reached up, sliding her hands along his arms, feeling all that muscle bunch and tense beneath her palms.

She lifted her hips against his cock and was rewarded with his deep, guttural groan. It felt good knowing he was as into this as she was, that he felt the same intense desire that swept her along like a storm.

She pulled her lips from his, staring up at his meltingly sexy brown eyes.

"How about we get totally naked?" she asked.

The corners of his lips tipped up. "I like that idea." He reached underneath her and with one deft movement had the clasp of her bra undone.

"Hmm. You're very good at that. I think you've done that before."

"A time or two." He pressed a kiss to her shoulder, then pulled the straps of her bra down her arms, removing it and tossing it aside, baring her breasts. He cupped them gently, then slid his tongue over one nipple, making her gasp.

"Oh, yes," she whispered, nearly dying from the excruciating pleasure.

Until he did the same to the other. Then "yes" nearly became "oh my God," and she was certain this was some kind of a near-death experience from having her nipples licked and sucked.

But, hey, it had been a long dry spell, and she desperately needed some action. And this was some serious action.

After thoroughly lavishing attention on her breasts, he kissed his way across her rib cage and down her stomach, lingering at the edge of her underwear. And then he gently started rolling them down, kissing her hip bone, the top of her sex, and finally peeling her panties down her legs. He made eye contact with her, his expression dark and delicious with intent before he spread her legs and went down on her.

She momentarily lost the ability to breathe when his mouth made contact with her clit. The only thing she could think of was to beg her body not to come too fast. But oh, she was getting there because Linc had apparently zeroed in on exactly the right spot, sliding his tongue over and over at exactly that place that felt so good. And she couldn't help herself; it was too good and she needed this orgasm so badly.

She might have screamed. She couldn't say for sure because she also might have blacked out when she came. All she could remember was lying on the bed like she'd just run a marathon, even though she was pretty certain that whole thing had taken no more than fifteen seconds.

Linc climbed up and braced his hands on either side of her. "Needed that, didn't you?"

"You might say that."

"Then let's see if we can give you another one." He climbed off the bed and dropped his boxer briefs, leaving him in his naked glory.

Wow. Just . . . wow. Lean muscle and beautiful all over. And that hard cock just waiting to slide inside of her. She rose up to a kneeling position so she could run her hands over his body, hearing his sharp intake of breath. She liked knowing she had that effect on him.

"I like the feel of your hands on me," he said.

She smoothed her palms across his chest, then slowly snaked them down his stomach. "I like touching you."

When she grasped hold of his cock, winding her fingers around the width of him, he let out a groan. She stroked him, gently, loving how he pushed against her hand.

"Enough," he said, his voice going low as he slid his arm around her and tugged her close. "You'll make me come, and I want to be in you when I do."

His words made her insides quiver. "Then let's do it. I'm definitely ready."

"Me, too." He reached over into the nightstand and withdrew a condom, tearing the wrapper. "I want you to know I don't have indiscriminate sex, Hazel. I'm pretty choosy about my partners and I'm always careful."

This shouldn't have been a sexy conversation to have while she watched Linc put on a condom, but hell if it didn't turn her on like mad. She scooted to the center of the bed. "I haven't been with anyone since my ex. And that was a while ago."

"It's been six months for me," he said, climbing onto the bed and parting her legs with his knee, teasing the skin of her leg with the tips of his fingers. "And that was a yearlong relationship."

Breathless with anticipation, she reached for him. "Then I'd say we're good, don't you think?"

"Oh, I think it's gonna be really good." He nestled his body on top of hers, and Hazel wasn't sure she'd ever felt anything so good. He kissed her, and it was deep and passionate. She lost herself in the sensation of his lips and his tongue and his wandering hands. And when he slipped his cock inside her inch by slow inch, she moaned against his lips, taking in the exquisite sensation of being filled by him.

She wrapped her legs around him and arched, wanting him deep. He began to move against her and it was so, so good. It was as if Linc's body had been made for hers. The barely functioning logical side of her knew that was ridiculous, but, hey, he was hitting all her happy buttons, so she could feel however she wanted about how perfect this was. All she knew was that this man was going to give her an awesome screaming orgasm, and there was zero logic involved in how she felt about that.

It was glorious to be in a man's arms, to feel tickling hairs as she ran her foot along his leg, to slide her hands across the sweat-soaked muscles of his back, and to reach up and tangle her fingers in the softness of his hair. His strong, masculine scent permeated her senses like the most powerful aphrodisiac, and the way he looked at her while he fucked her made everything inside her twist and tumble like an enthusiastic gymnast.

She felt both languorous with sensual warmth and amped

with energy and didn't know what to do with all these sensations bombarding her. She finally took a breath and decided to just go with it before she ended up crying from the utter joy of this experience.

Bottom line—this all just felt really damned spectacular, and she wanted it to last forever, but it was too good and she was so close. He swept his hand underneath her to grasp hold of her butt, which tilted her pelvis up, allowing him to drive even deeper and slide his magnificent cock against her clit, and that was all she needed to release. And oh, it was a good climax, making her cry out and dig her heels into him as she shuddered through waves of orgasm that sent him into his own climax. And when he gripped her hips and began to barrel into her with force, she kept going, surprising her with the intensity of sensation that seemed to go on and on. And on. And maybe on again. She'd lost all sense of time, so she really wasn't sure, because now she was floating on a cloud of satiated happiness.

"Hey."

She blinked to find Linc lying next to her, a sexy grin on his face. She turned on her side. "Hey."

"I don't know about you, but that was pretty amazing."

She shrugged. "It was okay."

He laughed and drew her against him. "You screamed. Twice."

"I did?"

"Yeah, you did."

"Huh. I don't remember that. Then again, I might have had an out-of-body experience. You're very good at this. We should do this again. A lot."

"Agree. But right now I'm sweaty. And thirsty."

She nodded. "Same. I'll get water, you turn on the shower."

She threw on her underwear and shirt and went downstairs, letting the dogs in and locking the door. Then she fixed two ice waters and carried those upstairs to Linc's bedroom.

The dogs had already found him, so he was leaning down and petting them.

"I don't hear the water running," she said as she handed him a glass.

He got up and took several long swallows before answering. "I thought if you wanted to get sweaty again, the shower would be a waste of time."

She took a few sips of water, then set the glass down on the nightstand. "Good point. We can shower later."

She pushed him on the bed and climbed on top of him.

CHAPTER THIRTEEN

*L*inc was covered in sweat. The problem with working in Florida, especially a high-humidity environment like Orlando, was that even in the fall, it was still fucking hot. But he had work to do today, and despite the sweat pouring like a river down his back, he still had to lay flooring.

It didn't help that every time he took a break to rest his back and knees and sat down, Gordon came over and plopped himself in Linc's lap, his furry little body pressing against Linc's sweaty jeans. But the dog went to sleep and started to snore, and Linc's bottle of water was nearby, so whatever. He leaned against the wall and pulled out his phone to check in on what was going on.

There were a few emails from his investment company, so he answered those first. He was lucky to be able to work remotely, and he had a great staff who handled everything so he could be out here doing what he loved. He only occasionally had to be in the office to handle in-person business, which suited him just fine. He'd spent the first five years building his company up and hiring all the right people who could do the job without him looking over their shoulders. He trusted every single one of them to get it done, and so far it had worked out perfectly.

He frowned when he saw a group email from his two brothers and some lame suggestion about fixing Mom up on a date.

Warren seemed to think Mom was lonely and it was high time she started dating again. Eugene thought it was a good idea and made some suggestions for dating sites.

"Good God," he whispered, shaking his head. He quickly answered with: *No. Bad idea.* Hopefully, that would put an end to it. If Mom wanted to start dating, he was certain she could find her own man without help from those two idiots Warren and Eugene.

"Comfy?"

He looked up to see Hazel standing there wearing her swimsuit cover-up. "As comfy as Gordon's going to let me get. Taking a dip?"

"I thought I might. I was scrubbing bathrooms and got hot, so I thought I'd cool off in the pool. Care to join me?"

What he should do was finish this section of flooring in the living room. But what harm would it do to take a break? He was sweaty, after all. Maybe a cooldown would help motivate him.

You want to hang out with Hazel, don't you? Maybe do a little kissing.

Hell yeah, he did. He got up and stretched. "I'll meet you outside."

Her lips curved. "Okay. I'll make us some lemonade."

"Sounds great."

He went upstairs to wash off the sweat and changed into his board shorts, happy to be out of those jeans. He could wear shorts to work, but being on bare knees to lay flooring? Not his idea of a good time. He'd rather sweat.

He went outside and was immediately bombarded by the dogs, so he squatted down to give them all some love. He saw that Hazel had left a glass of lemonade on the table and smiled. He took a couple of swallows of the icy, sweet drink before heading over to the pool. Hazel was already in the water just floating around.

It actually felt better outside than it did in the house, even though the air-conditioning was in working order. Out here there was a nice breeze. Add in the water and this was going to be great. He dived right into the deep end, the cold water immediately refreshing him. He swam underneath the water toward the shallow end, surfacing alongside Hazel. He smoothed his hands over his hair and smiled at her.

"Better?" she asked.

"Much."

"You were looking a little hot in there."

"Just a little?"

She laughed. "Correction. You're always hot. I meant you were sweating."

"Yeah, I was putting in the work today, for sure. This break is nice. Even better is spending it with you."

He put his arm around her and pulled her toward him. She immediately wrapped her legs around him and held on to him while he walked them around the water toward the shaded part of the pool. He quickly checked the dogs. Gordon and Lilith were underneath the palm tree curled up together, while Penny was asleep under the table on the porch. Freddie was digging up something in the far part of the yard. He made a mental note to fix the hole later. Right now he was more interested in the beautiful woman in his arms. He pressed her against the side of the pool, and she wrapped a cool, wet hand around the back of his neck, bringing her mouth to his.

Despite the coolness of the water, that kiss fired up every part of him to overheated levels. They'd only had that one night together a few days ago—so far. Then Hazel had seemed content to stay in her own room, which was fine. He didn't want to pressure her for more, but the long, hot looks they shared every day were driving him mad.

And now, with her lips moving under his and her body undulating against him, all he could think about was touching her, getting her naked, and putting his mouth all over her.

He scooped her up in his arms and started to slide his fingers into the cup of her bikini top when he heard a distinct cough above them.

"Well, Hazel. I see that you have company."

He didn't know who the woman standing there was, but Hazel nearly fell underwater as she scrambled to get out of Linc's grasp.

"Nat. What are you doing here?"

"I rang the bell but no one answered. Door was unlocked. I let myself in."

"I mean what are you doing *here*?"

The person named Nat shrugged. "You haven't answered my text messages or phone calls. Mom and I have been worried."

"I'm fine, as you can see."

"Oh yes, I can see all right. And who's this guy?"

Linc heard Hazel sigh. "Linc Kennedy, meet my sister, Natalie."

Her sister? Linc looked from Natalie to Hazel's extremely mortified face.

Well, shit.

CHAPTER FOURTEEN

*I*f there was one thing Hazel knew for certain about her big sister, it was that Nat had always had the worst timing ever. From the time she'd found Hazel masturbating in her room to when she'd caught her smoking weed with her friends in the backyard to that one—and only—time she'd snuck a boy into her room, Nat could always be counted on to make an appearance at the worst possible moment.

Like now, when Linc had just about had a handful of her breast and his mouth had been firmly planted on hers. Things had been hot and heavy—and going so well—until Nat had showed up.

How typical.

"Okay, so now I know his name," Nat said, looking suspicious and her typical holier-than-thou as she regarded Linc. "But who the hell is he?"

"I'm the handyman," Linc said, winking at Hazel as he hauled himself out of the pool. "I think I'll go work some more on the floor so you can visit with your sister. Nice to meet you, Natalie."

"Mm-hmm," was all Nat said, eyeing Linc critically.

Shaking her head while simultaneously rolling her eyes, Hazel walked over to the steps and out of the pool, then grabbed a towel to dry herself. She should make her sister stand there in the sun, considering Nat was wearing black capri pants and a short-sleeved blouse and pointy-toed canvas shoes, though she had no idea why she was so overdressed when it was eighty-something degrees outside. Then again, she'd never been able to decipher Nat, so why start now?

Hazel pulled her cover-up on and went to the table where she'd left her glass of lemonade.

"Something to drink?" she asked after she had a sip, then took a seat, motioning for her sister to do the same.

Natalie sat. "No, I'm fine, thank you. What I want to know is what the hell is going on here."

The dogs had come over to sniff Nat, but she shooed them away with her foot so they wandered off. Nat had never been a dog person, and she sure as hell wouldn't want any at her showplace of a house. Hazel had been surprised when Nat had popped out two children, seeing as how they were messier than dogs. Then again, knowing her sister, she probably had those kids well trained. Nat wasn't known to be relaxed or easygoing. Or fun.

"Nothing's going on here. Other than Linc is renovating the house and I'm still fostering dogs."

Nat literally looked down her nose at Hazel. "Really, Hazel. Playing house with the hot handyman?"

"We're not playing house and he's not a handyman. He owns this place."

"Oh, really. Since when?"

"Since he bought it from Ginger and Greg. He buys and reno-vates homes."

"And he's just letting you stay here. With the dogs. How convenient."

She could only imagine what her sister was thinking. The issue was—did she care?

Probably, since whatever was rolling around in Nat's head would soon be reported to their mother. And the last thing Hazel wanted was for Mom to show up here, so she needed to make the situation very clear.

"Actually, he employed me. I'm cooking for him."

"Obviously, that's not all you're doing for him."

Nat just had to see that, didn't she? She could try and explain what was happening between Linc and her, but it was new and she didn't exactly understand it herself. Besides, the last thing she wanted was interference from her sister.

"What I'm doing with Linc is none of your business."

"I'm worried about you."

Sister speak for *I want to know every sordid detail*, emphasis on *sordid*.

"Don't be. I'm fine. I'm putting money away so that I'll be able to get my own place soon."

"A place without the dogs, hopefully."

"Nat, it's what I love to do. So no, not without the dogs."

Natalie brushed her hair back from her face and sighed. "This so-called career of yours is getting you nowhere. Which is exactly what Mom told you, like when we warned you about Andrew—"

She shot Natalie a scathing look. "Do not mention my ex-husband's name to me again. It's over, and it's in the past. I'm moving forward now."

Natalie sighed. "I get it. He made some mistakes. Which doesn't mean—"

Nat had always been the one to list Andrew's shortcomings while simultaneously defending him, as if Hazel should hold on to him like he was the only man who'd ever want her.

"He cheated on me. More than once."

Nat waved her hand back and forth. "Men and their penises. You just have to learn how to control them."

She wasn't about to get into a discussion about the philosophy of a successful marriage with her sister, whose antiquated way of thinking about men made her blood boil. "Speaking of children, where are Cammie and Christopher?"

"Camryn is in school and Christopher has started preschool." She looked at her phone. "I'm due to pick Christopher up at three thirty, then we'll swing by and get Camryn, take her to ballet class, and make it home in plenty of time for me to get dinner started before Sean comes home from work."

She caught the tension in Nat's voice. "Everything okay between you two?"

Nat gave her what Hazel could only consider her fakest bright smile. "Of course. Why would you ask that? Everything is perfect. Sean's job is amazing and he's busy all the time. And the kids are so busy with all their activities that I barely have time to go to my yoga and Pilates classes, but Sean insists that I keep myself in tip-top shape."

And, again, that slight note of tension in her voice, no doubt the stress of trying to be the perfect wife and mother.

"Don't you miss being an interior designer, Nat? You were so good at it."

For a second there, the facade fell away and she saw genuine misery on her sister's face. But she quickly masked it again. "Of course not. I'm totally fulfilled. And very busy taking care of Sean and the kids."

"You know you don't have to be everything to everybody, Nat. It's okay to take a day for yourself every now and then to do what you love. Or maybe just relax a little."

"I don't know what you're talking about." She swept her hair back, though not a single hair was out of place, as always. "I am relaxed and my life is perfect."

"Uh-huh. I used to think the same thing until my husband cheated on me and ran off with all our money. But you do you, honey."

Nat stood. "I just stopped by out of concern for you. If you're going to pick a fight with me, I'll leave."

She had been doing that. "I'm sorry. I just felt . . . judged, and I took it out on you."

"I would never judge you. Worry about you? Absolutely. I only want what's best for you, Hazel. Mom and I both want what's best for you."

Hazel could already imagine the conversation Nat and Mom were going to have tonight after Nat filled her in on what she'd seen. But Hazel could only worry about the things she could control, and she'd learned a long time ago that she had zero control over her sister or her mother.

"Anyway, I'm glad you stopped by," she said as they moved through the side yard toward the front of the house. "Maybe we could have lunch sometime soon. We could invite Mom to come, too."

"I'll mention it to her and we'll make plans. You should call her, too. She'll worry less if she hears your voice."

What Natalie meant was that Mom would be happier if she could lecture Hazel about all the things she's doing wrong with her life. "Yeah, I'll do that."

They stopped at Natalie's car. "Thanks, Nat."

Nat patted her arm. "We'll talk soon."

She got into her car and drove away, and Hazel exhaled, realizing she held so much tension her shoulders were nearly covering her ears. She let them drop, then turned to see Linc watching from the garage, so she made her way toward him.

"Tense?" he asked.

"Normal."

"I noticed no hugs or 'I love you's. Did you have a fight?"

"Not at all. My family isn't affectionate."

He pulled her against him. "But you are."

She laughed and smoothed her hand over his chest. "Well, I had it all saved up."

"And I'm the beneficiary? Lucky me."

He kissed her, and all the tension she'd been holding immediately dissolved.

There was nothing like a passionate man to make you forget all your troubles. At least temporarily.

"I've got a fun idea that might cheer you up," he said.

She arched a brow, hoping said idea was hot sex and several orgasms. "I'm listening."

"I have to head home for a few days to take care of some business. I thought maybe you'd want to come with me."

So . . . not hot sex. And not at all doable. "I can't."

He shot her a curious look. "Why not?"

"Because of the dogs."

"You can't get someone to watch them for you?"

She opened her mouth to immediately say no, then realized that was wrong. "I . . . could."

"But you don't want to? And hey, it's fine if you don't want to come with me."

"No, it's not that." She rubbed her temple and immediately started pacing. "It's just complicated. I'd have to ask the director of the foster agency to keep an eye on the dogs. Which would mean they'd have to stay with her. She has a lot of acreage, so she has the space, but still."

"You're worried about the pups."

"Yeah."

"Hey, it's fine. Forget I asked. Of course the dogs and their needs have to come first." He picked up his hammer and went back inside.

Hazel grimaced, staring at the closed door where Linc had disappeared.

The dogs loved Sandy. They'd all been with her before they'd come to live with Hazel. She trusted Sandy with her babies. And Sandy would absolutely let her have this short break. The only one stopping her from going on this trip with Linc was . . . herself.

So why did she say no? Was she afraid of going away with Linc, or was she afraid if she let go of the dogs she might not get them back? Or that possibly Sandy would find someone to adopt them all while she was gone?

Wasn't that the objective, though? Didn't she want her babies to find happy, fulfilling lives—with other families?

Now she felt more conflicted than ever. But she couldn't stop herself from living her life. Or letting her pups live theirs, no matter where that road might lead. She took out her phone and sent a text message to Sandy, who replied almost right away, saying she'd be happy to take care of the dogs for as long as Hazel needed. And then she'd assured her that the pups would be fine while she was gone, which she was absolutely right about.

Okay, that part was done. Now to talk to Linc. She went into the house and found Linc working on the living room floor.

"So . . . about that trip."

He looked up at her. "Yeah?"

"Can I change my mind?"

He stood. "Always. Have you?"

"I have. I'd really like to go with you."

"Then it's done. I'll make the arrangements." He took out his phone, then looked over at her. "We can stay at my condo. It's a two-bedroom if you'd like your own room."

She cocked her head to the side. "Why would I want that?"

"I mean, I know we've been together, but I didn't want to assume."

She appreciated that he would do that. But when he suggested she take this trip with him, the only thing she could think about was sharing a bed with him. Unless . . .

"Do you want to have your own room?" she asked.

He walked toward her and leaned over, brushing his lips across hers. "Hell no."

"Then it's settled. I can't wait to see your place."

"It's not fancy."

"Perfect. Neither am I."

Suddenly, she was really looking forward to this trip with Linc.

CHAPTER FIFTEEN

*T*he last thing Linc wanted to do in the middle of a renovation project was fly home, but he had some client and staff meetings to take care of that couldn't be put off any longer, so he'd had no choice.

The benefit of doing so was bringing Hazel with him. He was happy she'd agreed, and he hoped like hell he could show her a good time. That she relaxed, had fun, and didn't think about anything back home. At least not all the time, anyway.

And now they were on a plane, making their approach to San Francisco International Airport.

"How much work do you have to do while you're here?" she asked as she looked out the window, watching the plane's descent.

"Probably just a day's worth."

"Not too bad."

"I can arrange for you to have a tour of the city."

She pulled her attention from the window and onto him. "I have a phone and a map and I've already looked up places to go— and to eat at. I'll be fine. But thanks."

"Sure."

He'd called his mom to let her know he was going to be in town, and of course she'd insisted he stay with her. Bringing Hazel with him would have made that incredibly awkward, so he'd told his mom he had a lot of meetings in the city, some going late at night, so that wasn't going to be possible. He hated lying, but there were just some things he wasn't ready to do, and pushing his family onto Hazel was one of them. His mother was heaven on earth, and she would welcome Hazel with open arms, no problem. But if he stayed at the house, his brothers would invariably show up, and then Hazel would be bombarded with an inquisition, so, no way was he going to expose her to his family.

But he hadn't been home in a couple of months. And since he wasn't full up with meetings with clients and staff, he'd have some time to see his mom while he was there.

She'd never forgive him otherwise.

After landing, they made their way to the rental cars, where he picked up the car he'd reserved, put their luggage in the trunk, and drove to his condo.

He'd bought a condo in the perfect location. He could walk to his office, plus there were several interesting sites for Hazel to see all within walking distance. They pulled up out front, and he gave his keys to the valet, figuring it would be a day or so before they'd need the car again, then walked inside. He'd also invested in a place with full amenities, including valet, a doorman, a gym, and an indoor pool. He made sure Hazel's name was added to his guest list so she could come and go as she pleased, and make use of all the facilities without question.

Keys in hand, they made their way to the elevator and headed up to the unit.

He held the door while Hazel walked in. She rolled her suitcase to the side and placed it against the wall.

"Wow," she said as she headed to the slate of windows. "This is really nice, Linc."

The open floor plan had been his number one requirement. "It's not huge, but I like to be able to spread out." He put his suitcase next to hers and joined her by the windows.

"You can see the bay from here," she said. "Oh, and there's a balcony."

"It'll probably be cool and windy outside. But at least you can get some fresh air if you want to."

"The sun's out. Let's chance it." She unlocked the sliding door and stepped out, pulling her cardigan together as the wind whipped around her.

Linc was used to the weather in San Francisco. The wind could be blustery, if not downright violent at times. Today it was actually fairly mild, but they were higher up and near the bay. It was sunny, not a cloud—or fog—to mar the day.

"It's beautiful," she said. "You must have loved growing up here."

"I was raised quite a bit inland, but trips to the city were always a treat. As far as working here? It doesn't suck, and my clients who live here like it. The ones who fly in enjoy being in the city. It's a win-win."

She looked around. "I imagine it's expensive for your employees to commute here. Or live here."

He nodded. "It's definitely one of the most expensive places to live in the country. Some of my people telecommute and only come in for critical meetings. Also, they're paid very well."

"I suppose that helps, too." She went inside so he followed, closing the door behind him.

She hadn't once asked him questions about his income, or how he could afford such luxury. She asked about his work and seemed genuinely interested in what he did for a living. Otherwise, she wasn't invasive about his money, and he liked that about her. He liked it a lot.

He busied himself with unpacking while Hazel made a call, obviously to the person who was watching the dogs, since he heard her mention all their names. When she finished, she grabbed her suitcase and came into the bedroom to unpack, turning to face him halfway through. "I'd love to explore the city," she said. "It would help me get my bearings for tomorrow."

"Sounds great. I heard you on the phone. How are the dogs?"

She shook her head. "Sandy spoils and pampers them. They'll be ridiculous when we get back and it'll take me forever to get them on a routine again."

"Yeah, but worth it."

"You're right about that."

He grabbed his jacket. "Are you ready to head out?"

She changed from her cardigan to a zip-up jacket. "Let's go."

He took her for a long walk, telling her where they were and all the places she could wander to tomorrow, like the Embarcadero, the Ferry Building Marketplace, and the Exploratorium, all of which were less than a fifteen-minute walk. Hazel made notes in her phone, and though he asked if she wanted to stop at any of the locations, she shook her head, saying she was just enjoying the walk and the fresh air for now.

"How about a cable car ride?" he asked as they approached one of the hop-on points during their walk.

"I'd love one."

They waited until a car arrived, then climbed on, along with several other people. He'd done this so many times since he was a kid, but it was still fun to ride the car, especially with someone who'd never experienced it before. Hazel held on to the pole along with grasping his hand, as if she half expected the car to catapult her like some kind of violent amusement park ride. He wrapped his arm around her to hold on to her, even though it wasn't necessary. Then again, holding Hazel wasn't exactly a hardship.

The ride was steady and not too fast as they made their way toward Pier 39 and Fisherman's Wharf. Along the way he pointed out spots she might want to stop and get off at tomorrow should she decide to ride the cable car by herself and explore. She nodded but didn't make notes this time. Her body was tense, but she was smiling.

"You okay?" he asked.

"Yes. This is amazing. Do people commute this way?"

"Some do, yes."

"Incredible."

When they made it to the wharf, they got off and he walked her toward the pier.

"I've read about this and seen it in movies," she said. "I've always wanted to come here."

They grabbed something cold to drink from a vendor and wandered along the pier. There were attractions and shops and just about anything and everything, but Hazel seemed content to just walk and watch, which suited Linc just fine.

"I hear the seals," she said, grinning at him as they got close to the end of the pier. She picked up her step and he did as well.

The pier was covered with seals of all sizes, their loud bellowing like an insistent complaint. Or maybe an urgent request for someone to bring them some herring.

Hazel leaned against the railing, pulled out her phone and started recording, then took some pictures. She was giving those seals the kinds of emotional, loving looks that made him feel kind of jealous.

"They're great, aren't they?" he asked.

She glanced over at him briefly before turning her attention back to the seals. "They're gorgeous. And so gloriously loud. I love them."

Of course she did. She'd probably want to slip one in her luggage and bring it home, where it could live out its days in the backyard pool.

Eventually, he pried her away from the seals and they made their way down the wharf, exploring a few shops where she wanted to buy absolutely nothing.

"Really? Not even souvenirs or a T-shirt?"

She shook her head. "The experience is all I need. Besides, I'm taking pics." She grabbed him and leaned in, snapping a photo of the two of them, then showed it to him.

They were both smiling, and Hazel had laid her head against his shoulder. It was a perfect picture of the two of them. He hadn't realized before how well they fit together.

"It's a pretty good shot," he said.

"I think so, too."

"Send it to me?"

She nodded. "Sure." She pulled up his number and texted it to him. When his phone buzzed, he brought up the pic and saved it, then realized he had no other pics of her, and hadn't ever taken any of her and the dogs. He made a mental note to rectify that when they got back home.

Home. He mentally paused when he realized that the house they currently shared wasn't his home. Or hers. It was a temporary thing, just like their relationship. So why had he called it home?

"I'm getting kind of hungry," she said. "How about you?"

"I can always eat." He looked at his phone, realizing it was nearly six thirty. "We can head back to the condo, change for dinner."

"Oh, we're dressing up for dinner tonight?"

"Hell yeah, we are."

She looped her arm in his. "Okay, then. Let's go get fancy."

*H*azel was relieved to have raided her boxes of stuff at Sandy's and brought a nice dress for dinner. It wasn't super expensive, but it was a gorgeous burgundy, hit just above the knees, and fit her perfectly. It would be suitable—she hoped—for any restaurant Linc decided to take her to. She'd combed through her hair, touched it up with a bit of wave, then put on makeup and lip gloss along with her heels. She felt good and more than ready to enjoy a night out in San Francisco with her guy.

Her guy. Was he, though?

He took you on a trip to another city, Hazel. That's got to mean something, right?

She supposed it did. What exactly it meant, she didn't know, and it wasn't like she planned to bring up the status of their relationship over dinner. This was a fun trip. Business for him, total relaxation and touristy stuff for her. Whatever else happened would just . . . happen. Right now she was looking forward to a relaxing evening of cocktails and dinner and hopefully an amazing view.

She came out of the bathroom, and Linc was dressed in black pants, a black-striped button-down shirt, and a jacket. He looked . . . Damn, he was a fine-looking man no matter whether he was in dusty jeans or dressed up like this.

"Wow," he said, walking over to her and taking her hands in his. "You are gorgeous."

"You're full of hyperbole."

"Not even lying. You look beautiful, Hazel."

"Thank you. You clean up nice, too." She laid her palm on his chest. "I guess we're both beautiful tonight."

"I'll take it. Shall we go?"

"I guess we shall?"

She grabbed her wrap and slung it over her arm, then slid her other arm through Linc's as they made their way downstairs to the lobby. Admittedly, she felt kind of special as she walked with Linc, certain that the people they passed by were staring at him. After all, he was tall and good-looking, and dressed up like this he was kind of perfect. But then she realized that couples were staring as well, so maybe it was both of them.

"People are staring," she said as they made their way through the lobby.

Linc looked around, then down at her, smiling. "Because you're hot as hell and have amazing legs."

"I don't think they're all looking at me."

"And I don't think they're all looking at me."

"Some might be."

He laughed. "Okay, I'll take that. How about everyone thinks we make a spectacular couple?"

She thought about that as they reached the doors, looked up at him, and grinned. "And I'll take that."

Their car was waiting for them outside, which was perfect timing. Linc held the door for her and she slid inside the back seat, Linc following her.

She had no idea where they were going. Since he was more familiar with the area, including places to eat, she trusted his judgment. Plus, she liked food in general, so she was up for anything. Mainly, she enjoyed the ride, sitting next to a hot man while taking in the incredibly beautiful city.

They ended up at Ghirardelli Square, right near where they'd been earlier in the day, at a restaurant called McCormick & Kuleto's. The restaurant was warm and atmospheric, and they were seated near the full windows that lent an incredible view of the bay, the boats swaying in time with the water.

"This is incredible," she said after their hostess left them with menus.

"I thought you might like a view. Plus the food here is amazing."

"I'm a fan of food." She opened her menu and started perusing, her stomach doing flip-flops over the amazing selections.

Their server came over and discussed drink orders.

"Would you like a bottle of wine or something more specific, like one of their craft cocktails?" Linc asked.

Hazel looked at the cocktails, immediately intrigued. "Hmm. I'm thinking I might like to try the prosecco sangria."

Linc nodded. "Good choice. I'll have a Guinness stout."

Their server nodded and disappeared.

"Thank you for taking me to dinner," she said. "This is lovely."

"I want you to enjoy this trip. San Francisco is all about good food and great sights."

"I'm really looking forward to sightseeing tomorrow."

He reached out and laid his hand over hers. "I'm sorry I can't go with you."

"Please don't feel bad. It's totally okay. You have work to do, which is why you're here, and I'm used to being on my own."

"Okay. But don't be surprised if I text you throughout the day to make sure you're doing all right."

She would not tell him how special that made her feel. "That'll be fine."

"And if you run into any problems, you call me right away."

"I will absolutely not do that. Again, you'll be working."

He gave her a stern look, which admittedly was kind of a turn-on.

"Hazel, you have to promise."

"Fine. I promise, but I won't run into any problems at all."

Their server came by with their drinks. Hazel took a sip, delighted by the sweet, bubbly flavor. "This is so good."

Linc took a swallow of his beer. "You like fruity drinks?"

She laughed. "I like all kinds of drinks. Beer, wine, cocktails, shots."

He arched a brow. "Shots, huh?"

"Of course. There's nothing like a smooth tequila on its own."

"I agree with that. We'll have to do shots sometime."

Hazel could already imagine how much fun that could be. "I'll make a note to put tequila on the shopping list."

"You do that."

She wondered if he was even aware that while they were talking he was drawing circles and other shapes on her hand with his fingertip. He might not notice, but every part of her definitely did. What was it about his touch that got to her?

"Your city is beautiful," she said, trying to disengage her sensory reactions to his skating fingertip. "How could you possibly want to leave it?"

He shrugged. "Yeah, it's really nice here. But so are other places in the U.S. and I wanted to see them."

She took a sip of her cocktail, studying him. "What made you decide to go into renovating houses?"

"I hate to be cliché, but I'm gonna do it anyway and say I've always liked doing things with my hands. Working in investments has been fun. It engages my brain in all the right ways."

"But not exactly a physical workout."

"No. When I got the business up and running and put the right people in place, I knew I could take off for long periods of time, popping in when needed. Which meant I could take six to eight weeks to renovate a house, then head back here, take a week or two to catch up before I start the process over again."

He was so confident about who he was and where he wanted to be. She wished she'd had that level of self-assuredness about any aspect of her life, instead of floundering for so long about . . . everything.

Their server came and took their food orders. After, Hazel took several sips of her outstanding cocktail while pondering her life choices versus how Linc seemed to have it totally together.

"You're staring," he said.

"I am? I was. I'm sorry. I was just thinking about your confidence level, how you seem to know exactly what you were meant to do."

He swirled his fingers around his glass. "You'd like to think that, but it wasn't always the case. I started out working in finance. I was good at it, but God, I was bored. I knew right away I didn't want to work for someone else. I had all these ideas about what I wanted to do, investments I wanted to make in real estate."

"And you obviously did."

"Eventually, yeah. But I had to save money. I lived at home for the first five years after college, banking every penny I could save. Then I took the leap and started my investment firm, hoping and praying and lying awake nights scared shitless that I would fail."

She cocked her head to the side. "You don't strike me as someone who's afraid of anything."

"Thanks for that, but trust me, I was plenty scared. But I plowed headfirst into this dream of mine, figuring I would either succeed fantastically or fail dramatically. I got lucky and the business took off, thanks to my amazing team."

She loved that he gave credit to the people around him instead of taking all the glory for himself. "I'm sure you had something to do with it, too."

"Maybe a little, but like I've told you before, I have outstanding people working for me. I couldn't have gotten this far without them."

"Then you are one of the lucky ones."

"Don't I know it."

Their server brought drink refills, and Hazel stared out at the gorgeous sunset.

"I could definitely live here."

"In the city?"

"Yes. It's teeming with life and excitement. I can't wait to get out there tomorrow and check it all out."

He laid his glass down. "Yeah, you should definitely do that. San Francisco is an amazing city."

"I like what I've seen so far."

"What are some of your favorite places you've been?"

"Oh . . . uh . . ." She swept her hair behind her ear. "I haven't exactly traveled all that much."

"That's okay. Where have you been?"

"My ex and I went to Miami for our honeymoon, and then one year in college I went to the Bahamas over spring break."

He didn't say anything right away until he realized she had finished talking.

"You know it's okay that you haven't been to a lot of places. Many people never leave their hometown."

"Well, I've definitely done that. I've driven all over Florida. I'm pretty sure I've been to damned near every beach in that state."

He leaned back in his chair. "You like the beach, huh?"

"I do love the beach. How are the beaches here?"

"The water on this side of the country is cold. Not like the Atlantic. But the beaches can be really nice."

"I just like being at the beach, not necessarily in the water."

"Same. Though there's good surfing here if you decide you want to take that up on your touring tomorrow."

She laughed. "I think I'll leave the surfing to the experts. Not that I wouldn't want to try it someday."

"Next trip we'll hit up Hawaii. Surfing is amazing there."

"Don't tease me."

"With what?"

"A next trip that we'll never take."

He frowned. "Why would you think we'd never take it?"

She opened her mouth to say that they were temporary and the likelihood of the two of them ever going to Hawaii was slim, but that was the negative side of her. "I don't know. It's so far from Florida. And you have business to take care of."

He shrugged. "It never hurts to think about an awesome vacation, now does it?"

"I guess it doesn't."

The one thing that scared her about Linc was that he kept giving her hope for a future that didn't exist.

Even worse, she was starting to want that kind of future. The kind that included an extremely good-looking, incredibly kind man who also loved her dogs. The problem was, Linc didn't exist in her future, because as soon as he was finished with the house, he'd be off on his next renovation adventure, and she'd be . . .

Well, she'd be out of that house and going somewhere. Where that was, she didn't know just yet. But it wouldn't be with Linc. Time was running out on this fantasy between the two of them, and she needed to get in the right headspace to make her next move. She was already searching for rentals, and had found a couple that were within her price range. If she saved all her money, she could do this. And that was all she needed to be thinking about. Real, tangible things, not fantasies about jetting off to Hawaii with Linc.

Their food had started to arrive, giving her respite from her tortured thoughts. She first had the lobster bisque, followed by the clam linguine. Linc also had the bisque, but for his main course he'd opted for lobster. She was happy when he offered her a taste. The food was incredible, the sauces were perfection, and she made mental notes about dishes she wanted to try making at home.

By the time their server cleared their plates and asked about their interest in dessert, Hazel was utterly full and ready to walk off dinner. Fortunately, it was a nice night with no breeze, so they took a walk around the wharf to digest a bit.

"Dinner was amazing," she said. "Thank you for bringing me here."

"You're welcome."

He grasped her hand and they walked.

"Do you hear the seals?" he asked.

She paused, then smiled up at him. "Yes. They're very adorable, aren't they?"

"I guess if you like loud, smelly things, they are."

She laughed. "Hey, they're sea creatures. And they can't help how they smell." She gave a gentle shove of her shoulder against his arm.

"You're right, of course, and I won't disparage their incredibly bulky beauty."

"Now you're just making fun of me. Or them."

"Neither." He paused and peered into one of the shops. "Come with me."

She wasn't much of a souvenir person, but she was interested in what Linc could possibly want in this quirky little shop of wharf gifts. She followed him down the center row.

"Pick one," he said.

"Pick . . . oh." Her emotions were about to have a meltdown as she looked over all the stuffed seals on the shelf. "That is not necessary."

"Oh, but it is. A memory from your visit. Plus, you love them."

She chose the fattest, ugliest brown one and cuddled it against her chest. "This one."

"Okay, then." He took it from her and went to the register, paid for it, and told the person they wouldn't need a bag.

After they walked out, he handed it to her. She took his hand and held tightly to the seal.

They finally decided to call for a ride back to the condo, which suited Hazel just fine since the heels she wore were so very pretty but not necessarily awesome for walking in for any length of time. When the car arrived, she was ever so grateful to slide into the back seat. If it had been her own car, the heels would have been off and she'd have been done with them, but she'd just have to wait. Instead, she cuddled her seal and laid her head on Linc's shoulder, looking out the window to take in the bright lights of the city as they made their way back to the condo.

Between the wine and the full dinner and all the fresh air from the walk, Hazel was decidedly . . . relaxed. Maybe a little too relaxed, because her eyes drifted closed on the ride, and Linc had to lightly jostle her when their car pulled in front of the condo.

"Taking a short nap?" he asked as they made their way across the lobby toward the elevators.

"Mmm, just very content right now." She lifted her gaze to his while they rode up in the elevator alone. "I had a very good night."

His lips lifted. "Night's not over yet."

She leaned into him, pushing him against the wall of the elevator, then lifted up to press her lips to his. He wound his arms around her and kissed her, taking her breath away with the passion in that kiss. The way he kissed her, taking possession, squeezing her hips, holding her as if he never intended to let her go—all those things made her toes curl in her very awesome shoes.

The elevator doors opened onto their floor, so she broke the kiss and Linc took her hand again, leading her down the hall toward his condo. Her heart was still pumping maniacally from that hot kiss when he used his key and opened the door.

She kicked off her heels as soon as she walked into the room, then turned to face Linc. He removed his jacket and tossed it. His mouth was on hers in an instant, all hot and desperate and exactly what she needed. She lifted up and dragged her fingers through his hair, moaning against his lips as he reached down to palm her breast, sending sparks of utter deliciousness even through her dress and bra. But she wanted so much more, so she cupped his erection through his pants, torturing him in the same way, making him groan.

He grasped her butt and lifted her. She wrapped her legs around him, the hard ridge of his erection hitting her at a perfect spot to make her wish they were both naked right now.

This was not happening fast enough.

He walked over to the nightstand and grabbed a condom, then pressed her against the wall, undid his pants and dropped his boxer briefs, then pulled her underwear to the side, teasing her into a frenzy with his stroking fingers.

"Now," she said through panting breaths. "Inside me now."

"Condom," he groaned.

"Shit. Right. Let me have it." She took it from him and tore it open, removing the condom. They managed circus-level balancing moves while he got the condom on, both of them laughing at how awkward it was.

Awkward, and yet oh so hot. Then he repositioned her, slid his cock inside of her, and began to drive into her.

"Yes," she managed as he slammed into her with forceful strokes. "More. Harder."

It was intense, and as she went from one deep climax to another, she thought she might be having an out-of-body experience. Except she kept banging her head against the wall and that hurt, so there was that aspect of reality, and Linc's fingers dug into the flesh of her butt cheeks, which made her all too aware that this was not some dream. Just awesome, hard-driving sex.

And when he shuddered, she quaked, going over with him while he held her tightly and kissed her so deeply she thought she might die from breathing so hard.

He finally turned and dropped her onto the bed, falling onto it next to her.

Linc stared up at the ceiling. "My fingers are cramping, my arms are shaking, and I think I might die."

She rolled over and propped her arm up, resting her head on her hand. "So what you're saying is that the sex was good."

He laughed, then rolled over to give her a quick kiss. "Uh, a lot more than good." He disappeared into the bathroom while she got up and changed out of her dress and into pajama shorts and a loose tank top. She grabbed a bottled water and took several long swallows.

When Linc came out of the bathroom, he gave her a critical look.

"Whoa, whoa, whoa. You changed clothes. Or put different clothes on."

"Yes. I wanted out of that dress. Mostly the bra."

"And I wanted you naked. That before was just a warm-up."

She curled up against the pillows on the bed. "Well, I'm plenty warm now."

He undressed until he was gloriously naked, then came over and took the bottle of water from her hands. After gulping down a few swallows, he laid it on the nightstand and climbed onto the bed next to her, pulling her on top of him.

"I might need a minute to gain my strength back."

He was already hard underneath her. She laughed. "Liar."

"Okay, fine." He started to flip her over, but she pushed on his chest.

"Oh no. I like this position. To start, anyway."

He leaned against the pillows and grasped her hips. "You're in charge, ma'am."

She liked where this was going. She leaned in and pressed her lips to his.

CHAPTER SIXTEEN

Linc's meetings, both with clients and with his staff—had all gone exceptionally well. And the team had managed to pick up a new client today, which had made the trip totally worthwhile. After client meetings he and his staff discussed managing the new client's accounts, then he was done for the day.

What he hadn't expected was a message from his mom on his phone.

He'd planned to take some time to meet up with her while he was in town, so maybe she wanted to make arrangements. He punched in her number.

"You must be done working," she said.

He smiled. "Yeah, all wrapped up. How are you, Mom?"

"I'm fine. Come to dinner tonight."

He grimaced. He hadn't told his mom about Hazel, and he didn't want to leave Hazel in the city by herself tonight. "Yeah, I don't think I can do that."

"Do you have dinner with a client?"

He rubbed his temple. He'd never lied to his mother, not once in his entire life. He wasn't about to start now. "Not exactly. I brought a guest with me on this trip."

"Oh. A girlfriend?"

"No. Sort of. I don't know. It's undefined at the moment."

"Great. Bring her with you. Dinner's at seven. Love you."

She clicked off, leaving him staring at the phone.

He wasn't sure Hazel would be up to meeting his mother—and, knowing his family, also his two brothers. She might be intimidated or upset about it. As he headed back to the condo, he thought about how he was going to handle this if she said no.

By the time he walked into the lobby, he still hadn't formulated a plan. But he saw Hazel standing to the side of the lobby, typing something on her phone, so said plan had better come together, like, now.

"Hi, beautiful."

She startled, then smiled. "I was just about to text you. For a second I thought you were some weirdo hitting on me."

"I am some weirdo hitting on you."

She laughed, then tucked her phone into her bag and looped her arm with his as they made their way to the elevators. "How was your day?"

"It was good. Got everything done I wanted to. How about yours?"

"Amazing. I feel like I went everywhere, though I know I didn't because there's just so much to see. But I went to Chinatown, Coit

Tower, the Exploratorium, Golden Gate Park. This is such an amazing city."

"I'm glad you had fun." They got out on their floor, and he slipped his key into the door and held it open for her.

"I had so much fun. I wish we had a week to spend here. There's just so much to do and see."

"There's tomorrow, so we'll do a few more things."

"Awesome." She flopped down on the bed. "I'm exhausted."

He winced, knowing she'd rather have a quiet evening, just the two of them. He sat on the bed next to her. "So, my mom called."

She rolled over to face him. "Yeah? Are you going to take some time to go see her while you're here?"

"I had planned to. The thing is, she invited me to dinner at the house tonight."

"Oh, that's fine. I can order delivery and stay in."

"Yeah, about that. I also told her you were with me, so now you're invited to dinner tonight."

"Really." She tilted her head. "How do you feel about me meeting your mother?"

"I feel fine about it. How do you feel about it?"

"I'd love to. What should I wear?"

She was currently wearing dark capri pants and a T-shirt along with tennis shoes. "What you're wearing right now is just fine."

She sat up and patted his arm. "No, it's not. Give me a few minutes to freshen up and change clothes, and I'll be ready to go."

She disappeared into the bathroom.

Okay, that went better than expected. Hazel hadn't freaked

out, and now he was going to introduce the woman he was currently sort of living with to his mother.

Should make for an interesting evening.

*H*azel was so excited to meet Linc's mother. He was such an
awesome human, she couldn't wait to see how he'd grown up and
who was responsible for helping to make him the incredible man
he was today.

Plus she had to admit she was extremely curious about where
he'd grown up, and he'd told her his mom still lived in his
childhood home.

"Is it just your mom we'll be having dinner with?" she asked
on the drive across the Bay Bridge over to the East Bay toward
Pleasanton.

"I have no idea. Mom probably told my brothers I was bringing
you. They're nosy bastards, so knowing them, they'll probably
show up."

She laughed. "Awesome." You could tell a lot about a person
when you met their family. Then again, he'd met her sister and
likely thought she was a flipping fruitcake.

At least he hadn't had the joy of meeting her mother, and
hopefully it would stay that way.

They pulled into a one-story ranch style with a wide driveway.
It was painted white with dark green trim and expansive front
windows. The yard was beautifully landscaped with colorful flowers
and incredibly tall trees. She could imagine Linc and his brothers
climbing those trees when they were kids.

"It's a beautiful house, Linc."

"Thanks. It's pretty much like it's always been. My dad and my brothers and I did some renovations a few years before Dad passed away."

"Which is why it looks so amazing on the outside."

He smiled. "Mom had been after Dad to paint for several years, and it did make a difference. And once we were done with that, we realized it needed a new roof, and after that, guttering."

"Like dominoes."

He laughed. "Pretty much. And Mom decided it looked so good we needed to freshen up the landscape, so that was next."

"Now it's perfect."

"Yeah, it is. It's home. Always has been, always will be."

Her heart did a tumble at the warmth in his voice.

They got out and went to the front door. Before he had a chance to ring the bell or turn the knob, the door opened and there stood a tall, stunning woman with whiskey brown eyes and the brightest smile directed at Linc.

They stepped inside and the woman hugged him.

"You stay away too long," she said, giving him a squeeze before letting him go.

"Yeah, I know. I've been busy."

"Too busy," she said.

"Mom, this is Hazel Bristow. Hazel, my mother, Lisa Kennedy."

Lisa shook Hazel's hand. "It's a pleasure to meet you."

"You as well, Mrs. Kennedy."

"None of that. Call me Lisa. Welcome to our home. I have coffee, iced tea, and all kinds of booze. Let's go get acquainted."

Hazel followed Lisa into a beautiful kitchen with a decent-sized island and some pretty great appliances. But there was nothing fussy about it. There was fruit on the island, some glasses, and a newspaper. It looked homey and comfortable, and Hazel felt instantly at ease.

"What will you have to drink?" Lisa asked. "I'm having wine."

"Wine sounds good to me."

"I'm grabbing a beer," Linc said, obviously making himself right at home by heading to the fridge to grab a bottle of beer.

"Love your kitchen, Lisa," Hazel said.

"Oh, thank you. The boys and my husband did this. It's my favorite place in the house. I love to cook."

"Do you? Me, too. I actually cook for Linc. It's sort of my job."

Lisa handed Hazel a glass of sauvignon blanc that she'd poured for both of them. "Really. Do you have a restaurant?"

"Uh, not exactly." She wasn't sure how to explain their current situation.

"She's staying at the house I'm renovating," Linc said, so matter-of-factly. "So I hired her to cook for me because she's amazing at it. She's also fostering several dogs."

Lisa gave her a genuine smile. "Really? I love dogs. That must be so fun."

"It is. I care about the dogs so much and want them to find good homes."

"I'm sure it's hard to let them go. You must get so close to them."

Hazel inhaled, then sighed. "It can be very hard. But I try to do what's best for them."

The front door opened and Hazel heard several footsteps. Suddenly, three tall, handsome men presented themselves in the kitchen.

"I heard there's an asshole here so I came to see for myself." The person who said it saw her and cringed. "Oops. Didn't know we had other company."

"Hazel, may I introduce you to my oldest son, Warren, and his husband, Joe. And standing behind them both looking sheepish for his crass outburst is the youngest, Eugene."

Hazel laughed, then stood so she could shake their hands. "Hi. I'm Hazel."

"She's with me," Linc said.

Both the brothers arched a brow, seemingly in unison. All three men were incredibly good-looking, including Warren's husband, Joe, though he didn't share the Kennedy dark hair and intense eyes. Joe had dark skin and dark eyes and the most amazing long lashes she'd ever seen. And was he a bodybuilder or what, because damn, he sported some muscles.

This was going to be fun.

"What does 'she's with me' mean, bro?" Eugene asked.

Warren pulled up a chair at the table, and Joe followed suit. "Yeah. I mean, apologies in advance for the third degree, Hazel, but Linc, are you two a thing? Or is it more serious?"

"None of your damned business is what it means." Linc sat at the table, twisted the top off his bottle of beer, and took a long swallow.

Mom just smiled.

"You look . . . tan." Warren gave him the once-over. "How's construction life?"

"It's good. You look like you could use some sun. You should get out of the office more often. You, too, Eugene. You look great as always, Joe."

Joe laughed. "Thanks, man."

"I get out plenty," Eugene said. "I was just down at Big Sur last week."

"For what?"

"What else?" Warren said with a shrug. "A girl."

Linc arched a brow at Eugene. "You have a girlfriend?"

"No. I had a date. The word 'girlfriend' sounds too . . . committed."

"Yeah, God forbid you should attach yourself to anything. Or anyone."

Eugene obviously wasn't at all insulted, since he grinned. "That's right. I've got things to do and places to go. Unlike you, I guess, whose relationship status has changed to . . . what, exactly?"

Linc wasn't about to tell them anything about Hazel. Besides, it wasn't really a relationship and she wasn't his girlfriend. They were just sharing a house. And having sex. And fun together.

Wait. No, he wasn't going to label what they were doing, and especially not tonight when he needed his wits about him. "Again, none of your business."

"You look good," Joe said. "Obviously something"—he looked over at Hazel—"or someone is making you happy."

"Thanks. I feel good." He reached under the table to squeeze

Hazel's hand, hoping like hell that bringing her here hadn't been a huge mistake. But she seemed relaxed, sipping her wine and smiling.

"Boys," Mom said, "there's some knocking noise in my car. Would you mind taking a look at it?"

"Sure, Mom," Warren said, then looked over at his brothers and Joe. "Let's go."

Linc looked over at Hazel. "I'll be right back."

"Your mom and I will be just fine."

The door to the garage closed, and Lisa started getting things out of the fridge. Hazel got up and went to the sink to wash her hands, drying them on a paper towel.

"What can I help with?"

"I'm making tacos and Spanish rice, so how about you get the rice in the cooker while I get the meat started?"

"You got it."

She found the rice cooker and got everything prepped there, then began to slice lettuce and tomatoes.

"Tell me about yourself, Hazel."

"I foster dogs, I love to cook, I recently got out of a disastrous marriage where my ex took everything including the house and left me completely without money and also homeless, so that wasn't fun, but I'm managing to put my life back together."

"Ouch. That must have been rough."

That had probably been way too much information. But now it was out there, and Lisa hadn't looked at her weird, so onward she went. "It wasn't fun, that's for sure. But it was a valuable life lesson."

"And what life lesson is that?"

"That I'm stronger than I thought I was, and that I'm more independent than I ever gave myself credit for."

"Two very good things. A lot of women don't realize how strong they are until they suffer some kind of major crisis or loss. When my husband died, I thought my whole world was going to crumble around me."

"I'm so sorry for your loss."

"Thank you." She stirred the ground beef while she talked. "You know, when Scott died, I didn't deal well with it."

"Does anyone when they lose someone they love?"

"True. But I had the boys and my friends, and they helped me to realize that I couldn't mourn him forever. And he'd have hated that for me. So little by little, I started to find joy in my favorite things again, and discover new things to love."

"I'm so happy to hear that."

"I'm sure you went through something similar with your divorce. I've had friends who went through a divorce, and they said it's like a death. You get married, you have all these hopes and dreams for forever, and you don't get that forever. It's so unfair."

Lisa had just summed up Hazel's heartbreak in one simple sentence. "That's so true. It was devastating. Our marriage wasn't perfect, but I had no idea he was such a bastard who was cheating me out of half of what I was entitled to."

"Like you said, a good lesson to learn."

"Very true. And now I'm standing on my own—well, sort of—but I will stand on my own again, thanks to Linc, who has given me a place to stay and a chance to save money so the dogs and I can move into a place of our own as soon as he's done with the house."

Lisa added spices to the ground beef, along with tomato sauce, then continued to stir while Hazel put the tomatoes and lettuce on a platter.

"How will you feel about moving out?"

"Oh. You know, it's just a temporary place to live, so we'll be fine."

"And Linc? How will you feel about leaving him?"

She didn't know how to answer that, because her feelings for Linc were a giant batch of mixed-up. "Honestly? I don't know. I like him—a lot. He's been very good to me and he's very easy to be around. But our relationship from the beginning has been so . . . unorthodox."

"Really? How did you and Linc get together?" Lisa asked as they worked side by side prepping the food.

"Oh, well. That's kind of a disastrous story." She filled her in on staying at Ginger's house, not knowing that her friend had sold it, and almost beaning Linc in the head when he showed up that first night.

She waited for Lisa to be horrified. Instead, she laughed. "Wow. That was some intro, wasn't it?"

"It was something." She took a sip of her wine. "I'm sure I scared the hell out of Linc. I thought I was either going to get arrested or tossed out on my butt on the street. But then I explained the situation, Ginger verified it to Linc, and he calmed down. And then I calmed down. And then I cooked him dinner."

Lisa let out a sharp snort. "You cooked him dinner?"

Hazel shrugged. "I was hungry. Anyway, he liked the food I made, so he suggested the dogs and I stay there—temporarily—and I suggested that I could cook for him so he didn't have to eat takeout every day, and I could earn some money since I didn't have any."

Lisa slanted a sympathetic look her way. "Your ex really put you through it, didn't he?"

"A lot of it was due to me not paying attention to what was going on under my very nose. That won't happen again."

"Good for you."

"Sorry to lay my messy backstory on you right off the bat, Lisa. Sometimes I blurt."

Lisa laid her hand over Hazel's and smiled at her. "You're frank and forthright and honest. I like that about you. I like you."

She exhaled, relieved to know she hadn't totally burned any bridges with Linc's mom.

She started the beans, then checked on the rice. While she was at it, she found some corn on the cob so she decided to grill it for roasted elote. Then she made guacamole and salsa.

Lisa leaned against the kitchen counter to watch her. "I can see why Linc enjoys your cooking."

"Oh, God. Am I doing too much? I didn't mean to take over your kitchen. I'm so sorry."

Lisa laughed and reached out to grab her hand. "Honey, you're doing great. I'm just amazed at how fast you work."

"Oh. I'm kind of an automaton in the kitchen. I get ideas and I start working and don't even think about it."

"That's a great skill to have. And everything looks amazing."

"It's a simple meal, but these are big guys so I figure they'll want a lot of food. I don't know how you did it when they were growing up."

Lisa's lips lifted. "Quantity."

Hazel laughed. "Understood."

"How about a refill on your wine?" Lisa asked.

"I'd love that."

"Great. Next I want you to tell me all about your dogs."

She liked Lisa—a lot. She was easy to talk to and made Hazel feel as if she was right at home, something she rarely felt with her own family. She saw a lot of Lisa in Linc. His warmth, his sense of humor, and his acceptance of her.

She was very interested in getting to know his brothers.

Tonight was going to be so fun.

Warren had grabbed his mom's keys and backed the car out to the driveway. Linc and the others followed. They turned the engine over and all of them listened for a while, even taking it out for a drive, but didn't hear anything. Not that any of them expected to.

"You know she just wanted us out of there so she could grill Hazel," Eugene said after Warren parked the car back in the garage.

Linc knew his mother, and she was a kind woman. There'd be no inquisition.

"Nah," Joe said. "Your mom isn't the grilling kind. She just wants some one-on-one time with Hazel without all of us knuckleheads arguing. She did the same thing to me when I first started dating Warren."

"No doubt to make sure you weren't an asshole," Linc said.

"Which everyone knows I'm not. Which is why she always makes my favorite vegetarian food."

"Butt kisser," Eugene mumbled, but he smiled.

"Hey, I can't help it if she likes me best. I'm her fourth son—sort of."

They hung around the car a little longer, even though there wasn't anything wrong with it. But, still, since Mom lived alone, it wouldn't hurt to check it over to make sure everything was in working order. And they could always refill the washer fluid, if nothing else.

"I wonder what she's making for dinner," Eugene said.

"You're always hungry," Linc said. "Though I don't know why since you don't do anything."

Eugene wiped his hand with a shop rag, then leaned against the side of the car. "Oh, I do a lot more than you think, bro. It's just all here in my mind." He pointed to his temple.

"Uh-huh. I think you live in your head. I'm frankly surprised you aren't still living in the basement."

"Old joke, asshole. And still not funny."

"Sorry," Linc said. "How's work going?"

"Writing code like I invented it. Oh, wait, I actually did invent it. Two new games coming out in the next six months."

"He's killing it," Joe said. "Which is what he tells me anyway and I assume is a good thing."

"It is," Warren said. "As much as Eugene annoys me—like he annoys everyone—dude is a master at video game design. And I keep telling him that instead of creating games for other people, he should start up his own company and use that big brain of his to create his own worlds."

"Yeah, yeah." Eugene started cleaning up the garage, tossing rags by the steps. "I've been thinking about it."

Linc had no idea Eugene had ideas to start his own business. The gaming industry was only getting more popular, and he'd played the ones that Eugene had a hand in. They were damned good. He knew from experience that his younger brother was kind of a genius. "I could help you with the start-up. So could Warren. And I know other people who could assist as well."

Eugene stared at both of them. "Well. Damn, guys. Thanks. I'll give it actual serious thought now."

"I told you they'd help you," Joe said.

"It never occurred to me to ask."

Linc rolled his eyes. "Hey. We believe in you. When you're ready to jump off on your own, ask."

Warren piled the tools into the tool chest. "What he said."

"How did your meetings go today, Linc?" Joe asked.

"They were all good. Met with some clients, then I had a meeting with my team."

"The business running smoothly while you're away?" Warren asked.

"Like a well-oiled machine, as always. I have two managers who are on top of everything and keep me informed of anything that goes on that I need to know about."

"So you don't have to be there," Eugene said. "That's how it should be."

"I dunno," Warren said. "It would make me . . . itchy if I wasn't in my office to oversee everything."

Linc pointed a finger at Warren. "That's because you're anal and have to have your thumb on top of everything and everyone."

Joe snorted out a laugh, causing Warren to shoot a glare at his husband.

Joe just shrugged. "He's not wrong, babe."

"You think I micromanage?"

"We all think it," Eugene said. "You've always been that way."

"Yup," Linc said. "Agree. If you hire all the right talented people, they can run your office and you don't need to be there every second of every day."

Warren started to object but then paused for a few seconds before speaking.

"I think it's because you're the oldest," Mom said. She'd been out on the step—with Hazel—and they hadn't even noticed. "You've always felt like you needed to be in charge of everyone, to make sure you had a handle on your brothers. You've been that way since you were a kid. It's only natural for you to have done the same in your business as well. It's not a flaw, just who you are. Which doesn't mean you can't make some alterations if you think the way you run your law practice could work better a different way."

Leave it to their mother to pump Warren up while also leaving him room to make changes if he wanted to.

"I'll consider it. Thanks, Mom."

"Look at us, considering life-altering changes," Eugene said. "Well, two of us, anyway." He looked at Linc.

"Wait." Mom looked them over. "Two of you? What did I miss?"

"Eugene is going to look into starting his own gaming company," Joe said.

"Well, it's about time. You're too smart to be giving other people your time and talent."

"Thanks, Mom."

"And what's up with you, Linc?" Mom asked.

"Me? Nothing. My life is just fine."

"Is it, though?" Warren gave him a direct look.

Linc leaned against the car. "Okay, hit me. What's wrong with my life?"

"First, you're never here," Warren said. "Sure, your staff can run the business, but should they have to while you're off playing Mr. Fixit with houses?"

Linc rolled his eyes. "I'm not playing anything. I run a legitimate business buying and renovating houses—for a profit, I might add. It all falls in line with the real estate investments I make. Some places I buy I turn around for a profit without ever touching them. There's no reason to change a business model that works, while also giving me an opportunity to do something I enjoy."

"Still, we would like to see you a little more often," Mom said.

"Mom would like to see you more often," Eugene said. "We don't care."

Warren nodded. "This is true."

Linc laughed. "Noted. I'll definitely try to make more trips home."

"That would make me happy," Mom said. "And as far as your

work? If you're happy doing it, and you're successful doing it, then stay the course."

"Thanks, Mom."

"But I'd really like some grandchildren, so one of you needs to get on it."

"You heard her, Warren and Joe," Eugene said.

"Actually," Joe said, "we're talking to a surrogate right now."

Linc pushed off the car. "Seriously?"

"Yeah," Warren said. "We interviewed several, and we're pretty sure we've decided on the one we want."

"Oh my." Mom put her hand to her heart. "That's very exciting."

"We weren't going to say anything because we didn't want to get your hopes up," Joe said. "But it's looking good. So keep your fingers crossed."

Eugene grinned. "Hey, this is great news. Keep us all updated, okay?"

"We'll do that," Warren said.

This trip home had been decidedly worthwhile. Besides the necessary business stuff, he loved spending time with his mom and his brothers. But now, with this news? He was really happy to have made the trip.

"Well, now that we've heard all this news," Mom said, "dinner's ready. And Hazel made most of it, so I think you're all going to be really impressed."

"Oh, I'm intrigued," Warren said.

"And I'm starving," Eugene said.

"You're always hungry," Joe said.

Linc shook his head, then slid his arm around Hazel. "You made dinner."

"I helped. Added a few small dishes."

"Uh-huh." He swept his lips across hers.

"I like your family, Linc. Especially your mom."

He smiled at her, that warm feeling settling somewhere around the vicinity of his heart. "Yeah, me, too."

They headed into the house.

CHAPTER SEVENTEEN

*H*azel opened the door to the local animal shelter. Sandy Patterson of Fluffy Fosters was in there talking with the head of the shelter, so she walked over to them. It had been a week since she'd picked up her dogs from Sandy after her trip to San Francisco. Sandy had, of course, spoiled them rotten.

Sandy smiled at her. "Hi, Hazel."

"Hi, Sandy. Hey, Rick."

"Nice to see you, Hazel," Rick said.

She had worked with Rick before, taking in a few animals from the shelter. She'd known Sandy for as long as she'd been taking care of animals. In fact, it was Sandy who'd gotten Hazel into fostering after Hazel had volunteered at several weekend events when she'd still been married to Andrew. After the divorce, she'd agreed to take in her first dog—Gordon—who was still with her. But he was old and, okay, kind of ugly with missing hair and protruding teeth. Also, he was somewhat set in his ways and not exactly a family-type dog, which meant he was difficult to adopt out, though Hazel found him sweet and lovable. That no one else ever saw how perfect he was, was not Hazel's problem. It was always difficult to place senior dogs.

"I'm glad you agreed to meet with us today, Hazel," Rick said. "Sandy said you have an opening now that one of the dogs you fostered was adopted."

"Uh . . ." She didn't know how to respond to that since she and Sandy hadn't communicated at all about her taking on another dog. She exchanged glances with Sandy, who just smiled at her.

Rick started walking back toward the cages, so they followed.

"She's small, and a senior, but very well-behaved. Her owner passed away recently, and the family couldn't take her in, so they surrendered her. She's fourteen years old, but our vet did a thorough exam and tests and she's in good health, though she could stand to get a little exercise."

They stopped at a cage where a small Chihuahua/dachshund mix was huddled in a corner. Hazel felt the sadness vibes immediately. Not only had—she checked the name on the card—Mitzi lost the person she loved most in the world, leaving her alone and scared, but the only other people she had any connection to had abandoned her. Once again proving to Hazel that humans mostly sucked.

"Would you take her out so I can visit with her?" Hazel asked.

Rick nodded. "Sure."

Rick opened the cage, and Hazel waited for Mitzi to come running out. Instead, she stayed pinned against the back of the cage.

The poor baby.

"Hi, sweetheart," Hazel said, crouching down so Mitzi could

see her. "I know you must feel so lost and lonely after losing your person. I'd really like to get to know you if you'll let me."

She sat on the floor in front of the cage and reached a hand inside. Mitzi leaned a little to give her a sniff. She left her hand there so Mitzi could get accustomed to her scent. She looked up at Rick and Sandy. "We'll be fine here for a while."

The two of them left, and Hazel got comfortable there on the floor. She talked to the dog in a low, sweet voice.

"We have four dogs at home right now. You'd love Gordon. He's older, like you. And Lilith is a Chihuahua, though she likes to be in the middle of all the action at all times. Penny is super fun and you'd enjoy lying under the palm tree watching her antics. Freddie is a long dog like you are, and he's just the sweetest. You'd have a whole bunch of dog siblings who would love and protect you. And I'd love and protect you, too, and try to find you a home with people who would care for you for the rest of your life."

Mitzi finally made a move, inching over toward the entrance of the cage. She was a beautiful dark brown with fuzzy ears, slightly on the portly side, and appeared to be missing quite a few teeth, which made her tongue hang out. To some people she could be considered a hot mess. To Hazel, she was gorgeous.

"Oh, you're such a pretty little girl. Who wouldn't want to love you forever?"

The pup licked her fingers and came to the edge of the cage, then, finally out, crawling onto Hazel's lap. Hazel fought back tears at how much this dog's heart must have broken at the loss of the person she loved. She ran her hand over Mitzi's back, stroking her fur.

"Don't worry, baby. You're coming home with me today. And you'll never be lost or alone or scared again. I promise."

She had no idea how Linc would feel about her adding another dog to the menagerie, but she'd worry about that later. Right now, Mitzi was her number one priority.

She scooped the dog up in her arms and carried her to the front where she saw Sandy filling out paperwork. Sandy cast a smile in her direction.

"I knew you were going to fall in love. I'm already doing the foster paperwork for you. All you have to do is sign."

She hated being a sure thing. Then again, Sandy knew her well. Maybe too well. She signed the form and walked out the door with Mitzi cradled tightly against her.

"Okay, girl," she said after she had Mitzi harnessed in the back seat. "Let's take you home to meet your siblings."

She just knew Mitzi was going to fit right in with the pack.

CHAPTER EIGHTEEN

*H*azel paced the length of the makeshift kitchen / living room area in the main house, all five dogs pacing back and forth with her. Linc had been out most of the day buying supplies for the house, which had given her time to get Mitzi in and settled.

The dogs had immediately surrounded Mitzi and sniffed her, and surprisingly, Mitzi had been very patient about the ordeal, then had fallen in order with the pack, following them around the house while Hazel had given her a tour. She loved the backyard, especially the shady trees, just like Gordon. In fact, Mitzi seemed to like Gordon the most, just as she suspected.

"Linc's not going to be mad, kids. He'll be fine with this." She wrung her hands together and hoped her stress wasn't vibrating off of her in waves. The last thing she wanted was to make the dogs nervous. She was carrying enough anxiety for all of them.

"Maybe I should have talked to him before I made this unilateral decision." She pivoted, looked at the dogs, who had all stopped and stared up at her expectantly, as if she always carried a handful of treats in her pocket. "No, this is not something to talk about on the phone. I need to see his face, to gauge his reaction.

After all, this is his house and I just brought another dog into it. That wasn't part of the agreement."

She started walking again, stopping to look out the front window as she made her way into the living room before pausing again. "But, I had five dogs when I met him, then Boo got adopted, and now I have five dogs again. So it's not like I added additional pups. It's simple math, right?"

Mitzi cocked her head to the side, and Gordon left the group to go lie on a pile of towels in the kitchen.

Hazel rubbed her hands together. "It's all going to be fine. Totally fine."

And if he threw her out, she'd manage. It wouldn't be the first time her world had fallen out from under her.

Except it would be different because she cared about the man who would be throwing her out.

She jumped at the sound of the garage door opening. Her heart thudded in her chest. Lilith growled and Mitzi started barking.

"Shh, shh, it's okay, it's just Linc. Everyone calm down." She opened the back door and let the dogs out, where they ran to bark at him at the gate, then she closed the door.

Linc walked in and laid several bags down in the kitchen, casting the kind of smile at her that lit her up. He headed over to her and immediately pulled her into his arms, surprising the hell out of her by planting one seriously hot kiss on her lips, making her momentarily forget her pent-up anxiety. She curled her fingers around the nape of his neck, letting them linger in the softness of his hair while she relished the feel of his body pressed against hers.

He pulled back. "Hi."

She couldn't help but smile. "Hi yourself. What was that about?"

"Missed you while I was gone. Where are the beasties? I thought I'd be attacked the minute I walked in."

"They're out back. I figured your arms might be overloaded with stuff."

"Nah. I'm good."

Before she could say anything or prepare him, he was out the door, and there were the dogs, including Mitzi. Linc immediately crouched down to pet them. Hazel held her breath.

"Hi, babies. I missed you, too. And I see we have a new member of the pack. Who are you?"

Hazel kneeled down next to him. "This is Mitzi. I got a call from the head of the foster agency this morning. Mitzi's human passed away and none of the other family members would take her."

"That's rough. Hey, Mitzi. You sure are cute."

Mitzi's tail whipped back and forth and she whined to be held, so Linc scooped her up and cuddled her to his chest. She settled in and laid her head against him, looking up at him adoringly. Obviously, it was love at first sight. Not that Hazel could blame her. Linc had a very nice chest. Among other things that were very nice about him.

"She's older?" he asked, as he stood and pulled Hazel up as well.

Hazel nodded. "Fourteen. Which makes her the oldest of this pack."

He looked at Mitzi and stroked her back. "I guess you'll be trying to lead things before long. If Lilith allows it."

That was it? No yelling, no recriminations? "I meant to say something to you, but I knew you were busy and I didn't want to talk to you about it in a text."

He laughed. "It's fine, Hazel. Don't worry about it. She's cute. And we were one dog down, anyway. I'm gonna grab a beer. You want one?"

"Uh, sure. Thanks."

He walked toward the guesthouse, still cradling Mitzi. The other dogs followed.

We were one dog down anyway. Hazel shuddered in a breath at Linc's words.

He'd made it sound like they were a pack. All of them.

Okay, then. She took a seat at the table outside and tried to get her wayward heartbeat under control. In the meantime, Linc resurfaced from the guesthouse holding two beers, all five dogs following behind him, Mitzi pulling up the rear. She made a mental note to get Mitzi involved with daily walks right away and schedule a vet appointment tomorrow.

He handed her a beer. "Thanks."

"No problem. So, you ended up having a surprising day."

She nodded. "Definitely unexpected, but that's how it often goes in the foster business."

"I assume there's a limit to how many dogs you can take on."

"Oh, definitely. Fortunately, I have a few small dogs so that makes it more manageable. And they're all well behaved, plus the homeowners on either side of this house don't mind the occasional barking. When I relocate it might be a different matter."

He took a long swallow of his beer, then nodded. "I guess you'll have to be super picky about where you live next."

"I will definitely have to do that. Of course, ideally, I'd love to have some land, plus a pool. But you know I'm not exactly in a financial position to dictate that."

"Someday you might be."

She laughed. "Yeah, as soon as I win the lottery." She sipped her beer and watched the dogs frolic across the lawn. Though Mitzi had stayed planted next to Linc, who casually scratched her behind the ears.

It amazed her how quickly her dogs had fallen in love with him. Then again, maybe it wasn't so amazing after all.

"Tell me your ideal place to live. When you leave here, if money were no object, where would you like to live?"

"Oh. Okay. Let me think about that for a sec." She conjured up her imagined nirvana in her head. "My first objective would be to have some land. Not a lot, of course, but enough for the dogs to be able to run freely without me having to worry about neighbors being close."

"Sounds reasonable," he said.

"And then, as far as a house, I don't really care."

"Sure you do. What do you want?"

She took in a deep breath, then let it out. "A fantastic kitchen, with a chef's stove and a huge refrigerator. Lots of room to prep so I could really stretch out and have the space to create. Let's see, what else. I guess if I was going to have all of that, I'd want to stay awhile. Or maybe forever, so I'd want an office and four bedrooms. And an amazing main bathroom with a huge shower. Oh, and also an outside shower for the dogs."

"Is that all?"

She laughed. "Isn't that enough? What about you? What do you want?"

"Everything you said, but also a pool and an outdoor kitchen."

"Oh yes, definitely, those as well. Draw up those plans for me, won't you?"

His lips curved. "Yeah, I'll get right on that."

She looked down at Mitzi, who had curled up at Linc's feet and gone to sleep. "She's cute, isn't she?"

"Damned cute. You sure know how to pick 'em, Hazel."

"I know." She sighed, looking at Linc, who had scooped Mitzi up and let her settle back on his lap so she could nap more comfortably.

Yeah, she for sure knew how to pick them, didn't she?

CHAPTER NINETEEN

*H*azel looked over at the newest member of the pack, who was napping next to Gordon in the corner of Sandy's house.

Linc was doing noisemaking work today, so Hazel gathered up the pups and told him she had things to do and places to go, so they'd be out of his way for the day. In actuality, she'd had zero plans, but she always knew she could count on Sandy's hospitality. Plus, she wanted Sandy to see how well Mitzi was adapting to her new pack.

Sandy had been divorced twice and was fifteen years older than Hazel, though she still looked like she was in her thirties, dammit. She might sport a few more wrinkles around her eyes, but she had amazingly toned muscles, no doubt earned from keeping this place up nearly on her own. It was one of the reasons Hazel admired her so much.

Sandy looked out over the yard. "How's Mitzi adapting?"

"She's doing great. She's settled in, gets along with all the dogs, and even Li—well, everything's going super."

Sandy cocked her head to the side and gave her a rather keen inspection. "You left something off that sentence. Care to elaborate?"

"Not particularly."

"This is about a guy, right?" Sandy took a long swallow of her herbal tea. "It's always about a guy. It's not your rotten piece of shit ex again, is it?"

One thing Hazel liked about Sandy was that, no matter what, she always took Hazel's side. The benefit of the two of them knowing each other for years.

Now Sandy had this sprawling five-acre ranch that was overrun with dogs, cats, chickens, goats, horses, cows, and any other fragile creature in need of love and rescue.

Basically, Sandy was living Hazel's dream. And doing it well.

"It's not about my ex. Thankfully, I'm unaware of his whereabouts. Hopefully, he's fallen off some cruise ship or something, never to be seen or heard from again."

Sandy snorted out a laugh. "That's my girl. So who's the guy?"

"Linc. He's this guy I'm living with—temporarily. He owns the house. It's . . . complicated."

"Complicated how?"

Hazel popped a grape into her mouth, chewed, and swallowed. "We sort of bumped into each other in the kitchen of the house one night. I tried to kill him with a cast-iron skillet, and he intended to throw the dogs and me out on the street. Instead, we came to an understanding and a mutually beneficial agreement."

Sandy arched a brow. "You're not—"

Hazel laughed. "Of course not. I cook for him so he doesn't

have to eat junk food, and in return he pays me a salary, and the dogs and I have a place to stay until we find something else."

"Sounds like a pretty great deal. So what's the issue?"

"We've gotten . . . close."

"Ah. So you are having sex."

"Yes. The mutually consensual kind. He's pretty hot, Sandy."

"If you're both open to it without sacrificing the biz end of your deal, I don't see the harm as long as both sides get what they need and want out of it."

"Except . . ." She let the sentence trail off, unsure of where she was going with that word.

Sandy arched a brow. "Except that now you're developing feelings for this guy?"

And there was the sentence she was afraid to say out loud. "I don't know. Maybe. I like being around him. Beyond just the sex part. He's awesome to talk to, he listens, and the dogs all love him."

"Dogs are stellar judges of a person's character, ya know."

"Yes, I know that all too well. Remember when I brought my first foster home, when I was still married to Andrew?"

Sandy got up and wound her way around her cat, Plato, who was lying on his back sleeping in a patch of sunlight on the kitchen floor. She grabbed an empty water bowl on her way to the sink, refilled it, then brought it back and set it down. Gordon got up from his nap, stretched slowly, and made his way to the bowl, taking a few delicate laps of water before heading back over to Mitzi and curling up beside her for his next round of naps for the day.

Sandy brought over some chips and salsa and set them on the table. "I will never forget you calling me crying, telling me how angry Andrew was because you, and I quote, defied his orders and brought a dog into the house."

Just the memory of it made a knot form in her stomach. "Yeah, he was a real peach."

"But you didn't back down and you kept Lucille for three weeks until we placed her in her forever home."

"Andrew pouted that entire three weeks. I knew then we were not going to make it. Too bad I didn't know about the money thing back then."

"Yeah, that part's too bad. But you're rid of him, and looking back doesn't do you any good. Besides, you learned a lot about yourself in the process, and now you're on the right path."

"Not yet, but I'm getting there. Since Linc is letting me live in the house rent-free, I'm putting away all the money he pays me so I'll have first and last month's rent saved up, plus be able to buy some essentials and get the dogs settled."

"And how's that going? The moving-on part?"

"Okay, I think. There are some rentals that could work, and the money Linc is paying me is decent, and since I don't currently have any expenses, I've been able to save it all. I think once he's done with the renovations and he's ready to put the house on the market, I'll have the money saved to do a lease on a house."

"That's great."

"Yeah." Saying the words out loud made her feel calm, that first realization that she really could do this on her own. "It'll be nice to have the dogs settled somewhere."

"Speaking of the dogs, we're doing an adoption event first of the month. You'll bring yours?"

She cringed inwardly. Adoption events were typically well attended, and often resulted in animals being selected. The thought of losing any of her babies . . .

But they're not really yours, are they, Hazel? The dogs, just like every other thing in your life that matters, are only temporary.

She shook it off, knowing it was the right thing to do for the pups. She offered Sandy a bright smile. "Sure. We'll be there."

She had to focus on the dogs' futures. And her own. Because she was starting to think she needed some permanence in her life.

It was time to think about setting down roots. And, now that she had a plan in motion, she knew she could get there.

CHAPTER TWENTY

*L*inc was trying to finish up flooring in the dining room and kitchen today, so Hazel had taken the dogs out for the day so they wouldn't be in the way. He'd told her they could just hang out outside, but she wanted to be sure to remove herself and the pups. He'd said that it wasn't necessary, but, hell, when the woman got an idea in her head, there was no arguing with her.

Still, he had to admit flooring was coming along faster than he'd anticipated, especially since he'd hired a guy to assist him. As it was, it looked like they'd have the living, dining, and kitchen flooring in before the end of the day, which suited him because flooring was at the bottom of his list of fun activities.

By the time they laid the last board, his back and knees were screaming. He paid Miguel and thanked him for working his ass off alongside him, then cleaned up his tools and went into the house to wash up. Then he changed into his board shorts, sent a text to Hazel to let her know he was finished for the day, and tossed his phone on the table. After that he made a beeline for the pool and dived in. The cool water felt amazing on his hot and tired body and revived him considerably, though if he were honest, he could have just as easily face-planted in the bed and passed out for the night, even though it was only six p.m. or so.

After he swam a few laps to stretch out his cramped muscles, he got out, grabbed a towel to dry off, and checked his phone, frowning when he didn't see a reply text from Hazel. Then again, she might be driving, so he figured it might take her a while to respond. Or she could be on her way home, which would be even better since he was starving. She'd fixed him both a breakfast and a lunch sandwich and put them in the fridge before she'd left this morning, but that had been hours ago. He decided he'd go upstairs and shower and then take her out to dinner.

The hot shower felt great on his sore muscles. He could have stood in that steamy water for hours, but he finally washed, rinsed, and dried off. He walked out of the bathroom, giving his bed a lingering, regretful look before getting dressed and going downstairs.

Penny greeted him at the foot of the steps, her tail whipping back and forth in her excitement.

Linc crouched down to pet her. "Hey, girl. Did you have a good day today?"

The back door opened and Hazel stepped in. "She did. We all did."

"Where are the rest of the pups?"

"Upstairs passed out in my room. We went to the dog park, then stopped off at Sandy's place where they ran amok with her dogs. It was hours of chaos."

He rubbed Penny's face. "But you're ready for more, huh, Penny?"

Hazel laughed. "No, she smells french fries and doesn't want to miss out on a chance for food."

His brows lifted. "Fries? There are fries?"

"I figured since you were doing floors you'd have a full day, and I sure as hell had a busy one myself, so I picked up some chicken sandwiches and fries for dinner."

His stomach grumbled at the description alone. "That sounds perfect. I'm so hungry right now."

"Same. I'll go pour us some iced tea. The food is on the table outside."

Fortunately, it had cooled off outside, which suited Linc. He spread out the sandwiches and fries on the plates, shoving a fry in his mouth as he did. Hazel came back from the guesthouse with two large glasses of iced tea, setting those on the table. They sat and started to eat while Penny laid her head on Linc's knee, looking adorable with her sad, begging eyes.

"Not a chance, girl," Hazel said. "You had treats today."

Linc picked up a fry that Penny tracked all the way to Linc's mouth. After he swallowed, he said, "Sorry, Penny. Mom said no."

With a look of disgust, Penny made her way to the shade and curled up, closing her eyes.

"Gee, thanks, Hazel. Now she hates me."

Hazel laughed. "Penny doesn't know how to hate. And the next time you have food, she'll be right back here, head on your knee, giving you her sad puppy eyes."

"She's very good at it."

"Of course she is, because sometimes it works. Don't think I haven't noticed how you slip her food."

He shrugged. "Can't help it. She's cute."

They finished their food, and Linc wrapped everything up and tossed it out. When he came back outside, Hazel was sitting by the pool, her legs dangling in the water. He went over to join her.

"The floor looks amazing, by the way. I love the flooring you chose."

"Thanks. I think it looks good and makes the rooms appear larger."

"Agree. So what's next?"

"I'll put cabinets in next, and appliances are due in soon. In the meantime, I'm going to start working on the bathrooms upstairs."

"Oh. You need me to get out of the way?"

"I'll do one at a time so we have one full working bathroom. I'll likely start with yours, but you can share mine as long as you don't mind."

"I don't mind. I'll move my stuff out tomorrow."

"Good, thanks. Fortunately, the floor tile's in good shape in both bathrooms, and it's modern enough that it won't need replacing. But the guest bathroom needs a new tub and wall tile, and I'll refresh the cabinetry and sinks along with the mirror and faucets. In the main bedroom I'm just going with a new shower like the one that's there now. No need for a tub."

"I'm sure it'll look amazing. How long will that take?"

He gave her a long, studying look. "Trying to get rid of me?"

She laughed. "Well, first, this isn't my house, so I wouldn't be getting rid of you. And, second, when you're done here, I'm out, so the longer you take, the more money I can save for my own place."

"Noted. I'll start working slower."

She nudged his shoulder. "You will not."

"Okay, I won't. I've actually got a line on a few new houses to work on."

"You do? Where are they?"

"One's in Flagstaff. Another in San Diego. And one just outside San Francisco."

"Oh. Close to home. That could be fun for you."

She didn't even balk or say she'd miss him. Then again, did he expect her to? They had never discussed their relationship. Did he even know how he felt yet? "Yeah. Fun. We'll see."

"How do you choose? Is it based on location or the condition of the house?"

"That's part of it. The area has to have good sales statistics. And it has to be somewhere I actually want to work. Plus I need to be able to turn around the house in a reasonable amount of time, without draining a lot of money in the process or having to bring in a sizable crew to do the project."

"That makes sense. Will you go to the houses to look at them?"

He nodded. "I have to do a walk-through to get a feel for each house. Then I'll decide and buy the right one. At that point I'll start ordering materials."

"Makes sense. So when will you be finished here?"

He thought about it while also trying not to think about how soon he'd be leaving Hazel. "Maybe four weeks?"

Her brows lifted. "Wow. That soon."

He thought he heard surprise—and maybe regret—in her voice. Or maybe that's just what he wanted to hear.

"Yeah, things are moving smoothly here, so it won't be much longer."

"Okay, then. I'll start making plans."

He reached for her hand. "You don't have to move out today, Hazel. We can enjoy the time we have together while we have it."

"You're right, of course. But at the same time I don't want to be blindsided like the last time. I've already been looking for a place to live, but it's good to have a timeline."

His stomach tightened. He wasn't looking forward to the day when he wouldn't be able to see her beautiful face anymore. But what the hell could he do about that? Their lives didn't mesh at all. He traveled around constantly, and she needed a place where she could put down roots and take care of the dogs. And that could never work. They could never work.

They were a perfect mismatch.

Didn't that just suck.

"A job like yours keeps you from getting bored," she said, her focus on the dogs as she said that. "You don't stay in one place too long, and you get to start over again all the time. That must be really nice."

"It's pretty awesome, I have to admit," he said as he leaned back on his hands. Mitzi came over and lay down between them. Hazel smoothed her hands over the pup. Then Lilith followed, climbing onto Linc's lap. He caught Hazel's approving smile. "But what about you and the dogs? Never a dull day with them around."

"That's for sure. They keep me entertained, and they're always a challenge. That's what I love most about fostering them. I only wish I could do more."

"You mean have more dogs."

"Yes. But that's a dream for far off in my future. Right now just finding a roof over our heads is paramount, and then a job for me so I can keep said roof. The job part is fairly easy because I can get one at a restaurant as a cook. And that'll give me enough money so I can keep looking after the dogs. After that, it'll be day-to-day. And someday."

"Understood." He'd love to be able to design a home for her that gave her everything she could ever want. God knew she deserved it after what she'd been through. But that wasn't his plan, and he needed to stick to the plan, which was to finish this house and move on to the next one.

Then again, wasn't he the one who'd told her they needed to enjoy each other while they had each other? So why wasn't he taking his own advice?

He leaned over and pressed his lips to her shoulder, earning a growl from Mitzi.

"Oh, look at you," Hazel said, sliding her hands under Mitzi to pick her up and cuddle her close. "Getting all comfortable and territorial already."

"Yeah, but was she growling at me or at you?" he asked.

Hazel grinned. "I don't know. But you should probably kiss me so we can find out."

"I'll gladly participate in that experiment." He leaned over, slid his arm around her, and tugged her close. Temporarily forgetting all about the dog, he put his mouth on hers, letting his tongue tease the seam of her lips. She opened for him and he slid his tongue inside.

She moaned. He groaned.

Mitzi gave a low growl, then climbed over onto his lap.

He broke the kiss and looked down at the pup, then at Hazel.

"Apparently, she likes you the best," Hazel said.

He shrugged. "And you're surprised? You've seen my charm, my magnetism. I'm fucking captivating."

She snorted out a laugh and pushed off of him to stand. "Okay, Mr. Magnetism. I'm going to go unload the car."

He hopped up. "I'll go with you and help. You can admire my floor work again."

"Yes, I'll be sure to do that, Sir Charm."

He couldn't help but grin.

CHAPTER TWENTY-ONE

Y ou don't have to be here for this."

Linc shot her a look. "Yeah, you've mentioned that at least twenty times—this morning alone. I want to help. Besides, I've never been to a dog adoption event. I'd like to see how they work."

"Don't you have work to do at the house?"

"I'm allowed to take a day off. Besides, I'm on schedule."

"Fine." Hazel pulled into the parking lot of the pizza place where the event would be held.

It was a lovely, cloudy Saturday morning, and the tree-lined parking lot was an ideal location. Which meant they'd likely draw a large crowd.

She should be happy about that. She wasn't, because that meant that someone might want to adopt one of her babies.

You have got to get over it, Hazel. These aren't your babies.

Fortunately, she'd left Mitzi and Gordon at the house today because not a lot of people wanted to adopt seniors, so they kept those to a minimum. Sandy was already bringing two of her seniors to show off today, which suited Hazel just fine.

Linc helped her unload the crates. Penny, Lilith, and Freddie were hooked up in the back seat, so she and Linc got them out and took them for a stroll around the grassy area surrounding the restaurant so they could stretch their legs and do their business.

"Looks like people are showing up," Linc said.

Hazel tracked where Linc motioned with his head, and sure enough, the parking lot was starting to fill up with cars. They made their way to the staging area, and she put the dogs in their assigned crates, which listed their names, ages, and breeds along with temperament and likes and dislikes.

"Okay, kids," she said. "Be on your best behavior and maybe you'll find a new home today."

She hadn't meant to end her sentence with her voice hitching like that. Hopefully, Linc hadn't heard. Instead, she smiled and greeted people as they walked by and bent down to greet the dogs.

Penelope, of course, liked everyone, her tail wagging profusely as she put on her brightest smile. Freddie barked loudly at every human, though he wagged his tail as he barked. Lilith, on the other hand, growled as each person passed by, causing Linc's lips to curve upward, though he did his best to hide his smirk from the gathering crowd.

"You shouldn't encourage her growling."

Linc shrugged. "I'm neither discouraging nor encouraging it. I'm just standing here."

"You haven't told her not to do that."

"She's not my dog."

Hazel rolled her eyes. "Oh, right. Like you don't scoop her up and cradle her against you every time you pass by her."

"Don't know what you're talking about."

"Can we see Penelope?"

Hazel turned to see a young couple who looked to be in their mid- to late twenties. The guy was already down on the floor having a conversation with Penny, who wagged her tail enthusiastically.

"Of course." She grabbed the leash, opened the crate, and took Penny out, walking her and the couple over to a fenced area where they could interact with the dog.

Linc walked along with them but stayed out of the fenced area so it wouldn't be crowded. Hazel noticed him frowning the entire time the couple played with Penny, until he finally walked away. She looked for him but didn't see where he'd disappeared to.

She wondered what had upset him? The couple—Cecilia and Kyle—were wonderful. They were both dog lovers and had recently gotten married and purchased their first house. They had a nice big backyard and were so excited about adopting a dog together. Cecilia had grown up with golden retrievers, so she was ecstatic when she saw Penny.

They played with her for about thirty minutes, then wanted to walk around the parking lot with her, so Hazel leashed her and strolled with the couple.

Cecilia and Kyle were lovely and sweet and obviously had taken a liking to Penny. They'd probably make amazing dog parents, providing they passed the home and reference checks.

And if so, Hazel would lose another dog. The pack would lose another dog. But Penny would have a forever home. Which was awesome and fulfilling and would make everyone happy.

She sighed, then continued to smile as the couple walked Penny around the grounds.

When they got back to the penned area, Sandy was waiting for them.

"I'm sorry to have to tell you both that someone has put in an application for Penelope ahead of you."

"Oh no," Cecilia said, clearly disappointed. "We were definitely going to apply to adopt her."

"You can still do that," Sandy explained, "and if the first application falls through, we'll consider yours. In the meantime, we have another retriever I think you'd really love."

"All right." Cecilia reluctantly handed Penny's leash over to Hazel, and Cecilia and Kyle wandered off with Sandy.

Just then, Linc made his way back over to her.

"Where'd you disappear to?" she asked.

He shrugged. "Wandered around to look at all the dogs. How's it going?"

"It's going . . . weirdly. This couple really liked Penny, but before they could put in an application, someone else did. Only I didn't show her to anyone else."

"Huh. That is weird. Maybe someone who met her at one of the other events?"

"Maybe. But unlikely. I think I'll go check out the applications."

But before she could, another person came by to inquire about Freddie, who wagged his tail and barked incessantly with glee. Linc offered to take Penny while she worked with the woman, who ultimately decided Freddie was too much for her and wandered off. And then someone else came by—a woman and man with a little girl who was just dying to hold Lilith.

Lilith was not thrilled and gave some growls, which immediately turned off the little girl, who turned her attention to one of Sandy's mixed-breed puppies.

"You did that on purpose, Lilith," Hazel said, reaching into the crate to scratch Lilith's ears.

"She's very smart," Linc said. "She knows a good thing when she sees one. She's got an awesome backyard with a pool, great shade, and people who love her."

"Uh-huh. I told her from the very beginning this was a temporary situation."

Linc cocked his head to the side. "Right. You're doing a stellar job trying to place these dogs with other families."

"Shut up. I'm doing my best here. It's not my fault that Lilith is growly and Freddie is barky and Penny is—well, I guess we might be saying goodbye to Penny." She fought the tears welling up in her eyes. But they were happy tears. They always were.

Linc scooped his arm around her. "She's not gone yet. Just because someone fills out an application doesn't mean it's an automatic yes, right?"

"That's very true. But oftentimes if people put in the effort to come to these events, they tend to be well qualified. I'd say we have about a ninety percent success rate with applicants."

"That's great. And if Penny gets adopted, another amazing dog will come along for you to rescue and give lots of love to, right?"

She laid her head on his shoulder. "Of course, you're right. I have to stop getting so attached."

"Nothing wrong with getting attached. It's what makes you who you are. If you didn't care about these dogs then it wouldn't hurt so much when you had to let them go. And if you didn't have a heart as big as the state of Florida, you wouldn't be as good at this fostering gig. But you do, so I guess the pain of losing them is part of it."

He'd summed up her entire heart in one statement. And complimented her as well. No wonder she—well, she sure appreciated the bejeebus out of him.

"I'm going to go inside and get us some pizza and drinks. How does that sound?"

"It sounds amazing. Thanks."

Linc went into the restaurant, so Hazel milled about, mingling with the visitors. She knew all of Sandy's dogs, and she was familiar with one of the other rescue organizations that was there tonight, so she got a chance to talk up a lot of the dogs—and cats.

But what she really wanted to do was see who had applied to adopt Penny, because it turned out that Cecilia and Kyle had fallen in love with Peg, Sandy's golden retriever, and ended up filling out an application on her instead of on Penny. Which meant if the person or persons who had applied for Penny was approved, she'd lose her sweet golden.

Which was fine, of course. Totally fine. That's what she was here for, after all. She'd gotten used to the revolving door of foster dogs. And if Penny got adopted, Hazel would be okay, because she'd know her sweet pup was going to be happy in her new home. Well, hopefully. She'd have to meet the people who wanted to adopt Penny first.

Linc came back a while later with several pizzas and drinks for everyone working, so when they weren't chatting with customers, they ate, which made Hazel so happy because she was starving. She ended up eating three slices of cheese pizza, then covered for Sandy, who hovered over the food table like she hadn't eaten at all today, which she probably hadn't.

They wrapped up about nine and started loading the dogs and all the equipment into various cars, trucks, and vans. Once they had the pups loaded into the car and had the air conditioner running, Hazel left Linc to watch the dogs and walked over to Sandy's van.

"How did it go?" she asked.

"Amazing. Six applications so far, and another two or three who said they'd come by the sanctuary this weekend."

"That's outstanding." She balanced on the balls of her feet, wanting to ask the question but knowing Sandy was likely anxious to get home. But she just couldn't leave it alone. "So . . . you'll let me know about Penny?"

Sandy frowned. "Uh, sure. But . . . Linc talked to you about her, didn't he?"

"Linc. Why would Linc talk to me?"

"Oh, uh, maybe you should ask him? Listen, I gotta go. We'll chat tomorrow, okay?"

Since Sandy was already climbing into the driver's seat of her van, Hazel had no other choice but to nod. "Sure, we'll talk."

She backed away and Sandy shut the door, effectively cutting off the approximately seventy-four questions she wanted to ask about why she should be talking to Linc about Penny.

Then again, Linc was currently leaning against the side of the car looking at her, so maybe she should just ask him. She turned and made her way to the car, started to say something, then realized the pups were likely tired and hungry and this conversation could wait.

"So, how was it?" he asked after they climbed into their seats and Hazel put the car into gear.

"It was good. Lots of applications."

"That's great news. Anything on your dogs?"

"Just Penny. And why did Sandy tell me to ask you about her?"

"Oh. Uh. Probably because I know the person who wants to adopt her. Pretty awesome guy."

"Really. Tell me more."

"I will when we get home. Any inquiries about the other dogs?"

She wanted to ask more questions about the person who'd applied to adopt Penny, but that could wait. "Freddie and Lilith are an acquired taste, and a lot of people don't have the patience or willingness to learn about and manage dogs who growl or bark."

He nodded. "That's for sure. But they're so lovable once you get past their barky, growly defenses. Too bad people are missing out on that."

He knew the dogs' personalities so well. One of the things she lov—really liked about him.

When they got home, she removed the pups' harnesses and they immediately ran into the house, greeting Gordon and Mitzi, then the entire pack ran out into the backyard together.

"I'm sure they're happy to be home," Linc said as he followed them outside. "Or, at least free to run the backyard."

He went to get them drinks from the guesthouse while Hazel put the harnesses and crates away. They met outside and sat at the table. She took a sip of the wine he'd poured for her, sighing in relief that today was over. And then it reminded her of something Sandy had said.

"Okay, talk to me about the person who applied to adopt Penny."

He took a long swallow of his beer. "I put in an application to adopt her."

Hazel's stomach did a weird flip-flop. "You what?"

"Something came over me when that couple seemed like they wanted to adopt her. She and I have kind of bonded, ya know? I couldn't imagine life without her."

And that weird flip-flop in her stomach gravitated to her heart. "You're going to adopt Penny? How are you going to manage that with all the moving around you do?"

He shrugged. "I don't know. I'll figure it out."

"And Sandy was okay with this?"

"She said you'll vouch for me and that's good enough for her."

She gave him a stern look. "And what if I don't?"

"What if you don't what?"

"Vouch for you."

He laughed. "Seriously."

"I'm serious, Linc. I have genuine concerns about how you're going to manage moving around the country and doing these home renovations with a sixty-pound golden retriever. And why wouldn't you have talked to me about this first?"

"Okay, I can see you're upset about this, and you're right, I should have discussed it with you first. It was totally impulse, brought about by the imminent thought of losing her. I acted without thinking, and I'm sorry for not talking to you about it."

All Linc's talk about not wanting to lose her—her being Penny—made her feel some kind of way. Hazel wondered how he was going to feel when he walked away from her. Would it be easy for him, or would he have a crushing sense of loss? Because he sure had attached himself to Penny in a short period of time.

Then again, who wouldn't? And this wasn't about her; it was about her dog. She needed to remember that.

"So we should talk about how you're going to handle traveling with Penny in tow, and how you're going to live with her at your home base."

"My home base is a condo, and I'm hardly ever there. As far as Penny traveling with me, I'll drive instead of fly wherever I'm going. Maybe I'll buy an RV."

She cocked a brow. "You're not serious."

"Why not?"

"And then park it where?"

"Wherever the hell I'm working. Or I'll store it while I'm in whatever city I'm working in and rent a truck for the duration of my work there so Penny and I have a vehicle to ride around in."

She shot him a long look. "You have an answer for everything, don't you?"

"Honestly? I'm thinking on the fly here. But I'll figure it out, Hazel, and I promise that it'll be good for Penny. You know I'd never do anything to hurt her."

She did know that. She trusted him. But still, she hesitated, and she didn't know why. Was it because she didn't want to give Penny up, or was it something else?

"You could always interview me," he said.

"What?"

"Don't you interview people who want to adopt the dogs?"

"Yes, of course, but it's not like I don't know you."

"But do you know everything? This could be your opportunity to ask serious, in-depth questions."

She laughed. "About you having a dog?"

He shrugged. "About anything you want to know, I guess."

"Hmm." She leaned back and took a drink of her wine. "This could be interesting."

He stretched out his legs, running his hands over Penny when she came to him. When Penny did a few circles and lay down underneath him, Hazel knew that the whole Linc-and-Penny thing was a done deal. That dog loved him as much as he loved her.

But the Q and A was still open, so she might as well dig in.

"Did you have pets growing up?"

He nodded. "Two dogs, a cat, and a rabbit. Not all at the same time. Oh, and a turtle."

"Nice. Who took care of them?"

"When my brothers and I were all really young, mostly my mom and dad. But as we grew up we were given more responsibility for animal care. Taking them on walks, making sure they had food and water, cleaning their bowls or cages, giving them plenty of playtime—which for a kid was easy."

"And who was your favorite?"

He frowned. "Aww, come on, Hazel. That's like asking a parent who their favorite kid is."

She laughed. "Good answer."

"Was that a trick question?"

"Maybe." She took another long swallow of her wine. "What do you do when you're in the middle of a date with a new woman, and your dog decides to throw up on your fancy rug?"

He arched a brow. "Have you had this happen?"

"I have yet to experience a date with a woman, nor have I ever owned a fancy rug, but the throwing up part during a party definitely happened to one of my friends."

"Ouch. Hope the poor dog was okay."

"Correct answer. And, yes, the dog was fine. He had eaten some gunk from the backyard that he shouldn't have. The timing wasn't awesome, but everyone at the party laughed about it since they all had either pets or kids."

"It happens. I think if you are going to have pets—or kids, for that matter—then you have to toss the idea of perfection out the window. If you've ever had some weird idea of perfection."

"I take it you don't have that idea."

He let out a short laugh. "No, I don't. I believe if you're expecting perfection in any aspect of your life, you're setting yourself up for disappointment. Life happens, and often that means disasters or things don't always turn out the way you want them to, so you have to be willing to roll with it."

"I agree. Though I do believe that it's okay to dream, and want your life to turn out the way you envision it."

He picked up her hand and started teasing his fingers along the top of it. "You're talking about more than the perfect party."

"Of course I am. I mean to be able to plan for a future and have grandiose dreams about what that future might entail. And if it doesn't turn out to be exactly that, it's okay. We all deviate from the road set out in front of us. Well, maybe not everyone. I imagine some people have a dream or outline for their lives and it turns out exactly as they planned."

He swept his thumb over the top of hers, making it difficult for her to concentrate. Not that she was complaining. His touch set her a little haywire, and concentration was overrated anyway. "You know, I don't think there are that many people whose lives turn out exactly as they plan. I think everyone has to pivot, even if it's just a little bit."

"You're probably right about that." She paused and thought for a minute while enjoying the way he continued to touch her. "Did you? Have to pivot, I mean?"

"Sure. When I was little I wanted to be an astronaut. Then a firefighter. Then a wrestler. None of that happened for me."

She laughed. "How sad."

"Seriously. But I did decide when I started college that I was going premed."

Her brows shot up. "Really. What made you want to be a doctor?"

"Television. I watched a lot of medical shows, and the doctors were so suave and cool, not to mention all that lifesaving shit they did. Then I got into medical documentaries and saw all the real medicine that was being practiced and decided I really wanted to do it."

"What changed your mind?"

"Too much work. The one thing I was always good at was doing my homework, research-wise. I didn't want to be paying off student loans for the rest of my life, and to be honest, I just didn't feel as committed."

"Maybe the TV aspect of it was more attractive than the reality of it?"

He snaked his fingers up her arm, and she wondered if he even realized the effect he was having on her. "You're absolutely right about that. And, besides, I decided I wanted to make money, and help other people do the same. That's when I got interested in finance and business, which is probably boring as hell to most people."

"I don't know about that, Linc. I think most people are very interested in making money. I know it's what motivates me to get out of bed every day. If I make money, I get to eat. The dogs eat. We get a place to sleep at night. See? Very interested in money."

"Ha. You're probably right. Anyway, we've gotten off the topic of my interview."

"You passed."

He looked genuinely excited. "I did? When?"

"When you answered the first question. But it was still fun, and I've gotten to know a lot more about you."

"I see." He continued to sweep his fingers up her arm, teasing her neck. "Does that mean I get to interview you next?"

She got up and took his hand. "I've got a much better idea, but it requires some in-depth exploration. Indoors."

"Yeah? I like exploring indoors."

He followed her inside. The dogs stayed out, no doubt enjoying the cool breeze that had whipped up, so she closed the door and led Linc up the stairs.

Oh yes, she definitely had some ideas for what to do with him.

Q and A was over. Now it was body exploration time.

CHAPTER TWENTY-TWO

*L*inc couldn't remember ever having as much fun just having a conversation with a woman, but Hazel was the kind of person that you could talk to about anything and everything. It didn't hurt that he enjoyed touching her, and it was obvious that she liked being touched in return.

Now they stood in his bedroom while they watched each other undress. He couldn't think of anything he'd rather be doing right now. Time for conversation was over, and as she dropped her underwear to the floor, his throat went dry. What was it about her that made him feel like some awkward teenager who couldn't get a handle on his hormones?

He stepped forward, smoothing his hand across the soft column of her throat, snaking his fingers across her collarbone and down toward her breasts, circling her nipples. Her sharp indrawn breath told him she liked what he was doing. He damned well enjoyed the feel of her silky skin, the way her nipples puckered at his touch, the way she intently watched his every move.

He got closer and palmed her breast at the same time he took her mouth in a searing kiss, unable to hold back the need to taste her. Hell, he wanted to taste all of her. He maneuvered her toward the bed and pushed her back.

She laughed, tilting her head back as she scooted fully onto the mattress. "In a hurry?"

"Yeah," he said, pulling her legs apart so he could climb between them. He nestled between her legs, pressing his lips to the side of her neck.

"Mmm," she said. "I like your mouth on me."

"I like the taste of you. And the way you smell. Like lemons or cookies . . . lemon cookies. Yum." He ran his tongue along her throat, raining kisses down her chest to her breasts, taking a nipple in his mouth to suck. She arched against him as he pressed it between his tongue and the roof of his mouth.

Hazel was the sweetest candy, and he wanted so much more of her. All of her.

He moved up, down, and across her body, using his mouth and his hands to explore, learning what parts she liked him to touch or lick, and where she had no reaction. She was sensitive all around her breasts and the crook of her left arm, and he was surprised to find that her right hip bone was an erogenous zone, so he spent some time there as well. She also shivered when he kissed her feet. She had beautiful, dainty feet, and he'd definitely spend some time exploring there, but later, because she moaned and arched and he knew exactly what she needed.

He gradually made his way up to her sex, lightly licking her inner thigh, taking in the soft sounds of her breathing.

And then he licked around her clit, sliding his tongue along her salty, sweet folds, following her sounds and movements as he used his tongue, lips, and fingers to take her right where she wanted him to go.

He loved a receptive woman, and Hazel was vocal, moving against him, telling him where to go, and letting him know she liked what he was doing. Her sweet sounds made his dick swell and ache with the need to be inside of her, but right now he wanted her to come.

And when she did, lifting against his mouth with a shudder and a gasp, he licked her fully, taking in every second of her orgasm until she finally settled against the mattress. He climbed up her body, rolling over to grab a condom and put it on, then taking her mouth in a deep, passionate kiss. He pulled her leg over his hip and entered her.

"Ohh," she said, sliding her hand across his jaw. "You feel so good."

"Yeah, so do you." He began to move, gently at first, her pussy hot and tight as it surrounded him. She made him feel out of control, making him want to pound hard and fast, intensify these sensations. But he reined it in, keeping his movements easy, at least at first, wanting to prolong every minute of being this close to Hazel.

But she was making it so hard for him to hold back, because every sound she made, every one of her writhing, undulating movements, made his need to come more and more desperate.

He grasped her hand, twined his fingers with hers, and stared into the depths of her mesmerizing blue eyes. "Do you know what you're doing to me?"

She gasped out a breath. "Same as you do to me. And don't stop."

He smiled down at her before taking her mouth in a deep, soulful kiss. Then passion took over and he couldn't think anymore. He could only feel every nerve ending in his body zapped by the electrical charges of lust and desire and desperate need for this woman. He suddenly wanted more hands, more tongues, more everything to touch her with, because her taste, her scent, the feel of her skin were all combining to drive him right over the edge.

And when she shattered, he lost it, too, both of them shuddering and holding on to the other like lifelines in a world-ending storm.

When it was over, all Linc could do was continue to hold her, shaken by the way she undid him. And not just physically shaken, either, but something deep inside of him that he didn't want to examine at the moment, because Hazel was running her foot alongside his calf and making noises he could only describe as yummy sounds.

He looked down at her. "Feel good?"

She smiled. "I feel very good. Let's do it again."

He left to dispose of the condom, then came back, gathering her into his arms. "Insatiable, huh?"

She rolled over on top of him. "What's wrong? Can't keep up?"

"I can do this all night. Can you?"

"I've got stamina for hours and hours."

"Let's see who gives out first."

"Yes. Let's."

As he smoothed his hand over her hip, he smiled up at her, then kissed her. Yeah, it was going to be a long night.

But a damn good one.

CHAPTER TWENTY-THREE

*H*azel and Linc had settled into a companionable routine over the past week or so. If she wasn't so grounded in reality, it would almost seem as if this was their house and they were a real-life couple. They'd get up early every morning and let the dogs out, then have coffee together on the back patio, watching the dogs frolic and roll around on the lawn. It was always so quiet and peaceful, and neither of them felt compelled to carry on a conversation. Hazel couldn't recall ever feeling that comfortable with anyone, especially a guy. But Linc made her feel . . .

He made her feel a lot of things. At times passionate, other times he'd make her laugh so hard she was afraid she was going to pee her pants. They'd even argued about something so inconsequential she'd already forgotten what it had been about. What she did remember was that not once had he been mean or unreasonable. And when the argument was over, that was it. It was done and they moved on, with a hug and a very warm kiss.

Safe. That's how Linc made her feel. She felt safe enough to be herself, to express her feelings when she was around him. Such a rare and delightful feeling to be that free.

But the reality of it all was that this wasn't their house, and they weren't a real couple. She was dreading the time when he told her he had completed the house and it was time for him to move on, because once that happened, it would be over.

They would be over. The very idea of it pained her.

She tried really hard not to think about it, but sometimes she couldn't help it, like now when she was returning from an afternoon walk with the dogs and Linc was outside in the driveway working on something. Whatever he was doing was loud, and water rolled down the driveway.

Tile, maybe? He'd been working on the downstairs bathroom, along with putting backsplash in the kitchen, so it could be either. But as she approached the house and snuck a peek at the boxes in the garage, the dark tile made it evident it was for the bathroom floor. She slipped the pups into the backyard through the side gate so they could get a drink, then started for the house where Linc had disappeared inside, but a car pulling into the driveway caught her attention.

She recognized her mother's car right away, and noticed Natalie sitting in the passenger side, which meant Nat had told Mom about her current living situation with Linc. She'd been dodging her mother's calls for a while now, and replied to texts with nebulous answers, which she had known would eventually come back to bite her in the butt.

No doubt Mom wanted to check the situation out for herself, and probably lecture her about bad decisions.

Well, shit.

She turned around and plastered on a smile as she made her way to the vehicle.

"Mom. Nat. This is a surprise. Shouldn't you be at work today?"

Her mother, dressed impeccably as always in an ankle-sweeping sundress and a wide-brimmed hat, was not smiling. "It wouldn't have to be a surprise if you'd answer your phone once in a while. All I ever get is vague responses to my text messages. I took the day off I was so worried about you."

"I don't know what you mean."

Nat smirked at Hazel, knowing full well an interrogation was forthcoming.

"Don't be obtuse, Hazel," her mother said. "You know exactly what I mean. Now, what's going on here?"

"Here? We're standing in the driveway, chatting. What's going on with you two? Out for a day of lunch and shopping?"

Her mother heaved in a deep breath and let out one of her infamous sighs. "Why must you always be so difficult? You know exactly the question I'm asking. You. Shacking up with . . . that man."

That man that her mother knew nothing about. Just like the situation that neither Mom nor Nat knew anything about. It was so frustrating, and, okay, maybe she could have answered her phone or at least informed her mother what was going on via text, but why did she always have to explain her life to her family? Was she really doing anything wrong?

Of course she wasn't. She was getting her life together, and not doing too badly at it, either.

"Well?" Mom asked. "Are you going to talk or are we going to stand here melting in the humidity?"

Melting in the humidity sounded like the best option to Hazel. Fortunately, she was saved—albeit temporarily—from having to answer that question when Linc opened the door and walked outside looking tanned and sweaty and utterly sexy in loose jeans and a sleeveless shirt. He beamed a smile at her mother and sister.

Mom, on the other hand, gave him the once-over, and Hazel could tell from her expression that she found him lacking.

Hazel knew better. Linc lacked for nothing. At least nothing she needed or wanted.

"Hi. I remember you, Natalie. So nice to see you again." He graced her sister with a million-dollar smile as he grabbed a cloth to wipe his hands. "I'm Linc."

Her sister immediately fluffed her hair with her hand. "Hello again, Linc."

Hazel rolled her eyes. "Linc, this is my mother, Melinda Burke."

Linc walked over to shake her hand. "Mrs. Burke. It's a pleasure to meet you. Hazel's told me a lot about you. She said you're a loan officer. I'm in real estate myself. I have investment and commercial properties, and I'll tell you, I could not do what I do without the help of a good loan officer."

Apparently, her mother also wasn't immune to Linc's casual, easygoing charm when it was turned on her. "Oh, well, thank you. I know what I do seems boring to a lot of people."

"Not to me it isn't. You help people realize their dreams."

"Well, aren't you sweet."

Linc looked around. "It's pretty hot out here. I could move the patio table inside and fix you all something cold to drink, if you'd like."

"That would be nice, thank you," her mother said.

Hazel followed her mother and sister, who had flanked Linc, the three of them engaged in conversation about something that clearly she was not invited to partake in.

Whatever. At least her mother wasn't turning her nose in the air whenever she looked at Linc, so Hazel was calling that a win.

Hazel let the dogs out back so they could get a drink. Mom had disappeared into the bathroom, making Hazel so happy that she'd just cleaned this morning. Linc brought in the table and chairs, then wiped them down before Nat took a seat.

"I'll be back with some iced tea," he said.

"You know," Hazel said, looking for any opportunity to escape for both of them, "I could grab the tea and you could get back to work."

"Nah. I'll do it, and you can visit with your mom and sister."

She offered up a tight smile. "Awesome. Thanks."

She took a seat, then Freddie and Penny scooted in while Linc opened the door.

"Ugh," Natalie said, patting each dog lightly on the head as if they had canine cooties. "Your dogs."

"Only two of them. The other three are outside." Avoiding her mother and sister like the smart creatures they were.

"You have five dogs now?" Her mother stared dramatically from the hall. "What could you be thinking, Hazel Elizabeth?"

Oh, she was getting middle named. Mom was in a mood. "I'm

thinking that it's my job to foster these animals and find them good homes."

"Really." Her mother made it down the stairs and pulled up a chair at the table. "And what kind of career is that for you?"

"I don't know that it's a career, per se, but I love doing it. Plus I'm Linc's personal chef."

Nat snorted. "Is that what we're calling it?"

"I make him three meals a day unless we go out to eat. I prepare said meals on the stove in the guesthouse or on the grill outside. I'm earning a paycheck that I'm putting into savings while I live here so that once Linc finishes this project I'll be able to find a place for me and the dogs to live."

"Uh-huh. And what else do you do for him, Hazel?"

"That'll be quite enough, Natalie," Mom said, then smiled as Linc came in carrying a tray filled with glasses and a pitcher of iced tea. Hazel started to get up.

"No, you sit and visit," Linc said. "Let me pour. I sliced some lemons, too."

"Aren't you so thoughtful?"

Her mother's sugary words to Linc were in direct opposition to the cutting tone she'd given Hazel a minute ago. Not that Hazel's feelings were hurt. She was used to her mother's judgmental attitude. For as long as she could recall, she'd been under a microscope, and no matter what she did, it hadn't been good enough for her mom.

Her dad, on the other hand, had been her friend and her confidant and her playmate when she'd been little. He'd let her get dirty when they played, he'd taught her sports, and he'd let her decide who she wanted to be and what she wanted to do with her life.

There wasn't a day that went by that she didn't miss his warmth, acceptance, and counsel. Or his ability to run interference with her mother.

Linc poured everyone a glass and handed them out. "I'll let you all visit."

"No way," Natalie said. "You should join us."

Her mother nodded enthusiastically. "Yes, you must. It'll give us a chance to get to know you. You are, after all, living with my daughter."

Hazel cast him a quick apologetic look.

"Sure, I'd love to get to know both of you as well. Did Hazel tell you that she met my family a few weeks back?"

Her mom shot her a benign smile. "She did not. Where did this occur?"

"I had some meetings in San Francisco, which is where I'm from, so Hazel accompanied me, and she met my mother and my two brothers."

"How wonderful. And what does your father do, Linc?"

Linc took a swallow of tea. "My dad passed away a few years back."

Mom gave him a sympathetic look, along with laying her hand on his forearm. "Oh, Linc. I'm truly sorry. I lost my first husband, too, though it was quite some time ago. How's your mother doing?"

"She's doing well, thanks. I think this is the first year where the anniversary of his death didn't totally wreck her."

Her mother nodded. "I understand. Grief has its own individual timeline. For me, it was several terrible years. Natalie and Hazel can attest to what a mess I was. There were days, especially in the beginning, where I couldn't face getting out of bed."

Linc nodded. "My mom went through that, too."

"I thought I was never going to make it without my love. But months passed, and then years, and friends and family made me put one foot in front of the other and start doing normal life things again. And then I met Paul. Well, he swept me off my feet, first as friends, then we fell in love. He was so sweet and kind and generous, and while he's nothing at all like the girls' father, he's his own person and loves me in his own unique way."

Hazel had never heard her mom talk about Dad that way, about how losing him had been so hard. She'd been wrapped up in her own grief, of course, so she probably hadn't noticed how much pain her mother had been in. Hazel was happy when her mom found Paul. He really was a great guy, and he treated Mom like gold.

"That's so awesome, Mrs. Burke," Linc said. "To find great love not once but twice in a lifetime? I'd say you hit the jackpot."

Her mother graced Linc with one of her infrequent genuine, warm smiles.

"Oh, you must call me Melinda. And, thank you. I feel very lucky, indeed. Just like my Natalie, who's married to a real prince of a man."

Natalie didn't meet her mother's eyes, instead staring at her glass of tea and giving a fake half smile. "Yes, he's a prince for sure."

Hmm. Definitely a tone of voice that Mom hadn't picked up

on. Hazel wondered what was going on there. Not that Nat would share anything negative about Sean even if there was something. Still, she hated seeing that look of unhappiness on her sister's face.

These were the times she wished she and Nat were closer. But they weren't, and they were both at fault. Nat knew where to dig the knife in on all of Hazel's failings, and Hazel didn't exactly step up to defend herself like she should, which made her resentful.

Whew. Sibling relationships were complicated. Or at least hers was.

"We should all go out to dinner," Linc said. "I'm pretty much done here for the day."

"That sounds fun. Paul is out of town at a conference. What about you, Natalie?"

"Um, I'll have to check with Sean and see if he'll watch the kids."

Mom gave Nat a critical look. "They're his children, too, Natalie."

"I know that, Mother. But he's very busy, and tired when he gets home. Excuse me while I go make a call."

Hazel rolled her eyes but figured it was wise to keep her opinions to herself since she had neither a husband nor children. But as Nat argued on the phone with Sean in the background, she wondered how bad it really was, and suddenly felt a surge of empathy for her sister. Hazel might have gotten surprised and dumped by her ex, but she hadn't had children to consider. What the hell was going on with Nat and Sean?

She exchanged glances with her mother, who shook her head and looked just as clueless as Hazel.

Linc stood. "I'll go clean up. Be back shortly."

Once he disappeared, Mom inched closer to Hazel, lowering her voice so Natalie couldn't hear. Not that that would happen since she was currently in a whispered argument with Sean.

"Do you know anything about that?"

"About what?" She was going to try her best not to plop herself in the middle of her mother's need to know everyone's business and whatever was going on with Nat and her husband.

"You know what." She nodded her head toward where Natalie was pacing back and forth, clearly irritated while she continued her phone conversation.

"Oh. Well, no. It just seems like they're talking. Why? Do you know something?"

Mom shook her head. "Nothing. I was under the impression that she was a Disney princess living a perfect life."

That pretty much summed up what Nat had always led Hazel to believe.

They separated when Nat returned.

Mom shifted in her chair to face Natalie. "All right. Tell us. What's going on with you and Sean?"

Natalie lifted her chin. "Nothing's going on, Mother. We're fine."

"You can try and tell yourself that, but I don't believe it. I can feel the tension in you. Can't you, Hazel?"

Hazel shifted her gaze between her mother and Nat, who gave her a pleading look. "Honestly? I don't feel a thing. But what would I know anyway? My marriage failed and Nat's is perfect."

"Exactly," Natalie said.

Their mother gave them a look that told Hazel she wasn't buying it. Then her phone rang. "Oh, it's a client. I need to take this." And then she wandered off and out the front door.

"Thank you," Nat said. "I appreciate you taking the heat off of me."

"Anytime. But you know if there's anything you want to talk about, I'll always be here for you, Nat."

Natalie opened her mouth, no doubt to object and say everything was fine, then sighed. "Things aren't great between Sean and me. He and I are trying to work it out, but I'm just not sure I want to be the dutiful stay-at-home wife anymore. I want a career, but Sean is very traditional and wants me to be home to take care of the kids."

"Natalie. I'm sorry. Have you tried counseling?"

"We're doing that now. Sean's not as enthusiastic about it as I am, but I'm going, so he can either follow suit and go with me or—we're finished."

Hazel knew exactly how devastating it was to end a marriage. "Oh, Nat. I'm sorry."

"Thanks. Me, too. Please don't tell Mom."

"Of course not. But I'm serious about having someone to talk to. I'm here for you if you need me. Or to watch the kids."

Natalie laughed. "I think you have your hands full right here."

"Hey now. Cammie and Christopher love dogs. If you need a break or a babysitter, you bring them here."

Nat reached over and squeezed her hand. "Thank you. I appreciate that."

And that had been the truest, warmest exchange she'd had

with her sister in . . . as long as she could remember. Hopefully, it would continue.

Linc came back downstairs right as Mom returned from outside. He had put on a camel-colored pair of shorts along with a cream button-down, his hair was slicked back, and he looked utterly gorgeous. How could he dress so casually and look primed for a night out at the same time?

Linc had some kind of *GQ* magic in him.

Now it was her turn to sigh.

Natalie leaned toward her. "That man is gorgeous."

"That he is," she said.

"Where would you all like to eat?" he asked. "Hopefully, not a suit-and-tie place, because if so, I'm underdressed."

Mom laughed. It might have actually been a giggle. She and Natalie looked at each other.

"Oh, you choose," Mom said. "We like everything, don't we, girls?"

"Sure," Nat said.

"Okay. Do you want to ride with us or—"

"No, we'll follow you," Mom said. "That way we can head home after."

They climbed into their separate vehicles and pulled out of the driveway, Mom and Nat behind them as Linc led them out of the subdivision and toward whatever restaurant he was taking them to.

"Your mom and sister are great," he said.

"You think so?"

"Yeah. Melinda speaks her mind and I appreciate that, and Natalie seems to just go with it."

"Yeah, she goes with it, I guess. But, actually, we had a good conversation today. First one we've had in . . . a very long time."

"That's good, right?"

"It's amazingly good, and a step in the right direction for our relationship. Well, to be honest, we haven't had much of a relationship at all for a lot of years. We haven't had much in common. She has her husband and kids, and I—"

He merged onto the highway, then gave her a quick glance. "You what?"

"Floundered, I guess. It always seemed as if she had it all together, while I was busy blowing up my life."

"First, you didn't blow up your life. Your ex did. And, second, most people don't have it all together. They just give the illusion that they do."

She laughed. "And you know this how?"

"Let's just say I've seen plenty of evidence of it. I mean, yeah, some people manage to eke out their little corner of happiness, but a lot of people hide behind this happy facade, when in reality they're fucking miserable."

"Whoa. Where did this come from? I thought you were living your dream?"

"Oh, I am. But I haven't always been this way. I had to go through some misery. And I'm not exactly where I want to end up yet."

"Is that right? And where do you want to end up?"

"I don't know. I just know I'm not there yet."

"So . . . you'll know when you get there, or is it one of those things you figure out as you go along? Because I'd for sure like to know where the hell I'm going to find my peace of mind and happy zen."

He took the exit, glancing in his rearview mirror, no doubt to make sure her mom was still behind them. "I don't honestly know if there's a perfect happily ever after, Hazel. I just think when you find that peace, that utter happiness? You'll know it. And you'll do anything and everything to keep it."

She stared out the windshield as the last brightness of the day began to fade under gathering clouds and an orange-hued sunset. "I don't know if I believe that, Linc. I think you can't just wait for happiness to fall into your lap, or for your future to come to you. You have to work for it."

"I don't disagree with that." He pulled into the restaurant parking lot. "But I also believe in destiny, in things happening for a reason."

He unbuckled his seat belt and came around to her side of the car, taking her hand to pull her out. "Like you and me and that crazy way we met. Destiny put us together for some reason." He wound his arm around her waist, tugging her against him. "And I'm damned happy whenever I'm with you, so I try to never second-guess the universe."

And then, right in front of her approaching mother and sister, he slipped his hand around her neck and planted a long, hot kiss on her, melting her right to the spot.

She didn't know much about destinies and meant to be's, but

she did know about long, toe-curling kisses that made her forget all about her mother and sister standing two feet away.

And one just didn't discount those kinds of kisses. Because they meant something.

What that something was, she didn't know, but what she did know was that Lincoln Kennedy was someone special.

And, right now, he was all hers.

Nat cleared her throat—then coughed, loudly. Linc pulled away and gave her a promising smile.

Yeah, she planned to hold him to that promise. Later.

CHAPTER TWENTY-FOUR

With cabinets and flooring in, the kitchen was starting to take shape. Now was the time Linc got really excited about the direction of a house reno. Appliances had been ordered and should be in this week, which meant he could get to work on lighting, and that should almost wrap up the kitchen. There wasn't a whole lot left to do in this room.

He had finished the downstairs bathroom, so it was time to work on the two upstairs. He had planned to start them sooner, but the downstairs projects had taken up more time than he'd planned, so those had to wait. But now he was ready to dive in to the bathrooms. Since they needed to be able to shower, he'd do one at a time. Kind of a pain in the ass and would cut into the timeline, but still doable.

He hadn't planned to redo the bathroom floors, but the more he looked at them, the more he thought new tile would complete the look. So today he was removing the old and outdated tile floor in both bathrooms, since the concrete floor would work fine for showering purposes. He'd convinced Hazel to move into his bathroom so he could work on hers first. Hopefully, it would convince her to also move into his bed, since she spent most of her time in it anyway. There was something intimate about her toothbrush sitting near his, her shampoo next to his in the shower. It felt right, like that's where her things were supposed to be.

He didn't know what to make of it, and decided thinking too hard about it was a bad idea, because that sent his brain off into all sorts of wild "what if" scenarios, so instead, he went back to tile removal. It was sweaty, hard work, but he had his dog—wow, Penny was his dog now—to help him. And by "help" he meant she was lying outside the bathroom woefully staring at him.

He paused to swipe at the sweat dripping down his face. Penny ran off, coming back a minute later with a tennis ball.

"You think it's playtime, huh, girl?"

She dropped the ball on his foot, making her intent clear.

He picked up the ball and looked down at Penny. "Okay, fine. I need a drink anyway. Let's go outside." Based on the breeze blowing the palm fronds outside the window, it was probably cooler out there than it was in here right now. He headed down the stairs and outside, through the pool door and toward the lawn. He tossed the ball to the far side of the grassy area, then made his way to the guesthouse for a drink.

Huh. He thought maybe Hazel would be in there cooking, but she wasn't. Maybe she went to the store and didn't tell him she was leaving—not that she needed to keep him informed of her whereabouts or anything. Then again, it was unusual for her to leave the house while he was working without giving him a heads-up so that he could keep an eye on the pups. He made his way back out to the yard and did a canine head count.

All the pups were present, including Penny, who had retrieved the ball and was now following him around the yard while he re-filled the dogs' water bowl and checked on each one of them. After determining they were all doing fine, he threw the ball a few times for Penny, who had to wrestle with Lilith for it, even though Lilith couldn't retrieve the ball because it didn't fit in her tiny mouth. But Linc gave her points for trying.

His phone buzzed so he pulled it out of his pocket. It was a text from Hazel.

> With my sister. She's having some issues. I'm bringing her kids home with me. Hope that's okay.

He frowned, worried about Natalie. He hoped she wasn't hurt or something. He sent a quick text letting Hazel know it was fine to bring the kids to the house, then went and picked up his tools, put them away, and did a quick cleanup, checking the surroundings for dangerous items. Nothing in sight, so he figured it was safe enough to bring children in here, though he had no idea how old Natalie's kids were.

Then again, there was a pool, and hopefully they'd like that. He went upstairs and changed into his board shorts along with a sleeveless top, slipped on his sandals and headed back downstairs, walked across to the guesthouse, and peeked inside the fridge, knowing that Hazel typically kept it fully stocked.

He was right. He sliced up a couple of cheeses and a few different fruits, grabbed some crackers and cookies, and set them all on a tray, hoping it was good enough for the kids.

He started out the door and then stopped. "Dammit. Drinks. They'll want juice." He pivoted and went back to the fridge, grabbed orange and apple juice and a few glasses, and put them on the tray as well, then balanced his way around the pool toward the back porch. Just as he laid the tray on the table, he heard the sounds of kid voices.

Suddenly, two kids—an exceptionally cute boy and girl—burst through the back door and there was a cacophony of squeals and dogs happily barking. Hazel stepped through the door with an apologetic smile.

"Sorry about this. Nat had a huge argument with Sean, she's in meltdown mode, and my mom isn't available, so I sent her to the spa for the afternoon to unwind."

He reached out and grasped her hand. She was no doubt stressed, too. "It's all going to be fine. Now let's entertain these kids."

He walked over to the two little ones, who were happily playing with the dogs. "My name is Linc. What are your names?"

*F*or the past four hours, Hazel had watched in awe as Linc managed to enthrall and entertain two small children as if it were the most natural thing in the world for him to do.

Camryn was an incredibly intelligent and curious six-year-old girl and asked Linc a million questions. Unfazed, he answered her calmly and honestly, even when Cammie asked about his relationship with Hazel.

Any normal man would have cut and run. Not Linc. He'd kicked a ball around with three-year-old Christopher, followed by the two of them engaging in a rather in-depth discussion about dinosaurs before Cammie intervened to talk to Linc about her favorite TV unicorn. He'd fed them, played in the pool with them, and let them climb all over him. And not once had Linc tapped out.

The kids were splashing in the pool at the moment, so Hazel pulled up a spot next to Linc, who was sitting on the side of the pool watching them.

"You're so good at this," she said, watching Cammie laugh as Christopher paddled along on his floating ring, kicking his feet wildly behind him.

"At what?"

"This. Kids. You dived right in—literally and figuratively. The kids fell instantly in love with you. How do you do that?"

He shrugged. "They're awesome. And easy."

Hazel knew from personal experience that Cammie and Christopher were anything but easy. Christopher could be a total hellion and Cammie a pouty diva. And yet they had been well-behaved and enthusiastic around Linc.

"Linc! Linc! Watch me do a somersault underwater."

Linc grinned at Cammie. "I can't wait. Hit it."

Cammie did her best effort at somersaulting, her little feet flailing above the water as she performed the maneuver. She surfaced sputtering and grinning while Linc and Hazel clapped.

"That was outstanding," Linc said. "Do it again."

"Okay!"

Christopher just laughed and continued to paddle his way

around the pool, occasionally yelling to Linc to watch him splash, which Linc told him was awesome.

It had never been this easy to entertain the kids.

"You must have that magical quality," she said.

He cocked his head to the side. "No magic. You just gotta like kids and treat them like humans."

"I see." Maybe that was her issue. Not that she didn't love children. She did. But maybe she had harbored a little jealousy toward Nat and her perfect life and her beautiful children, so it had held her back from forming a bond with Cammie and Christopher. If so, shame on her. Children shouldn't have to suffer a lack of affection just because the adult had some screwed-up personal issues. She was going to fix that immediately.

She'd put her swimsuit on as soon as they arrived home because the kids had been so excited about swimming in Auntie Hazel's pool. So she slid off the side and into the pool, the coolness of the water refreshing her heated body. She swam over to Christopher.

"What's up, buddy?"

"I'm swimming, Auntie Hazel. See my feets?"

"I do. You're so good. Want me to take you around the pool?"

His smile brightened. "Yeah."

She leaned back and grabbed hold of his floatie, sailing him around toward the deep end.

"Paddle with your arms, too, baby."

He slapped his little chubby arms into the water—okay, mostly into her face. But he was so cute and excited she didn't care.

She glanced across the pool area to see Linc tossing a ball back and forth with Cammie, the two of them engaged in animated conversation. She swore that Linc—and Cammie, for that matter—could have a conversation with a wall and talk for hours.

After another thirty minutes of splashing around, Hazel made the kids get out. They wrapped up in towels and sat at the table having a drink. Then she took them upstairs to change into dry clothes while Linc started the grill. He made hot dogs and burgers, and Hazel fixed a fruit salad and corn on the cob.

They feasted, and the kids ate really well. She remembered from her own childhood how swimming in the pool always worked up an appetite.

After they ate, they took all the dogs for a walk, though Christopher got tired out halfway through and Linc had to carry him the rest of the way home. It was a good thing Linc was a strong guy, because Christopher was a tiny chunk.

When they got home, Linc took Christopher upstairs and laid him in her bed. Cammie went up there, too, and lay down to watch a kids' show on Hazel's iPad, exclaiming that she was going to watch three of her favorite shows. Hazel was certain Cammie would be asleep in five minutes based on her yawns and drooping eyelids.

She went downstairs, found Linc outside in the dark sitting in the chair with a beer in his hand. She noticed he'd put another cold beer on the table.

"Is that one for me or did the kids terrorize you into two fisting those beers?"

His smile was warm and gentle as he motioned to the chair

next to his. "The kids didn't terrorize me. They were awesome. The beer's for you."

She grabbed the beer and opened the top, took a long swallow of the cold brew, and sighed, leaning back in the chair. "Needed that."

"How's your sister?"

"She's okay. She had a spa day and that helped. I told her we'd keep the kids here overnight, so she got a room at a hotel for the night to clear her head—and get some distance from Sean. He's totally freaking out that she and the kids aren't there."

"Good. Maybe that's what he needs. Though to be honest, I don't have any idea what's going on between them, so I probably shouldn't comment at all."

"That's okay. And you're right. It's exactly what he needs. He's always treated Nat more like a babysitter slash cook slash personal errand person than a wife and equal partner in their relationship."

Linc frowned. "Not okay. Marriage is between two people—a partnership." His lips curved. "My dad never made a decision without talking to Mom about it. They were a team, ya know?"

Hazel felt his sadness in that moment. "You miss him."

"All the time. I wanted him to be around longer. I wasn't always . . . When I was younger . . ." He shook his head. "It's not important."

She scooted her chair closer and wrapped her arm around his. "They're your feelings. They are important. Tell me."

He dragged his fingers through his hair, letting out a sigh as he did. "I was a shithead teenager, always testing my boundaries, talking back to my parents. I wanted to do what I wanted to do whenever I wanted to do it. I wasn't much for rules, and my dad and I butted heads all the time. I refused to back down, and it drove my mom crazy. My dad was always calm, trying to get me to see reason. The things I said to him—I wish I hadn't."

"You were a kid. I'm sure he understood that."

"He did. I apologized to him over and over again when I became an adult and smartened up, but I still put him—and my mom—through hell. Even got arrested once."

Her brows shot up. "You got arrested?"

"Excessive speeding."

"How excessive?"

"Ninety-four in a forty-five zone. I wanted to see how far I could push it. Which was the story of my life back then."

"Oh, Linc."

"Yeah. The cop actually called my dad and told him he'd let me off with just a ticket because he could see how scared I was, but my dad said to haul my ass off to lockup and he'd come there and pick me up. It was terrifying sitting in that cell, wondering if I was going to end up staying in jail. Then my dad showed up and I was mortified and embarrassed and also more than a little scared shitless that he might just kill me."

"So what happened?" she asked.

"He asked how I felt about what I had done. I told him I felt stupid. I told him I was scared and I was sorry. And then I cried in the holding cell. The other prisoners laughed at me."

"That must have been humiliating."

"It was. But I didn't care. I'd never needed my dad more than

I did at that moment. I threw my arms around him and cried. Sobbed. He hugged me. And then he bailed me out. We grew a lot closer that day. Though he did take my driving privileges away for a month."

Her lips curved. "You deserved it."

He laughed. "I really did."

They went silent for a few minutes, and Hazel took a breath, leaning back to take a couple of swallows of her beer. She listened to the sounds of the crickets and birds as the night took over.

"This is nice," she said. "Sitting here, the kids upstairs asleep. The dogs lying here at our feet, asleep. This is what I want for my life."

He looked over at her. "You want the dogs and your sister's kids?"

She laughed and shoved her shoulder against his. "No. But I want this. A life. A home. A family. The dogs. For the first time in a very long time I can clearly visualize a future for myself."

"And that future looks like this."

She inhaled, then let it out, smiling. "Yes. A lot like this. I mean, not exactly like this. More land. But definitely a pool. The dogs like the pool. The kids would like the pool."

"How many?"

She looked over at him and frowned. "How many pools?"

"No. Kids."

"Oh." She shrugged. "I don't know. Two. Three. Four."

He laughed. "Better get started."

She reared back, glaring at him. "Was that a remark about my age?"

"Hell no. I was just . . . What I meant to say was . . ." He grimaced. "Shutting up now."

"Smart." She leaned her head on his shoulder, suddenly exhausted. Linc put his arm around her and drew her close. Her eyelids felt heavy, and after a few minutes of cuddling Linc's broad shoulder she couldn't stay awake.

She felt his hand smoothing down her back, which gently roused her awake.

"Hey," he whispered. "Let's go to bed."

"Mm-hmm." Like a zombie, she took the hand Linc offered, all the dogs following as she walked up the steps hand in hand with Linc. With her eyes barely open, she brushed her teeth and washed her face, then undressed and climbed under the covers, hardly cognizant of anything but the sound of Linc's voice as he got all the dogs settled in their sleeping spots.

The last thing she remembered before falling into sleep was Linc's body pressed against hers and the rhythmic sound of his breathing.

She smiled and drifted off.

CHAPTER TWENTY-FIVE

*L*inc painted the guest bathroom, and placed a bigger bathtub. Yeah, it would be a good tub for the kids, or for the adults to take a good soak if they wanted. He was perusing vanities and tiles for both the floor and the wall, unable to decide which direction to go, when he looked out the window and caught sight of Hazel bringing the dogs into the backyard after a walk.

He grinned, feeling a spike of joy as he watched her frolic around the yard with the pups. Penny chased after Hazel while she crawled around on her hands and knees in the grass with Gordon, Lilith, and Mitzi, Freddie barking and running circles around her. It was comical to watch. It also gave him a punch to the heart to see how much those dogs loved her. How much they counted on her.

Kind of like he was starting to—

Nope. Not going there. He went downstairs and outside, following the sounds of laughing and barking. Hazel was sitting up now, playing tug-of-war with Freddie while throwing the ball for Penny. Mitzi sat on her lap, and Lilith was chasing a very slow-moving Gordon toward the shade trees.

"Busy?" he asked.

She tilted her head back, offering up that thousand-watt smile. "No. I'm playing. What are you doing?"

"Going to pick out tile and stuff for both the bathrooms. Wanna come?"

"I'd love to." She held her hand out and he hauled her off the ground. They corralled the dogs, which took about ten minutes because Freddie was more interested in play and Lilith wanted to be the chasee instead of the chaser, so they had to indulge. But, finally, they got all the pups into the house where copious amounts of water were imbibed and all the dogs headed upstairs for a well-deserved afternoon nap.

Hazel had gone into the bathroom to freshen up. He stood there for a moment, admiring her in her pink underpants and white bra. Nothing memorable about either, but he was kind of into her body. Plus she had a great ass.

But they had plans, and he was distracted by a cute ass in pink underwear, so he needed to focus. He walked into the bathroom, staring over the top of her head while he washed up and changed into a fresh shirt as she wound her hair up into a bun on top of her head.

"How can you possibly look even prettier than normal with your hair all like . . . that?"

She laughed and pivoted to face him. "Not a fan of buns?"

"I like your buns." He swept his hands around her and grabbed a handful of her sweet-ass cheeks. "The hair's nice, too."

She arched against him, and his dick went instantly hard. He scooped her up and sat her on the counter, swept his hands across her neck, then grasped her nape and drew her lips to his.

There was something about kissing Hazel that was spell-binding to him. Her taste, the intoxicating scent of her, the way her nails felt raking over his arms as he deepened the kiss, the sounds she made as he moved closer, their bodies touching as intimately as they possibly could with clothes on.

He licked her throat while he lifted up the cups of her bra to tease and tweak her nipples. She moaned and bit the skin between his neck and shoulder, making him groan. He snaked his fingers along her ribs and down across her belly, her sexy sounds making him rock-hard and aching to be inside of her.

He slipped his hand inside of her panties and stroked, sliding two fingers inside of her. She was hot, wet, and drove him nearly over the edge.

"Oh no," she whispered.

He started to pull his hand away, but she grabbed hold of his arm, her gaze intense as she looked at him.

"No. Don't stop. Keep going. Right there."

The words "don't stop" were like music, urging him on, giving him permission to continue to stroke her slick flesh as she writhed against his hand. And while he busied himself with trying to get her off, he had his mouth firmly glued to hers, soaking in her moans and little cries of pleasure.

He rained kisses along her jaw to her ear, whispering, "Come on, Hazel. I know you want to come. Let me see it."

"Oh, God. Oh, God. Yes. Yes."

There it was, that moment when she hung, suspended for a fraction of a second, then let go, her entire body shaking like she was lit up by some electrical current. She rode that current for a good long minute, then relaxed against him. And by now he was so hard he felt like he might explode. He drew her underwear down and dropped his pants, reached around her into the cabinet for a condom, and as soon as it was applied, he eased into her.

She wrapped her legs around his hips and lifted, drawing him in, allowing him to feel every part of her. And every part of her was perfect, as if she'd been made for him.

He knew that was all bullshit and romance, but hell, that's how he felt, and in the moment he wasn't about to question it. He wanted to feel it—feel her—for as long as this lasted.

She moaned against his lips and he drove in deeper. Then she lifted her gaze to his and gave him a pleading look with her bright blue eyes. He reached underneath her and brought her closer, grinding against her until he felt the way her body seemed to close around his dick. She tilted her head back and cried out.

That was his undoing. He came with a hard shudder, gathering Hazel close to him while he rode that hot wave of bursting pleasure until he was spent and she was limp against him. He caught his breath, rubbing his hands over her back, sliding over the soft slickness of her skin.

"I'm sweaty," she murmured against his chest.

"Same. How about a quick rinse-off in the shower?"

"Sounds ideal."

He pulled out of her, disposed of the condom, then turned around to find Freddie lying there outside the bathroom.

"You like to watch, huh?" he asked.

Freddie continued to stare.

"Kinky, dude." He grinned and Hazel laughed. He turned on the shower. They got in and did a fast wash and rinse and hopped out, drying off.

They got dressed, and Hazel went downstairs to get the pups some fresh water while Linc made some notes and measurements and took pictures of the upstairs guest bathroom. He met Hazel outside by the truck. She handed him a metal tumbler filled with ice water. He took several sips.

"Thanks. I needed this."

"I knew you did, what with all that yelling."

As she climbed into the truck, he leaned over to whisper in her ear. "I wasn't the one doing all the yelling. I believe that was you."

"Hmm. Maybe." She tipped her finger under his chin, and he bent to sweep a kiss across her lips. She responded by smiling. "We could go for round two in the truck."

He laughed. "And I'll never get anything accomplished today. But I am bookmarking round two for later."

"Suit yourself."

He closed the door and went around to the other side and climbed in. They drove first to the tile store. He had some ideas in mind, but he wanted a second opinion, so he gathered up the samples and set them on a table in front of Hazel.

"These are for the shower?" she asked.

"Yeah. Look those over and tell me what you think, and I'll grab the ones I was considering for the floors. Be right back."

He found the three sets of tiles for the floor and came back, laying those out as well.

Hazel spent about ten minutes studying all the tiles, then pushed one aside.

"This one's too busy for your wall and it'll be hard to decorate around." She studied the other two. "These are both close. I like them, but . . ." She pushed back from the table, looked again, then walked away.

He followed her toward the front of the store where she stopped and picked up a tile. It was similar to the two finalists. A nice gray backsplash, but this one had a white slash.

"This one's brighter, and the gray is a bit more subtle. It'll stand as background instead of overwhelming the space, but will wow any potential buyer. Plus it's less expensive than the other one but still looks just as good."

He was impressed that she'd not only chosen a good tile, she'd also paid attention to the budget. "You're right. It'll look amazing in the master shower, too."

"Agree."

"Okay, then I'll go with this one."

She grinned. "Perfect. Now let's go look at those floor tiles."

It didn't take her long to zero in on a muted gray with flecks of brown in the floor tile. "It's dramatic, and it calls back to the wood flooring. I think it'll blend well with the wall tile as well. And it's the least costly of all three, which you wouldn't know by looking at it."

Linc knew it was a sturdy tile that would stand the test of time, which was what mattered most, and Hazel was right about the design, so he agreed. "Okay, now on to the countertops for both baths?"

"Let's do this."

That turned out to be the easiest since Hazel decided white would go best so as not to mess with the other colors. They chose a nice quartz together and he went to the counter to order everything. After they checked out they headed to the kitchen and bath store.

"This is way more fun than I thought it was going to be," Hazel said, her eyes gleaming as they walked through the doors.

*T*hey chose vanities in black for both bathrooms, though they had more drawers than he had originally intended. She hadn't gravitated to bargain-basement stuff, but not the most expensive items, either. She stayed within his budget, and that worked for him.

"There's never enough bathroom storage," she argued. "In fact, the primary bath has enough space to add a linen closet, which would be invaluable. You should do that."

"Where?"

"South wall. You could place it just behind the door. It doesn't have to be huge. It just needs to have shelves for towels and such."

"Okay. I see your point. Linen closet it is."

She grinned. "Perfect."

After they picked out sinks for both bathrooms, along with faucets and hardware, they decided they were hungry, so they ended up at a nearby Mexican restaurant.

Hazel took a long swallow of her iced tea. "That was fun. Shopping for things with you. For the house. I think it's going to look amazing when it's finished."

"I think so, too. And thanks for your help. You have an eye for this kind of thing. You know, I could use an apprentice. I could finish these jobs in half the time."

She laughed. "Trust me, you don't want to be around me when I'm wielding a hammer. You'd be risking your life."

"Not your area of expertise?"

"I've tried it. I can manage with tools, but that's about it. I'm certainly not apprentice quality."

"Too bad. I guess I'll just have to relegate you to shopping and design."

She grabbed a chip and scooped it in the salsa. "Now that I can do. Clearly, you need me."

He ate a chip and chewed thoughtfully.

Yeah, he needed her all right. The question that kept hovering around in his head was—exactly how desperate was that need getting, and when the time came, would he be able to let her go?

As he watched her draw her hair back from her eyes, he couldn't imagine not seeing her again. But he hadn't broached the subject of his feelings. Or asked about her feelings, for that matter. At some point they were going to need to have a conversation about said feelings. And since Hazel hadn't yet brought it up, he supposed he was going to have to be the one to do that.

Except—he wasn't a feelings kind of guy. Or at least a talking-about-feelings kind of guy. But maybe it was time to be that guy.

Because he couldn't plan his future—and maybe their future—without having a serious talk with Hazel.

He made a mental note to do that. Soon.

You're avoiding.

He popped a chip into his mouth. Shut up.

It's the truth and you know it. No time like now.

She sat across from him, smiling and finishing the last of her taco while she went on about how much fun she'd had today. They'd had a good day. Nothing was stopping him from bringing up the topic now.

But how, exactly, did one talk about feelings? About love? About a potential future in the middle of a Mexican restaurant?

He'd do it later.

Coward.

Fuck off.

"How about dessert?" he asked her, and she smiled, and he knew that later was the best idea.

CHAPTER TWENTY-SIX

Something wasn't right. Hazel could tell the minute they got up this morning. He wasn't acting like his usual self. He was normally so upbeat, so happy. Instead, he was grumpy and unwilling to play. And that just wasn't at all like Freddie.

He wouldn't eat this morning, and he was usually the first one to the food bowl. He didn't seem to want any water, either. After she fed the other dogs, she brought him upstairs and climbed into bed with her cup of coffee and Freddie. He lay in her lap, looking tired and listless. Normally, he'd want to be with the pack, right in the middle of anything going on with the other dogs.

She ran her hand over his soft fur. "What's wrong, baby boy? Not feeling well today?"

He looked up at her with his sad, soulful brown eyes, breaking her heart because she knew he didn't feel good.

Linc appeared in the doorway. "I didn't see you downstairs with the pups. What's wrong with Freddie?"

"I don't know. He's . . . off. I think he might be sick."

To prove her point, Freddie popped up and promptly barfed on the bedspread.

Linc grimaced. "I'd say he's definitely sick. Poor guy."

She put Freddie on the floor and stripped the bed. While she was cleaning up, the poor pup threw up two more times. Linc cleaned up the floor while she got the bedding started in the washing machine. She put the other pups outside to keep them away from Freddie. She took Freddie's temp. It was higher than normal. She decided to call the veterinarian's office, and they told her to bring him in right away. She went upstairs to get dressed, wound her hair on top of her head, slipped into her shoes, and went downstairs, finding Linc cradling Freddie in his arms.

"He really doesn't feel well, does he?" he asked, slowly stroking Freddie's back.

She shook her head. "I'm hoping it's nothing serious, but the vet's office told me to bring him in."

"Want me to go with you?"

"What? Oh, no, it's not necessary. You have work to do. But thanks for offering."

"Okay. If you need me, though, let me know."

He had no idea how much she appreciated his offer to be there for her. She was so used to doing things on her own, especially with the dogs. She wouldn't know how to ask for help.

"I'll be back as soon as I can."

He grasped her hand. "Take all the time you need. I've got the other pups."

She squeezed his hand, then lifted up to press a quick kiss to his lips. "Thank you."

She got Freddie into his crate in the car and headed to the vet's office, trying to think positive thoughts. At a stoplight, she took a peek into the back seat. Freddie had settled in on the blanket in the crate, asleep.

At least he seemed relaxed, so that was good.

The vet's office was crowded, and the receptionist told Hazel she'd squeezed her in, so there would likely be a bit of a wait. Hazel didn't mind, grateful that she could get in at all today. She took a seat, and Freddie, who normally would be anxious and excited at the vet's office because of all the strange animals there, curled up on her lap and went back to sleep.

Yes, there was definitely something wrong with her dog. Now she was the anxious one. But she kept her anxiety at bay by observing all the animals in the waiting room. There was a white fluffy cat in a carrier sitting in the chair across from her. The cat was giving sweet little mews, and the woman and little girl there with the cat whispered comforting words to it.

In another chair there was a big, burly guy holding a tiny brown puppy. Hazel stared, trying to figure out the breed of the pup, and honestly had no idea, but the guy cuddled the pup like it was pure gold, and that made her heart squeeze.

Every few minutes a tech would come out and call a name. The cat and its family went into a room, and the guy with his small puppy disappeared as well, their seats taken by new people and new animals.

Busy place.

She waited, and Freddie continued to sleep, fortunately.

"Freddie?"

She looked up to see Malina the vet tech smiling down at her. "Hi, Malina."

"Hi. Come on in." Hazel got up and carried a now-awake Freddie. "What's up with Freddie today?"

She had always brought the dogs to this clinic, so everyone knew the animals, something she appreciated. She told Malina what was going on.

"Poor baby," Malina said, taking Freddie from her and running her hand over his head. "We'll get his vitals and then the doctor will see him. Doc also asked for a fecal test and blood work."

"Yeah, I brought a fecal sample with me." She knew the drill when the dogs were well and not well. She'd been through this before.

Malina was bright and friendly and gave Freddie a lot of pets and attention, the two things Freddie loved most. She set him on a towel on the table and did her work efficiently. "Doc should be in shortly."

"Thanks, Malina."

She closed the door and Hazel stood over Freddie, absently running her hand over his back as she surveyed the room. It was painted brightly, had dog cookies on the counter—no doubt treats for after shots—and felt cheerful.

The door opened and Dr. Amanda Harrison came in.

"Hi, Hazel. What's up with Freddie today?"

She explained Freddie's symptoms to Dr. Harrison, who then did an exam while speaking in soft tones to Freddie. "His abdomen isn't distended, so I don't think it's a foreign body. His fecal was negative for parasites, and we'll have to wait on blood work results. My guess is some kind of bacterial infection. I'm going to give him a shot for the nausea, and I'll send you home with antibiotics and nausea meds. That should help him feel better right away. If the results are any different I'll let you know. Withhold food today, but if he's up to it you can give him some light food tomorrow."

"Got it."

Dr. Harrison gave Freddie his shot, which didn't bother the pup at all. The doctor cupped Freddie's chin. "Stay out of trouble, mister. Everyone loves you." Freddie licked her nose and Dr. Harrison laughed. "Yeah, he's a lover all right."

"He sure is," Hazel said.

"Let me know if you need anything else."

"I will. Thanks, Doc."

Feeling so much better about her pup, she gathered him up and went to the front desk to pay for the services, which the foster organization would cover, fortunately. They got back into the car, and she sent a text to Linc, letting him know what the doc said and that they were headed back to the house.

Linc was in the driveway when she pulled in. He took Freddie's crate while she gathered up the paperwork and meds, and they went into the house. Linc freed Freddie from his crate, and all the dogs surrounded him, sniffing him all over. She let them out back, and Freddie looked improved already as he dashed out to the grass to pee. She breathed a sigh of relief when he went to play with the other dogs, even though he wasn't as animated as he normally would be. At least he had more pep than earlier, and that was a good sign.

"He seems better."

She nodded at Linc. "He got a shot and has some meds to take. Doc said it's probably a minor infection. I've got some meds to give him as well. And we can't feed him today. But as long as he's good, he should be back to normal routine in a couple of days."

He put his arm around her and pulled her close. "That's not too bad. I know you were worried."

"I was. But I'm happy he's okay."

"Are you hungry? I made breakfast burritos. I know you didn't eat this morning."

She tilted her head back to look at him. "You. Made breakfast."

"I'll have you know I'm an amazing cook."

"Is that right."

"It is. As long as it's eggs or steak. Or burgers."

"I'll hold you to making me a steak, then."

"You got it."

He left to go to the guesthouse and returned with a tray with an amazing breakfast burrito and some orange juice. She'd been so caught up on getting Freddie taken care of this morning, she hadn't paid the slightest attention to herself. Now, though, she realized she was ravenously hungry.

"Thank you for doing this. I was going to fix food when I got back."

He leaned back and unwrapped one of the burritos. "Now you don't have to."

She took a bite, then another, and didn't utter another word until she'd consumed the entire burrito. She polished it off with several swallows of juice.

"That was delicious. Thanks for including the bacon."

"Wouldn't be an awesome breakfast burrito without bacon in it."

She laughed. "I'll make a note of that for future breakfasts. Sausage would be good in it as well."

"I like either." He reached over to squeeze her hand. "Are you feeling better?"

She cocked her head to the side. "I feel fine."

"I mean about Freddie. You were so worried this morning. And then I was worried about him and you."

Her heart did a little flutter in her chest. "Oh. I'm good. And, yes, I was worried about him."

He leaned back in the chair. "What would you do if someone called today and wanted to adopt him?"

"Today? I'd tell them he's not feeling well and a meet and greet would have to wait a few days."

"And then?"

She didn't understand why he was asking the question. "I guess I'd take him to meet his prospective new parents. Why are you asking?"

"No reason. What about Gordon? What if someone wanted Gordon?"

She snorted out a laugh. "I think Gordon's a permanent member of my family. Not too many people want to adopt senior dogs."

"Some people do. Would you give him up? Would you give up Freddie?"

Now her heart fluttered for an entirely different reason. "It's my job to give them up."

"It was hard on you to let go of Boo."

She shuddered in a breath. "It's hard to let any of them go. But it's not like I can take them in and keep them all. I knew that when I first decided to foster. My job is to get them comfortable and happy and confident so that they are ready to be adopted."

"Huh. You make it sound easy."

She looked out over the yard where Lilith was lying protectively next to Freddie, who was napping under the palm tree. Gordon and Mitzi were fussing over a toy together, and Penny was sitting on the top pool step intently watching the pool vac snake around the bottom.

"It's never easy. I love them."

"What if you could keep them?"

She jerked her head toward him. "What?"

"If you had the opportunity to keep them, would you?"

"There's no point in even thinking that way since it's never going to happen. So I just . . . turn that part of myself off."

"You know it's okay to allow yourself to feel things. Even the hard things."

"I've felt a lot of hard things the past few years, Linc. More than my share."

He paused, then smoothed his hand down her arm. "Of course you have. I'm sorry. I can see why you'd want to shut down your emotions."

"I didn't say I was shut down. I feel . . . things. Just maybe at a less intense level than other people."

He studied her, frowning. "That doesn't even make sense."

"Maybe because it hasn't happened to you. Maybe someone hasn't shattered your heart to the point where you resolve not to feel anymore."

He scooted his chair around, then hers, so they were facing each other, her legs pinned between his thighs. "No, I mean it doesn't make sense in that I've never known anyone who has bigger feelings than you, Hazel. So if this is you with your emotions repressed, I'd sure as hell like to see you with full feelings."

"Oh."

She realized her one-word answer didn't suffice in relation to his thoughtful, beautiful words, but she didn't know how to respond to Linc, to her own overwhelming thoughts, and to her—yes, fine—feelings about all that he had said. Admitting some of those things to herself would be painful, might tear her apart. But Linc seemed to actually know her heart.

Could she trust that? Could she trust how she felt about him?

She'd trusted Andrew, once, and look where that had gotten her.

It was obvious that she knew nothing about love.

So what was she going to do about these burgeoning feelings she had for Linc? Stuff them deep inside and pretend they didn't exist?

Yes. Let's do that. We'll be safer that way.

Her inner voice was probably right. Better to be safe than to be hurt again.

Linc might be hot and gorgeous and kind and generous, but she had to guard her heart. At least until she reached the point where she could trust herself and her instincts again.

And who knew when that might be.

Maybe never.

CHAPTER TWENTY-SEVEN

*H*azel was being weird, and Linc didn't know what was going on with her. Hazel was being neither dark nor cranky. She was being polite and quiet, not her normal perky and funny self.

Since the guest bathroom had been finished, she'd moved back into the guest room, declaring without a word that she lacked interest in sharing his bed. Admittedly, that had hurt, but that was her choice to make, so he went with it, though he intended to talk to her about it.

Soon.

Coward.

Pretty sure I've told you to fuck off.

But he had been busy finishing off the main bath, and the appliances had come in, so he'd dived right into that project as well, keeping him working from sunup to sundown most days. And Hazel had been spending a lot of time with her sister and the kids, so they'd been mostly ships passing in the night the last week. Though she'd made sure to leave him prepared meals, which he'd told her she didn't need to do and she'd told him with a benign smile that was her job and she was going to make sure he stayed well-fed.

Having his stomach filled was the least of his worries at the moment.

He needed some advice. Eugene was useless since he wouldn't know a good relationship with a woman if it smacked him across the face. He made himself a tall glass of ice water and sat outside, watching the dogs busy themselves by sniffing things in the yard.

He pulled out his phone and punched Warren's number.

"Hey, what's up?" Warren asked.

"Not much. How are you and Joe?"

"We're good. I think we've found a surrogate."

"No shit, really?"

"Yeah. She just got her bachelor's degree in economics and wants to get her master's and then a PhD. But she doesn't want a mountain of debt, and she really wants to help us. She's smart as hell, Linc, and articulate and has done all her homework on surrogacy. She's not at all interested in having a kid of her own—at least not right now."

"She sounds kind of perfect."

"Yeah, let's hope so. We still have quite a few hoops to jump through, but hopefully this will work out."

"I really hope for you and Joe it does. You'll both make amazing dads."

"Thanks, bro. So what's up with you? How's the renovation going?"

"It's going great." He filled Warren in on where he was in the process.

"Sounds like it's moving along. It won't be long before you're done and ready to move on to the next project."

"Yeah." He really didn't want to think about that. Not yet. Just the mere thought of it made his stomach drop.

"And how's Hazel and her dogs?"

"She's . . . fine."

"Uh-oh. 'Fine' doesn't sound great. What's going on there?"

"That's the thing. I don't exactly know. She's being . . . not herself. Not angry or anything, but . . . distant."

"Did you do something wrong?"

"No. And that's what's bothering me. Things between us were going great, and then suddenly she's started pulling back. I don't exactly know what to do about it."

"You could try talking to her, telling her what you've noticed. And have you told her how you feel about her? How *do* you feel about her?"

"I have feelings. Deep feelings."

"Did you tell her that?"

"Not exactly."

He heard Warren's derisive laugh. "Which means you haven't told her shit. Tell her how you feel, Linc."

He leaned forward and dragged his fingers through his hair. "What if she doesn't feel the same way?"

"Then you'll know. Isn't it better knowing?"

"No. The one time I tried to tell a woman how I felt it blew up in my face."

Warren's voice softened. "She wasn't the right person. And ever since it's been one wrong woman after another. So maybe you've found the right one this time?"

"I dunno. Maybe."

He heard Warren's sigh. "I think you might be surprised by Hazel. I got a really good vibe from her when we met her. Give her a chance. Open up to her."

"Okay. I'll try. Hey, thanks, Warren."

"That's what I'm here for. I'm always right."

"Wow. Does that bullshit work in court?"

Warren laughed. "Hell yeah, it does. I gotta go. Love you."

"Love you, too. Later."

He felt immensely better and a lot more positive after his conversation with Warren. And maybe Warren was right. Money didn't ever seem to be an issue with Hazel other than her wanting to make it for herself, not looking for someone to provide it for her. They were on the same page on a lot of things, and the rest of it? They'd have to talk about it so they could work it out.

No, they would work it out.

Now he just had to hope that spike of positivity carried over when he talked to Hazel.

Penny came over and plopped a paw on his knee. He smoothed his hand over her head.

"What's up, girl? You ready for some playtime?"

She whimpered and gave him her best golden smile, which of course was a resounding yes.

"Okay, then. Let's do it."

He stood and headed out into the yard, pushing thoughts of Hazel to the background for now.

But soon, he and Hazel were going to have a conversation. And then he'd know for sure where this relationship was going.

CHAPTER TWENTY-EIGHT

Oh, Nat. A divorce? Are you sure about this?"

Natalie nodded her head. "I'm sure. Sean and I tried counseling sessions, but it became clear—to both of us—that we want different things. And no amount of counseling is going to change that."

Hazel sipped iced tea in Natalie's kitchen. Mom had taken the kids today, so it was nice and quiet. Nat had finally broken the news about her and Sean last week. Mom had freaked, of course, but then had gotten down to the business of telling Natalie exactly what steps she should take to put her marriage back together. Fortunately, Nat had ignored every bit of their mother's advice.

"What different things?" Hazel asked.

"He wants a dutiful woman who will spend her entire life being a stay-at-home wife and mother. I love the kids, but that's not my only identity. I want to go back to interior design, Hazel. I used to be really good at it."

"Used to? You still are. Look around here, Nat. Even with two small children, this house is a showplace."

Nat eked out a smile. "Thank you. I love this place. I'd like to stay here—the kids love it here and the school district is ideal—but there's no way I'll be able to afford it on my own after the divorce."

"You left a promising career to support Sean while he got *his* career off the ground. Now it's his turn to support you. Fight for what you need in the divorce, Natalie. He can afford to pay alimony and child support."

Natalie gave her an uneasy look. "I don't know . . ."

Having had a man take everything from her, the last thing she wanted was for the same thing to happen to her sister. "You won't be taking anything from him that you don't deserve. Do you have a good attorney?"

She nodded. "An excellent one. She was recommended by one of the women in my moms' group who recently went through a divorce. She got a very nice settlement."

Hazel grabbed her sister's hand. "I'm so sorry, Nat."

"Oh, it'll be fine. This is for the best. And then I'll . . . I'll . . ."

Hazel waited, knowing that Natalie always had her shit together—until she didn't. And then Nat burst into tears, crumpling into Hazel's arms. She wrapped her arms around Nat and smoothed her hand over her hair. She held her, letting her cry it out until she had nothing left.

Then she handed her tissues to wipe her tears and blow her nose. She grabbed her by the shoulders and made eye contact.

"Natalie. You are a big bully, and you've been standing up to Mom and pushing me around your whole life. If anyone can win this divorce battle and take back control over your life, it's you."

Nat batted wide, wet eyes at her. "That's the nicest thing you've ever said to me."

Hazel grinned. "You've got this."

She nodded. "I've totally got this."

After Nat settled, Hazel made them chicken salad sandwiches for lunch and they sat outside on Nat's gorgeous back patio. Plenty of shade, amazing trees and bushes, and a babbling brook winding through the back of the yard with decorative rocks. It was peaceful and glorious.

"You could also add in landscape design to your repertoire."

Nat glanced around the yard. "That would be so fun."

"You'd be excellent at it. When I have a huge, cool yard—which I absolutely will someday—you could design a gorgeous retreat spot for me, and then a beautiful place where I can house all the dogs I plan to foster."

Natalie stared out across the yard for a while without saying a word. "How many dogs?"

"I don't know. Ten, maybe fifteen."

Instead of wrinkling her nose whenever the dogs were mentioned, Nat nodded. "You'd need several acres. Lots of trees and greenery for the dogs as well, so they'd have shade and space to run around."

"Yes."

"And then a beautiful oasis for yourself and your—well, whoever, if you want that—to lounge and play." She got up and went into the house, coming back outside with her pencil and sketchbook.

Hazel watched in awe as her sister began to draw out a

backyard sketch. And with every half hour that passed, Hazel's vision for her future began to materialize on the paper. It was as if Nat had crawled into her brain and pulled out every single one of her dreams.

There were copious trees and a huge play yard with toys, exercise and play equipment for the dogs, plus a small pool. Any dog would be happy to call that their playland.

And the adult playland was perfect. A large patio with an outdoor kitchen, a covered pool with rocks and a waterfall, and so many trees beyond that looked so rich and thick and . . . She just sighed.

"It's so beautiful, Nat. In a perfect world, where I had money."

"Hey, it's okay to dream big. And you can always do this in stages, you know. Or modify it so it works for you."

"That's true."

Now it was Nat who laid her hand on Hazel's arm. "Don't give up on your dreams, Hazel. Not for any reason or for anybody. Not ever again."

Hazel lifted her chin. "Believe me, I don't intend to."

"Speaking of anybody, how are things with Linc?"

"Oh, they're . . . fine."

Her sister raised a brow. "Just fine? Is something wrong? Did he do something?"

She shook her head. "He didn't do anything. He says all the right things, does all the right things. It's me. I have feelings for him, Nat. Big, deep feelings."

"Oh, honey. How did that happen?"

"I don't know. I wasn't planning on it. It just happened. And now that it has, I'm scared to death and I've been avoiding him."

"As you should. The last thing you need is to get involved with someone again. Andrew hurt you, worse than I have ever seen anyone hurt. You need a long time to heal, to become the independent person you're meant to be."

Wise words. But were they meant for her or for Natalie? Hazel didn't know.

And she still didn't know what to do about her feelings for Linc.

CHAPTER TWENTY-NINE

*T*onight was the night. Linc wasn't going to let Hazel ignore him any longer.

It was a cool day, with rain on and off. She'd taken the dogs for three walks. Really long walks. The poor pups were exhausted and currently avoiding her so they could nap. When she wasn't harassing the dogs, she had closed herself in the guest room, saying she would be busy doing "important stuff" on her laptop. She'd only surfaced to feed him breakfast and lunch, taking both meals up to her room to eat alone.

In other words, she was avoiding him.

He was ending the freeze-out one way or another tonight. He finished up his work by five, which worked well for his plans. He put his tools away and headed upstairs, pausing outside her bedroom.

Just knock, jackass.

He inhaled a deep breath and let it out, then knocked. Once. Then twice.

"Busy in here."

Irritated, he said, "I'm coming in."

He opened the door. She was sitting cross-legged on the bed, Gordon on one side of her, Mitzi asleep at her feet, laptop on her lap. She didn't even look up.

"I said I was busy."

"I'm taking you to dinner tonight. We need to talk. Nice steak and seafood house. Seven p.m." He closed the door before she could object and headed to his room and straight to the shower, hoping she wouldn't burst in and tell him to go straight to hell.

He took his time in the shower, scrubbing off the day's grime, then stood in the closet deciding what to wear, as if that was the most important decision of his life when it very likely wouldn't matter at all. Knowing Hazel and her mood lately, she wouldn't even want to go to dinner with him. But he was still going through with the preparations. He chose brown slacks and a white button-down shirt, went downstairs, fed the dogs, and took them outside, grateful for the uncharacteristic cool breeze that had swept through today. He didn't know how long it would last, but he'd take it right now.

The door opened, and he held his breath as Hazel walked out wearing a copper-colored sleeveless dress that clung to every curve, highlighting her moonless-night black hair, which fell in dark waves across her shoulders.

"Damn," he said. "You're stunning."

"And you're demanding."

"Yeah, sorry. But I really want to talk to you."

She didn't smile, but she didn't punch him, either. Instead, she shrugged. "Fortunately for you, I'm hungry."

"Then let's go."

He didn't want her climbing in his dirty truck, so they took her car. The dead silence was uncomfortable, but he'd endure it because she'd agreed to come. She stared out the window while he drove. He tried to make small talk, but she only responded with one- or two-word answers.

Okay, so this wasn't going to be easy. But he was determined to break through this wall she'd put up between them.

When they got to the restaurant, he told the hostess his name and they were seated right away. He'd chosen this place because it was quiet and private, so they could have a conversation without other people around to eavesdrop.

They'd gotten lucky and scored a corner table even further removed from the other guests. It had a view of the water and felt cozy and private.

"This is nice, huh?" he asked after their server left the wine list and food menu.

"Yes. Very."

He studied the wine menu, then slid it over to Hazel. "Thoughts on wine?"

She looked at it for a bit. "We could do a merlot. It would go well with either steak or seafood. Or a sauvignon blanc if you prefer a white."

"Either works for me. You choose which one you want."

She pursed her lips. He was dying to kiss her. He missed kissing her, missed the feel of her skin against his. Even a chair away he could smell her.

Peaches. He loved peaches. He could lick her neck right now. At least he'd start there, then pull that dress off of her and taste her all over.

"The merlot, I think," she finally said, pulling him from his dirty fantasies.

He ordered a bottle of the merlot when their server returned. When he turned back to Hazel, her face was buried in the menu. A big, thick, leather-covered menu.

He'd been menu blocked. Okay, he could still talk to her. He'd make her talk to him.

"Hazel."

He heard a muttered *hmm* in response.

"You've been avoiding me."

The menu dipped, just enough for him to see her eyes. "I have not."

"Come on. Yeah, you have. Why?"

"Because . . . well, the reason doesn't matter." She still hadn't fully dropped the menu.

"It does matter. Everything was going fine."

"And that's the problem. I don't trust 'fine.'"

"Explain, please."

Instead, the menu block continued, so maybe it was time for him to speak up.

"I have feelings for you, Hazel. And they scare the hell out of me."

The menu dipped, showing her eyes, all wide and surprised.

"I have feelings, too," she said. "For you."

She'd said the words softly, but he heard them clearly. Loudly, as if she'd shouted them all through the restaurant. He couldn't help but smile.

"You do?"

She finally set the menu on the table. "Yes. And I'm scared, too. I don't trust my feelings."

"Why not?"

"Because I'm not a good judge of men, or character. Andrew was awesome when we first started out. We had all these grand plans for our future, and it all blew up in my face."

"But that's on him. He's the one who changed, not you. He was the one who broke all of his promises. How could you possibly have seen that coming?"

Their server returned with the wine and poured it out for both of them.

Hazel took several swallows of her wine. "In answer to your question about my ex, I don't know. But I should have known. I was unaware of everything going on behind my back. I was so focused on myself and my life and my needs, or maybe afraid to face the truth of what was happening. If I didn't say it or realize it, then it wasn't happening, right?" She shrugged. "I don't know. All I do know is that he snuck around behind me and took everything. All my hopes and dreams and self-confidence."

Linc dipped his head down, then back up again. "And look at you now. You're strong and confident with a new dream for your future. And you're going to make it happen, aren't you? You're never going to take shit from anyone ever again, and you'll never let any man take what's yours away from you again, right?"

She just stared at him for a few seconds, then gave a quick nod. "Yes."

"I believe in you, Hazel. You can do anything you set your mind to. And you don't need any man to help you get there."

She inhaled and let out a huge sigh. "Thank you for that. And I'm sorry for the way I've been acting. I need to work on trust."

"You can trust me, Hazel. I won't hurt you."

He could tell from the look on her face that she was wary. He couldn't blame her. He'd just have to continue to prove to her that he was the guy she could count on.

*H*azel took a sip of her coffee, savoring the tangy flavor. She'd had the most amazing lobster—ridiculously expensive, but Linc had insisted. He'd had steak *and* lobster.

So decadent.

Plus, he'd told her he had feelings. Feelings. And then he'd pumped her up and told her she could be anything and do anything. Live her dreams.

And then she'd proceeded to have a whole lot of wine, while Linc had made amazing small talk about the dogs and his progress on the house as if he hadn't just turned her world upside down.

She'd also had cheesecake. Exceptionally good cheesecake, too. Kind of an awesome topper to an amazing night.

She felt good. Not completely inebriated, just . . . calm and relaxed. And happy.

Linc paid the bill and they walked outside. The wind had picked up, and Hazel smelled rain in the air, saw lightning across the water. She tilted her head back and let the beauty of it roll right over her.

Linc slipped his hand in hers. "Feel like taking a walk?"

She looked over at him and nodded. "Sounds good."

There was a walkway by the water, and every quarter mile or so there were benches where you could sit. Linc sat them down at the first bench where they could watch the lightning across the water.

There were so many things she wanted to say to Linc. Spill out all her fears, and talk about how she felt about him. In detail. But she couldn't make the words come out.

"Thank you for dinner," she finally said, knowing it was woefully inadequate.

"It was good, wasn't it?"

"Exceptionally good. And totally extravagant. I mean, we could have gone somewhere else. You don't have to impress me with fancy dinners. It's not like you're a millionaire, you know."

He coughed. "Hey, it was just one night out, right?"

"I guess so."

"And I said we needed to talk. I didn't want to do that at a greasy burger joint."

Her lips curved upward. "I like greasy burger joints."

He grinned. "Me, too. But tonight was special."

"You're not going to propose or anything, are you?"

He laughed. "No. Not yet, anyway."

Now it was her turn to cough, because her breath had momentarily left her body. "Just for future reference, I am nowhere near ready to get married again."

"Duly noted. I'll table the proposal for some random date in the far future."

"You are a vicious tease, Lincoln Kennedy."

He picked up her hand and pressed a kiss to the back of it. "And you are too beautiful for words, Hazel Bristow. Is it all right if I kiss you? I promise no proposal implied."

"Yes. Definitely kiss me."

He leaned in and brushed his lips across hers. She sighed into the kiss, and he drew her into his arms, opening his mouth, his tongue sliding inside to flick against hers.

She wanted him. Right now, on this bench, with the wind whipping around them and thunder rolling in the distance.

But then he pulled back. "Storm's getting closer."

She swept her hand across his jaw. "I'll say."

He let out a husky laugh, then stood, taking her with him. "Come on, let's go home."

He hadn't been kidding about the storm getting closer. They'd no more than gotten inside the car when the skies opened, dumping heavy rain and wind, the thunder cracking so loud it seemed as if it was trying to get them.

She'd never feared storms; in fact, she loved them fiercely. They always revved her up, and tonight's was no different.

"We might have to sit here for a while," Linc said, staring out the windshield. "Can't even see to drive."

She reached over and walked her fingertips down his arm. "Whatever will we do while we wait?"

He arched a brow. "Seriously? Here?"

"What? Suddenly shy?"

Before she knew what was happening, he grabbed her and pulled her over to his seat, at the same time pushing his seat all the way back, giving her room to straddle him.

"I am never shy."

"Oh, good. Now if only we . . ." She reached between them and rubbed his already hard cock. "Never mind. No problem there. Got a condom?"

He arched and dug into his pocket. "Always."

They both maneuvered while he unzipped his pants and Hazel helped slide the condom on. And then she moved her underwear to the side and slid down over him, feeling every glorious steely hard inch of him entering her.

His cock pulsed. Oh, that was so good. She quivered, then began to move forward and back, her clit dragging against him. She was already so close to coming, that feeling of being on a rocket ready for takeoff. And with every thrust the fuse burned down a little farther.

"Oh yes," she murmured, raising her hands up to press against the ceiling, rocking against Linc to give them both what they needed. "Oh yes, right there. I'm right there."

He grabbed her hips, his fingers digging in. "Right there with you, babe."

And she was climaxing with a deep moan, falling against Linc's chest to dig her nails into his shoulders as she rode out these incredible sensations, absorbing his release as well while the storm raged all around them.

She was out of breath and utterly satiated.

Linc held her like that for a while, stroking her back, kissing her, until the storm began to ease up. She finally lifted off of him and made her way back to her seat while he removed the condom and tied it off, sliding it into an available plastic shopping bag that was in the back seat.

"Remind me to toss that when we get home," he said.

"I definitely will."

They put their seat belts on and Linc put the car in gear. Hazel leaned against the headrest and was out cold in less than five minutes.

CHAPTER THIRTY

Now that they had talked things through—at least initially, things between Linc and Hazel had smoothed out and were back to the way they had been before. She got up and made him breakfast, they ate together, and they made love—a lot—which put both of them in a good mood.

Today he was painting the living room. Hardware for all the cabinets was ready to be installed, as well as the new faucet for the kitchen and all the light switches.

It wouldn't be long before he was finished. He should have already purchased a new property, and as of yet, he hadn't.

He knew why, too.

Hazel.

He wanted a future with her. But things were going so well between them right now that he didn't want to do anything to fuck it up.

Like also telling her about the money?

His conscience was getting to be a giant pain in the ass.

He didn't think she'd care about that part, anyway. So he had a lot of money. What difference would that make?

Maybe that you never told her.

Of course he never told her. He'd learned that lesson painfully. Never tell them you have money because then you never know whether it's you they want, or the money and the lifestyle.

He didn't live rich. He lived comfortably, sure, but most often he renovated empty houses. He hadn't put down permanent roots anywhere.

Not yet, anyway.

So, again, what difference would it make?

Anyway, that was the least of his worries. Right now he needed to do two things—finish this house so he could put it up for sale, and buy another property to renovate. Then he and Hazel could have the big conversation.

Aren't you doing it backward? Shouldn't you have the big conversation with Hazel first?

He lifted his head, letting the paint roller slide down as he thought about that.

His conscience was probably right about that part. But that part would be really hard, which was probably why he was delaying doing anything at all.

Coward.

"Oh my God, would you go fuck yourself already?"

"Are you angry at the paint?"

He flipped around and smiled at Hazel. "No. It looks great. Doesn't it look great?"

"I love the color. It's not a blinding white but it's not a dark gray, either. It's good. Neutral. Any buyer would be happy with it."

"That's what I wanted to hear."

She came up to stand beside him, staring at the wall. "So who were you cussing at?"

"Just running some ideas around in my head, and I have this internal voice that sometimes—well, often—disagrees with my brilliant ideas."

"Oh my God, you do? I have an internal voice, too. It's very annoying."

He laughed. "Good to know I'm not entirely losing my mind."

She leaned into him. "No, it's not just you. So what were your ideas?"

This was not the time or place for that conversation. "How about we talk about it over dinner?"

"Okay. I'm making fish tacos and rice."

"That sounds so good."

"Good. I'm going to take the dogs out for a bit. I'll see you later."

"Okay."

She rose up on her toes and pressed a kiss to his lips, smiled, then left the room.

Yeah, his conscience was right.

They needed to have the big talk tonight.

*H*azel had finished cooking the fish and had all the other ingredients for the tacos ready to go. She warmed the soft tacos, put them in the container so they'd stay warm, then arranged everything on the tray and carried it to the table.

It was incredibly nice to be able to cook inside in the kitchen again, a spectacular kitchen, she might add, now that it was completed.

She was really going to miss this house when they had to move.

A pang of something she knew was fear and longing gnawed inside of her at the thought of all of this coming to an end soon, but she pushed it aside, refusing to think about it right now. And all those fears had to do with Linc instead of herself.

She had a plan for her future. Not a firm plan, but she had options. And money saved, which was more than she'd had before. So for the first time she felt—if not overly comfortable, at least . . . safe. And safe felt pretty good.

What didn't feel so good was the thought of losing Linc. And that's what she didn't want to think about.

Tell him you love him.

Yeah, that was easier said than done. It was one thing to have a fun romp while he was here renovating. Another thing entirely to talk about what happens next, and if he had room for her in his life after this house was finished.

And that's what caused the gnawing in her stomach most days.

Linc had cleaned up and moved a long folding table and chairs from the guesthouse storage into the kitchen so they could eat in the house, so that's where they ate some of their meals since he had already finished all his work in the dining area. He was upstairs showering and changing, so she poured them glasses of iced tea and set the table, finishing up just as he made his way downstairs.

The dogs were outside enjoying the cooler weather, all of them grouped together in a cuddle pile and snoozing under the palm tree.

"That smells so good."

She looked over and smiled at Linc. "Thanks. I don't know about you, but I'm super hungry."

"Me, too. Let's eat."

He pulled out a chair for her and she sat. They busied themselves filling their tacos with the slaw and fish, along with the special sauce she'd made.

Linc took a huge bite, chewed, and swallowed. "Damn, Hazel. This is great."

She couldn't help but grin. He always complimented her food and it always made her feel good. "Thank you. The garlic lime crema felt right to me."

"It feels right to my taste buds for sure." He took another huge bite, nearly polishing off the first taco in two bites.

She was glad she'd made a lot of fish and slaw because she really liked this dish. She made a mental note to type it up and add it to her recipe file.

"You're going to make this again for me, right?" he asked after they both finished.

"Of course. I'm adding it to my recipes."

"Have you ever thought about writing a cookbook?"

"Me?" She pointed to herself. "No. I'm just an average cook, Linc."

"You might think that, but you're not. You have a gift with food, Hazel. And I would know because I've eaten at a lot of fancy restaurants. You know just the right ingredients to make basic food into a tasty delight."

"Ooh. Tasty delight. Maybe you could write the forward in my nonexistent cookbook."

"Funny. But I know people that I think could hook you up with a book deal."

She cocked her head to the side. "Don't tease me. And also, no thank you."

"Why not?"

"I don't know." She shrugged. "It's scary to even think about? What if I failed?"

"What if you succeeded? Can you imagine that?"

"No. I've never even thought about it. I mean, yes, I have thought about writing a cookbook, but just for myself, you know? To keep my favorite recipes in a pdf file. All organized and such. Not for other people to see."

He crossed his arms. "What if I invited some people to taste food you cooked?"

She snorted out a laugh. "Where? Here, at our folding table in the kitchen in the house you haven't finished yet?"

"No. In a restaurant. I know a guy here who's the chef and owner of a pretty amazing restaurant. I'd bet he'd be happy to let you go in and cook for him."

"Thanks, but no. I'm happy doing what I do. Cooking because I enjoy it. Working with the dogs. I don't need more than that. Besides, cookbooks are written by people who have a following, who are already in the limelight. That's not me. And I don't want to be some restaurant star, either. I'm happy where I am, Linc. I occasionally work as a chef and it helps me make money doing what I really love. If that seems beneath you—"

"Whoa." Linc held his hands up. "I never said that. I admire the work you do with the dogs, Hazel. It takes so much self-sacrifice to foster animals, to put your heart out there and see to their well-being and futures. Don't ever think that I see you as anything less than admirable for the work you do. I was only making suggestions that I thought you might find interesting and fun."

She realized she might have overreacted. "Okay. Sorry I flipped out."

"You didn't. I pushed. I just want you to know I believe in you, no matter what road you choose."

Of course he did. He always did. "Thanks for that."

"Sure. Anyway, there's a property I'm interested in, and I was wondering if you'd look at it with me."

"It's local?"

"Yeah."

She couldn't help the smile that crossed her face. "So, you're thinking of renovating another property in Orlando?"

"Yes. I just found it this afternoon, and it's kind of perfect."

She was intrigued. And very excited that he'd consider staying on here. "Are you sure you want me along?"

"Absolutely."

"Okay. Just let me know when and I'll go with you."

They cleaned up the plates and stood side by side at the sink, one of them rinsing and the other one loading the shiny new dishwasher.

"Hey, you were going to tell me why you were cussing at the wall this afternoon."

"Huh?"

She wasn't buying his confused look. "Come on. What was it that upset you?"

"Oh, I wasn't upset. Just throwing some ideas around in my head. One of them was the idea of staying here. It just brings about its own set of . . . not problems, just . . . opportunities. And I got irritated because I didn't have all the solutions right then."

"Can I help?"

"You are. You're going to go look at that house with me. And then . . ."

She waited. He took her hand.

"Then we'll go from there, okay?"

She nodded, knowing there was a lot more he wanted to say. But she could wait.

"Okay."

She wished she knew what it was that he wanted to say to her, or what was bothering him. She hoped that someday very soon he'd trust her enough to unburden himself and open up his heart.

Because she was in love with him.

CHAPTER THIRTY-ONE

*L*inc was up to his eyeballs in computer work, talking with his local Realtor about possible properties to purchase, as well as fighting with a particularly annoying wiring problem in the upstairs primary bedroom.

How could a ceiling fan be such a pain in the ass? He did not have time for this.

Hazel had been busy poring over paperwork related to the foster organization, some annual reporting or something that she had been grumbling about. He'd kept his distance because he knew what kind of a nuisance paperwork could be.

The one house he'd wanted to show Hazel had sold before he could even get a showing, but there was another he really liked that was about to come on the market, so he was making plans to go see it soon. Hopefully, that wouldn't sell out from under him. In the meantime, he had a lot to do to keep himself busy.

Like figuring out why this damned ceiling fan wouldn't work.

His phone buzzed and he picked it up, then grinned at the FaceTime call from his brother Eugene. "Hey, asshole. What's up?"

"Just missed your sweet face," Eugene said, leaning back in a chair in his office. "How's it going? Got that house finished yet?"

"Just about."

"Where are you off to next?"

"I'm . . . not sure. Maybe I'll hang out here for a while."

Eugene looked surprised. "No shit. You like Orlando that much?"

"It's nice here and I can't complain about the weather."

Eugene gave him a wry smile. "Or maybe it's the company you're keeping?"

"Maybe."

"How is Hazel?"

"She's good. What are you up to? Designing a new, previously unknown way to play video games?"

"Actually, I might have something bigger in the pipeline. That's why I'm calling. I wanted to get your feel for Orlando. For the real estate out there."

This was a surprise. "You're thinking of moving out here?"

"I have a tasty job offer that might be too good to pass up."

"No shit. Tell me about it."

"Can't just yet. Not until I sign on the dotted line. But if I do, it's a five-year contract and I'm not going to do that in a rental."

"Ah. So you want to purchase property. I just happen to have a house that's almost ready to go on the market."

He laughed. "Maybe. Is it a nice house?"

"It's a perfect house." Linc told him about it.

"Sounds great. But I have specific needs that don't come with most houses."

"Like what? A sex dungeon?"

Eugene snorted. "No. Just a lot of tech stuff. And a soundproof room."

"Huh. Well, not sure this house could accommodate that, but the pool is nice."

"Good to know. But you'd look around for something for me?"

"Hell, if I do end up staying here, I'll renovate it for you. How much fun would that be? The two of us together again?"

Eugene laughed. "I can't say I'd hate that. One of the biggest drawbacks to taking this job would be leaving Mom. And Warren. And pretty much everyone I know. Not that I like you or anything, but it'd be nice to have family nearby."

"Yeah, it sure would. Have you talked about it with Mom and Warren yet?"

He shook his head. "Not until I know more. But you know how Mom is. She's big on all of us having our own independent lives, even if she misses us when we're not around."

"That's what airplanes are for, Euge."

"Yeah."

"Let me know as soon as you decide, okay?"

"Will do. Gotta go."

"Love you, bro."

"Love you, too. Later."

They hung up and Linc put his phone back in his pocket, smiling as he thought about the possibility of Eugene living close by.

He and his brothers rarely saw eye to eye—on anything. They all had distinct personalities. But in the end, they were family. And family was everything. The idea of having Eugene here, of building something permanent here?

Yeah, that appealed.

The day was really looking up.

He glared at the ceiling fan. "And you are going to start fucking working, or I'm taking you apart and burning you in the driveway, got it?"

He grabbed the remote, clicked the on switch, and the blades started rotating.

"That's what I'm talking about."

One disaster averted.

Now he felt really damned good about the rest of the day.

CHAPTER THIRTY-TWO

*H*azel had amused herself all day with the pups. They'd gone for a long walk this morning, though Mitzi and Gordon's walk had been shorter and then they'd finished off in the stroller.

Currently, Lilith was on a roll trying to micromanage all the dogs. Gordon and Mitzi ignored her, preferring the company of each other—which mostly consisted of napping together. Penny was adorably in love with Linc and followed him everywhere, so she didn't pay much attention to Lilith's attempts to herd her back to where Freddie was busily trying to dislodge a rock from the grass.

Freddie seemed to be the only one who toed the line where Lilith was concerned.

"At least one of them listens to you, girl," Hazel said as she washed down the walk around the pool.

Lilith looked up at her, her skinny little tail thumping wildly as she followed Hazel around the yard while Freddie had found a bug to bark at.

Her phone buzzed. She thought it was Linc since he'd been out all day running errands, and they'd made plans for her to go with him to look at a couple of houses he was interested in purchasing for his next project.

It wasn't Linc. It was a text from Sandy.

Awesome news! I think someone wants to adopt Freddie.

Her heart clenched. She punched the call button and Sandy answered.

"Isn't it exciting? They're an amazing couple. They already have a dachshund, and they're so excited about the idea of adopting another. I've already run background and done the home visit. I think Freddie would love them."

He loved her, too.

Hazel flopped down to sit right there on the grass, Freddie crawling into her lap, followed by Lilith. She swallowed, though her throat was dry. "Great."

"When can you arrange to bring him for a meet and greet?"

How about never? She shook her head. Keeping these dogs wasn't her job, no matter how much she loved them. "Um . . . can I get back to you after I check my schedule? I was just about to run out."

"Oh, sure. Just let me know. I gotta run, too. Later."

Hazel clicked off and tried to breathe in, but her chest felt tight. She looked down and smoothed her hand over Freddie's soft back, her eyes filling with tears.

Dammit, she sucked at this.

Shaking her head, she pushed all thoughts of Freddie to the back of her mind. He was still here, for now, and he was still hers.

She needed to get ready to head out with Linc, who told her he'd be back around three o'clock, and it was already two thirty. Since she'd spent time in the pool with the pups today, she was kind of a wreck, not to mention the tears.

She picked Freddie up, unable to resist pressing a kiss to his long snout before setting him back on the grass. He bounded off with Lilith hot on his heels.

After she took a quick shower, she towel dried her hair and ran through it with a comb, then blow-dried it and put on a quick touch of makeup. It was too humid right now for anything else.

She put on a sundress and her sandals and went downstairs.

Linc was there, wearing shorts and a short-sleeved shirt, his hair still damp.

"I didn't even know you were here."

"When I got home I saw you were busy getting ready so I showered in the other bathroom."

"Oh. Okay." He could have stepped in the shower with her. Maybe he was preoccupied. She certainly was. She wouldn't hold it against him.

"Ready to go?"

"Absolutely."

She brought the pups inside, refilled their water bowls, and gave them all a treat, and they headed toward their respective happy places for their afternoon nap in the cool air-conditioning.

Then Hazel and Linc got into his truck and buckled up.

He looked over at her. "You look pretty. I like that dress."

For the first time in a couple of hours, she smiled. "Thank

you. I figured if we were meeting with a Realtor, I should look decent. Plus it's humid and a dress is cooler."

"Well, you might be cool, but looking at you is making me all kinds of hot."

She laughed. "I guess you'll have to suffer through it."

"I could take you back inside and take that dress off."

"Not a chance. I've been looking forward to seeing these houses."

He shrugged. "Not as much fun as wild sex."

"True, but still, you're all but finished with the house. It's time to put it up for sale, and find a new place, right?"

"I guess so."

She hid her smirk at the disappointment on his face by looking out the window.

They arrived at the house. To say it was underwhelming was an understatement. Linc's Realtor, Jennifer, let them inside and told them to look around, that she'd wait out back.

Hazel stayed quiet during the walk-through of the four-bedroom, two-and-a-half-bath home, making mental notes as she wandered through the kitchen and living area, and down the hall to investigate the bedrooms and bathrooms. When she stepped outside, she was wowed.

A decent pool and a lake view.

Jennifer was seated in one of the chairs out there, going through her phone.

"We're going to do another tour inside," Linc said.

Jennifer nodded. "Sure, of course. I'll be right here."

They walked inside and he closed the door. Linc leaned against the kitchen counter. "Thoughts?"

"The kitchen is a gut job. You could open up this wall and it wouldn't feel so closed in, and it would give a more open feel into the living area." She stepped into the living room. "It's nice and spacious, but these floors have seen better days. What do you think?"

His lips curved. "Everything you just said, plus more. But you're good at this. Ever thought about becoming my assistant?"

"You're funny." They moved down the hall to the primary bedroom. "I like that it's nice-sized and has a walk-in closet. But carpet?" She wrinkled her nose. "No. The bathroom needs serious help. So does the other full bath and the half bath. And the exterior needs painting and some good landscaping. Backyard is awesome, though. Can you imagine the sunsets out there?"

They headed back toward the kitchen. "Agree. It's a huge selling point, and once this place is updated it'll be amazing—and worth a lot more money. I just need to have an inspection done for electrical, HVAC, and so on to make sure I'm not in over my head. Otherwise, the rest is doable."

They stood in the kitchen. "Plenty of space in here for an oversize island."

"Agree. Okay, then, let me tell Jennifer we're leaving so she can meet us at the second place."

Jennifer didn't ask any questions about how they liked the house, just said she'd lock up and meet them at the next one.

They stopped for a drink at a gas station, then drove somewhat out of the area for the next house. They'd gotten to the point where she didn't see neighborhoods. Instead, there was space, a lot of land, with just a sprinkling of homes here and there.

"This is interesting," she said.

"I hope you think so."

He pulled down a long gravel drive toward the largest, most sprawling house that Hazel had ever seen. They got out of the truck, and Hazel stood there and gaped. It was an L-shaped one-story in a color she could only describe as musty gray. And it had two entrances for reasons she couldn't imagine. She didn't even know where to start, other than this place needed a makeover. But, wow, was it ever huge.

"How big is this house?" she asked Linc as they watched Jennifer's car pull down the long drive.

"Uh, not exactly sure."

She gave him a curious look but turned to smile at Jennifer as she got out of her car.

"I'm so excited to show you this house. It's been on the market awhile, so I think you could get a great deal. And all this land is incredible." She pulled two sheets out of her briefcase and handed one to each of them. "Shall we go inside?"

"Yeah," Linc said.

Hazel followed, taking in the information sheet.

Six thousand square feet? Five bedrooms and four baths? All the places she'd ever lived in her entire adult life could fit inside this house.

The first thing she noticed when they walked inside was no carpet. No flooring of any kind, actually. No furniture, either.

"As you can see, the owners had started on a renovation, but that fell through when one of the owners became ill. They thought it best to sell the place and move somewhere more . . . convenient."

Hazel felt immediately for the owners. "I'm sorry to hear that."

Jennifer nodded. "I'll let you look around."

Jennifer was good at disappearing.

Linc looked over at her. "First impressions?"

"Humongous."

He laughed. "Yeah, it sure is. Come on, let's go explore. Try to visualize what could be."

"Okay." This should be fun. After all, it wasn't her house. But as they walked through the amazing oversize living area with its cathedral ceilings, she could already imagine a tall Christmas tree in the front window, and beautiful wood floors throughout. Or maybe wood-looking tile if the new owners had a bunch of dogs.

The kitchen was enormous, but very nineties, with oak cabinetry, laminate counters, and dingy white square floor tiles. Yuck. "I can already see a wall of cabinets over here, and here," she said. "Plus there's room for an oversize pantry. The area on this side is big enough for a chef's stove and refrigerator." She studied the space, getting her first glimpse of the actual size of the property behind them. "Oh. You could put bifold doors over here to let in light and showcase that yard and pond."

"That's a great idea."

She wandered to the back door and opened it, her jaw dropping at what appeared to be miles of open land, something she never saw in the city.

"Wow," she said as Linc came up beside her. "Does this belong to the house?"

"And then some. There's twenty acres."

She tried hard not to let her jaw drop. "Twenty . . . seriously?"

"Totally serious."

"Wow," she said again. "The possibilities are endless."

"What would you do? You know, if this were your place?"

"Oh, well. My wants are a lot different from the average home-owner."

He shrugged. "Maybe. Maybe not. But if this was your place, what would you do out here?"

She couldn't help but let her imagination run wild, recalling that incredible drawing Natalie had made for her. "A place for the dogs, of course, since there'd be plenty of room for them to run." She started walking. "You could fence in maybe a few acres for them in that grassy area to the left, to include the woodlands. The dogs would love that, especially if you put in some trails for walks."

"I like that."

"And then right outside the house I'd want a pool. Maybe even a pool in the dogs' area as well, just not as nice so we wouldn't have to worry about them getting dirt in the pool. And so many of the dogs love water."

An image of Freddie covered in mud popped into her head. A pang hit her stomach, but she pushed it aside, concentrating instead on this unrealistic dream.

"And a big covered patio with an outdoor kitchen, with extra space for entertaining. Lots of cushy seating so everyone would have a spot."

"So far it sounds great."

She took his hand and brought him back inside, already visualizing the kitchen that would never be hers. They turned down the long hallway and saw several bedrooms, all of them spacious with nice-sized closet areas. The main bedroom was huge. Like, ridiculously huge. So was the bathroom.

"A spa bath would be nice, with a soaker tub and a huge shower. And two vanities, that way you don't have to share."

He frowned. "Don't like sharing, huh?"

She laughed. "You leave beard hairs in the sink."

"I do not. And you're a toothpaste hog."

She wasn't at all insulted. "See? No sharing."

"Fine. Two vanities."

They walked outside and through another set of doors, and into what seemed like a second house, only much smaller. But it still had a kitchen, two bedrooms, and a bath.

"Guesthouse," he said.

"Oh. That's nice." She lifted her gaze to his. "Would you keep it a guesthouse?"

"I don't know. Would you, if this were your place?"

She thought about it, then nodded. "I think I would. It's nice to have a place for family or friends to stay other than one bedroom and a bath. Gives them some privacy and independence."

"Agree. We'll keep it as it is—and definitely update it, like the rest of the house needs."

She laughed. "Oh, 'we' will, huh?"

He turned to face her. "What would you say if I wanted to buy this place to live in?"

She blinked. "What? You want to buy this? It's huge, Linc. What are you going to do with all this space? And did you see the price? Not to mention what the renovations would cost."

"Okay, so here's the thing. I want to live with you, Hazel. I also want you to have your dream. A place to call your own so you'll never be without a house again. Plus, plenty of room for the dogs, and space for an office to write your cookbook or manage the foster paperwork or whatever you want to do with your life. What would you think about that?"

She frowned. "Are you drunk?"

He laughed. "No. I'm perfectly sober and know exactly what I want to do."

She wasn't sure she understood what he was asking. Or suggesting. She'd never been more confused in her life. "You want to buy this place to live in and renovate. And you want me to rent it from you?"

"No, Hazel." He took her hands. "I want to live here. With you. Not as a roommate, but sharing a bed with you. A life with you."

"Oh." She thought about it, ecstatic for a moment, confused for another, and then it all started to sink in. "You deliberately brought me here because you thought it's what I wanted."

"Well, kind of. I like this place, too. There's lots of storage for my renovation stuff, and it's close enough to the city that I can either work there or hop on a plane when I need to."

"And you'll still be able to afford to do that after you get a mortgage the size of Ohio for this place?"

He scratched the side of his nose. "Uh, no. I intend to pay cash for this place."

"You . . . what?"

"I have money, Hazel. A lot of it."

The shock hit her so hard she felt dizzy. "How much is a lot of it?"

"Lots of millions."

She heard a buzzing in her ears and wished there was a place to sit down, because dizziness overcame her.

Millions? "Wha . . . Why didn't you ever tell me that?"

"It's . . . complicated."

"Having money isn't complicated, Linc."

"It is when women use you because of it."

"Oh. I see." She took a deep inhale and let it out, suddenly unable to comprehend what was happening here. Linc was a millionaire. Or more than a millionaire. Something he'd left out of every conversation he'd ever had with her. And why was that? Did he think because she was broke she'd latch on to him like a barnacle and never let go? She had figured out that he was probably well-off, financially. After all, he owned a company that he managed well. One that gave him enough time to indulge in doing this side business, which probably also offered a decent profit.

But, millionaire? Never in her wildest imaginings did she expect that.

And then he throws out buying this place. For her. Because, obviously, she'd never be able to make a go of it on her own. What he must think of her. Well, she knew what he thought of her.

Inept. Useless. Unable to stand on her own two feet.

"Hazel, let me explain."

She held up her hand. "No, I think I've got it. Can we go now?"

"Babe, if you just let me explain, I think I can—"

"Oh, I think you've done enough for today. I'd like to leave."

He paused, and she refused to acknowledge the look of hurt on his face.

He'd lied to her. And more importantly, he'd invited her out here to this . . . this mansion, claiming he was going to buy it and he wanted her to live there with him. He hadn't included her in his decision-making, in his thoughts about the future.

How typical.

And not once had he told her how he felt about her. Not. Once.

She had to get away from him.

The drive back was in silence. Hazel spent the entire time with her focus squarely on the passenger side window so she wouldn't have to look at Linc. Fortunately, he stayed quiet as well until they pulled into the garage at the house. She got out of the truck immediately and went into the house.

"Hazel, please talk to me," he said as she went into the kitchen to let the excited pups out into the yard. "Or at least let me explain my reasoning for not telling you about the money."

She turned to face him. "Do you think I care about your money? That I've *ever* cared about your money? I don't. As far as money goes, I only need enough to feed me and the dogs and put a roof over our heads. And that's all I've ever needed. And if you didn't figure that out within the first couple of weeks of knowing me, then you're the dumbest man on the planet."

He held up his hands and stepped closer to her. "I know, I know. I should have told you. But by then things between us were going so well. I didn't want to say or do anything to screw that up."

She gave him a look of disbelief. "I've kept notes of everything you've spent on me, intending to pay you back out of the money you've paid me. The pots and pans and dog food and dog toys and anything else. My goal has always been to be independent, Linc. Were you not paying attention?"

"Of course I was. I am. But you don't have to pay for any of those things. I bought them because I wanted to."

She shook her head. "And I will move forward in my life on my own. Without anyone's help."

She turned and headed up the stairs, Linc right on her heels. She ignored him, pushing the hurt down until it was so far into the dark depths of her subconscious that it didn't exist anymore.

Now she had to make a plan for her future, one that she could control. She went into her room and shut the door, right in Linc's face.

Linc paced in front of Hazel's door, listening to her talk on the phone to someone, but he couldn't hear who, or what was being said. He wanted to knock, to get her to talk to him, but she was so upset he figured giving her some time to calm down would be the wise choice.

But after fifteen minutes, she hadn't opened the door yet. So he went outside and hung out with the dogs, tossing the ball to Penny, chasing Freddie around the yard, and watching Lilith attempt to herd Mitzi and Gordon to places they absolutely did not want to go. He laughed when Mitzi nipped at Lilith when Lilith pushed her toward the pool.

"I don't think Mitzi wants to go swimming right now, Lilith."

Dejected, Lilith came over and climbed into his lap. He petted her until she decided to go bother Penny.

The slider opened. "Come on, pups," Hazel called.

Linc got up and followed the dogs inside, surprised to see Hazel leading the dogs outside to her car, even more surprised to see all her bags along with her cooking pans sitting beside the trunk.

"Going somewhere?" he asked.

"I'm moving out. The house is done anyway, so it's time for me to go."

"Hazel." He stepped over to her. She scooted away. "Please, let's talk."

"We've talked enough. Or, maybe not enough. Obviously, you didn't talk enough. I don't even know you." She threw a bag in the trunk and closed it with a hard thud, then got all the dogs hooked up in the back seat.

"Don't leave. Not like this. We can talk through this. I made all these plans—"

"Oh, *you* made plans, huh? Is that how you rich guys do it? I mean, my ex wasn't rich, but he sure managed my life for me. I don't intend to do the same thing again, so thanks, but no thanks."

"Hey, that's not fair. And it's not the same thing. I'm not taking anything away from you. In fact, I was giving you your dream."

She moved closer to him, glaring up at him with eyes that were both sad and angry. "The fact that you can't even see all the things you did wrong tells me you have no idea what my dreams are, Linc."

She handed him a check. He looked at her and frowned.

"That's the money I owe you."

"Hazel, come on." He tried to hand the check back to her, but she ignored him. "Where are you going?"

She didn't answer as she buckled her seat belt.

"Hazel. Where are you going?"

She didn't look at him when she answered. "Anywhere but here."

He wanted to stop her, but maybe a cooling-off period would be best. Still . . .

"Hazel."

"What?"

"Penny is my dog."

She gripped the steering wheel for a few seconds, then got out and unhooked Penny, letting her out, along with a small bag of her favorite toys. She handed him the bag and her leash, then looked up at him, her eyes filled with tears.

"You . . . you take good care of her, okay?"

"You know I will. Please don't go."

She hesitated for a fraction of a second, then slid into the driver's seat, buckled up, and pulled out of the driveway, taking his crushed heart with her.

CHAPTER THIRTY-THREE

*H*azel grabbed a tissue—one of the thousand she'd already cried in over the past two days. She was going to need to buy Sandy several boxes to make up for the ones she'd used up.

She sat outside on Sandy's porch. Her pups were running amok outside with Sandy's fosters, having a fantastic time. For the dogs, it was like being on vacation. For Hazel, it was like being right back where she was two months ago. Broken and homeless.

And she desperately missed Penny.

The only good thing about her falling apart was that Sandy cancelled the meet and greet with the people who wanted to adopt Freddie. Hazel supposed Sandy figured she was already enough of a mess without adding to her sadness.

Sandy came out with lemonade, handing one to her before taking a seat.

"Thanks," she sniffled.

"Still crying, huh?"

"Yes. Sorry."

Sandy shrugged. "I have plenty of tissues. Cry away."

Hazel shook her head. "Nope, I'm done now. No more crying."

Sandy took several swallows of lemonade. "You sure?"

"Absolutely." As soon as she said it, the tears bubbled up again, spilling over. And just the act of tears rolling down her cheeks made the pain feel fresh again, the waterfall coming in waves that she couldn't seem to stop.

Sandy handed her more tissues. "I can see why you'd be blubbering. Walking away from all those millions."

"Oh, shut up." She blew her nose. "You know I don't care about his money."

"No, you don't. You care about him."

"No, I don't. Not anymore. Not after what he did."

"That's true. After all, he was going to buy you twenty acres and renovate a dream house for you and all the dogs you wanted to foster. How awful of him. I can see why you left him."

Hazel swiped angrily at her eyes. "Dammit. I didn't ask him to do any of that. I was saving money to do it all on my own. How dare he assume—"

"Assume what? That instead of taking baby steps, he had the ability to give it all to you right now?"

She flipped her attention on Sandy. "Why would he do that?"

Sandy gave her a sympathetic look. "Oh, honey, because he loves you. That's why."

But he'd never told her he loved her.

So how was she supposed to believe him, believe in that love? And if he did love her, he would know what she really needed more than anything.

His faith in her ability to forge her own future.

He hadn't given her that. Not by a long shot.

*L*inc smiled and nodded as the Realtor and the staging people milled about the house, talking amongst themselves. He was barely paying attention to what should be an important component of getting this house sold. All he could think about as he wandered the house was how Hazel had filled this place with laughter, with heart, with joy.

With love.

Dammit.

But the Realtor knew what she was doing, and she said the people staging the house were experts and the best in the city, so he'd let her handle it while he figured out how he'd screwed things up with Hazel so badly.

He'd tried calling and texting her for the past several days. She wouldn't answer. The worst part was he didn't know where she'd gone. And even if he did, he knew that chasing after her would only piss her off more.

He'd bungled this, but he couldn't figure out how. He'd thought it through thoroughly, every step.

Penny had been glued to his side ever since Hazel and the other dogs had driven away. She, too, knew something had gone terribly wrong. And it was all his fault that she felt abandoned.

She missed her pack.

So did he.

He'd taken her on daily walks, played with her as much as he was able, but no doubt she had picked up on his sadness. She even slept in the bed with him at night, and she normally liked the cool floor. He ran his hand over the top of her head, needing her as much as she needed him right now.

"I think we're finished here," Jennifer said. "We should be ready to stage within a couple of days."

"Great, thanks."

Jennifer walked out and shut the door behind her. He started to walk off but the doorbell rang. Figuring Jennifer had left something behind, he went to answer it, shocked to see his mother standing in front of him.

"Mom. What are you doing here?"

"I heard that Hazel left. I came to see if you needed help. Or just a hug."

"How— Oh, Warren." He'd talked to Warren right after it had happened, knowing his brother would offer a sympathetic shoulder. He had no idea Warren would tell their mother. Though he shouldn't be surprised. There were no secrets in the Kennedy family.

"Yes, Warren, though I'm disappointed you didn't call me yourself. And who is this sweet baby?"

"This is Penny. She was one of Hazel's dogs but I adopted her."

"Well, hello, sweet girl." Mom bent and swept her hands over Penny, who wagged her tail enthusiastically.

"I— How about some iced tea? And where are your bags?"

"I already checked into a hotel. And I'd love some tea."

He fixed them both glasses of iced tea and took them to the

table. Mom sat and took a few sips, leaning back in the chair. "Okay, Lincoln. Spill it. All of it."

He told her everything, about how their relationship had progressed, about her love of animals and fostering, about what an amazing cook she was, and how he wanted to give her everything. He told her about his plan to stay in Orlando and buy the twenty acres so she could have everything she ever wanted. And then he told his mother how Hazel had reacted, how upset she was when he told her about the money he had, and how she'd walked out on him.

"You lied to her."

"I didn't . . . Okay, I withheld information. But, Mom, you know what happened in the past with other women. How they treated me differently. I didn't want that to happen with Hazel. I had planned to tell her; it just never seemed the right time."

"Uh-huh." Mom sipped her tea and regarded him the way she always had when he'd done something wrong. "And when did you tell her that you loved her?"

"I—" He paused, thinking back to that day, to all the days before when they'd discussed their relationship.

Feelings. He'd told her he had feelings. He'd never said love.

"Oh, shit. Sorry. But oh, shit, I never told her I loved her. In all those conversations, and on that last day, I never said it."

"Why not? Is it because you don't feel it?"

"No, I do. God, I love her so much. How could I have not said it?"

His mother reached across and laid her hand on his. "You forgot the most important thing, Lincoln. Actually telling the woman you love that you love her."

"I love her. And nothing else matters." He laid his head in his hands, unable to believe how badly he'd handled it all. Finally, he looked up, blowing out a frustrated breath. "I have to find her. Even if she hates me, I have to at least tell her."

She patted his cheek. "Yes, you do. But first, take a breath. Take me to dinner. I'm only here for one day. Show me around this amazing house that you've renovated."

"I'll do that." He reached across the table. "I'm so glad you're here, Mom."

He'd needed his mother to help him find clarity. Now that he had it, it occurred to him that he knew who to ask about where Hazel might be.

CHAPTER THIRTY-FOUR

*O*n her way to buy dog food, Hazel realized she needed a plan. She'd already taken up enough of Sandy's generosity. Now, she and the dogs were going to have to move. It was time to carve out that independence she'd been talking about for so long.

But, first she needed to talk to Linc. Now that she'd had some time to come down from her abject anger, she realized she was in love with him. And, maybe things weren't going to work out between them, but she owed him at the very least a thank-you for housing her and giving her a job and a paycheck so she could move forward with her life.

Tell him you love him. Work things out.

Absolutely not. It was over. And she was going to be calm and rational and tell him that.

As soon as she got brave enough to make that phone call, or go see him in person.

Just the thought of seeing him made her legs shake.

What would she say? *Oh, Linc, thanks for handing me my world of dreams right before I threw them back in your face. Would it help if I told you I loved you?*

That would sound exactly like a woman who just found out

her guy had tons of money, and had decided she wanted a big chunk of that cushy, comfortable life.

This was a no-win situation.

Tough. Woman up, Hazel, and have the conversation. No matter which way it goes, you'll have told him how you feel.

She changed lanes and headed over to Linc's house.

*L*inc studied his phone, smiling at Jennifer as she went over the multiple offers on the house.

"One day, Linc," she said. "We were on the market for one day and got three offers, each one better than the last. One's lower but it's cash, so something to consider."

"Uh-huh." He studied the offers, making note of the family with two kids and a dog. The husband and wife had included a sweet note about how the place felt like home the minute they walked in. They also mentioned how much the kids loved the pool. They had financing in order, and he could see how this place would be an ideal family home.

He slid that offer back to Jennifer. "This one. Accept this one."

She looked up at him. "Really? But it's five thousand—"

"I don't care. That family loves this house, and I want them to have it."

She shrugged. "Okay. I'll let their Realtor know. They'll be thrilled."

He smiled and signed the papers, then showed Jennifer out, walking with her to her car as they discussed details.

When a car pulled up alongside Jennifer's in the driveway, he couldn't contain his shock.

It was Hazel.

Jennifer looked from the car to him. "I'll talk to you soon."

His gaze was fixed on Hazel. "Yeah. Thanks."

Jennifer left and Hazel got out of her car, walking over to him. "The house is for sale?" she asked.

"I accepted an offer today, actually."

"Wow. That's fast."

"Yeah. How are the dogs?"

"They're good. We've been at Sandy's."

"I called her. She told me to leave you alone until you were ready to talk. So, I tried to respect that."

"Thanks. I don't know if that helped when all I really needed was to talk to you."

Relief washed over him. "I want to talk to you, too. Come inside?"

She nodded. "Okay."

He wanted to take her hand, but he didn't, instead followed her as she went through the front door.

Penny greeted her with wild wags and whimpers. Hazel crouched down and gave her copious amounts of love. "Penny. I've missed you so much."

"She's missed you, too." So had he.

She got up and looked around. "Oh, wow. The house looks so different with furniture in here."

He glanced around the house, at how the stagers had put

furniture and decor in all the rooms. Nice furniture, too. It made the house look like a home.

"Yeah, the stagers did a good job."

"And it's probably why the house sold so quickly. I hope you got what you wanted out of it."

"I got three offers, but I chose the family with two kids and a dog because they wrote a sweet note telling me how the place felt like home to them."

Her eyes welled with tears. "That's . . . so nice."

"You know this place is built for a family—for a family with dogs and kids who'll love the pool and the yard."

She looked over at Penny, who lay contentedly at Linc's feet, then shuddered out an exhale. "Yeah, it's perfect."

He could talk bullshit about the house or he could do what was necessary to fix things with her. And maybe it wouldn't work, but it was up to him to try.

He picked up her hand. "Hazel, I love you. I stupidly forgot to mention the most important thing when I dragged you out to that property. I want to build a life with you because I love you. And I'm so damned sorry I didn't mention my financial situation to you earlier, because I trust you more than I've ever trusted anyone before in my life outside of my family. I can't make up for how badly I screwed up. I can only hope that someday you'll forgive me, because I would really like my future to include you. I love you. I need you. I've missed you so much I can barely breathe."

Linc's apology was everything to Hazel. His admitting fault meant more to her than she could convey. Telling her he loved her? Everything. But still, she needed more.

"I need you to understand that I can't have you giving me the life of my dreams, Linc. I have to have control over my destiny. And I know you have all this money and, wow, that's great and all, but I've taken some steps forward to be independent, and while not super successful, I'm standing on my own two feet for the first time in a long time."

He leaned forward. "Okay, tell me what you want."

"I love that property. It's my dream. But I am not ready for that yet. If you want to move in together that sounds great. Let's start small and let me get my business going. I can work and foster. We'll build up to the twenty acres, if that works for you."

He nodded. "Whatever makes you happy works for me. I want to give you the world, Hazel, but I'm willing to work on that world alongside you. I will do whatever it takes to earn your trust. I hope you can trust me to do anything to make you happy."

Her heart swelled and tears streamed down her cheeks. "Of course I trust you. And I love you, too, which I should have said the minute I felt it. I was afraid." Her voice wobbled so she stopped talking.

"I was afraid, too. Love is scary. But I think if we want to be with each other we're both going to have to be a little brave. Because we can do amazing things together."

She nodded. "I think you're right. I've been miserable without you, and I want to be a part of helping you do what you love, and letting you help me achieve my dreams, because that's what people who love each other do."

Linc's heart pounded so hard, blood rushing so loud through his veins he could hardly hear himself think. But he felt such joy at having this amazing woman forgive him, give him another chance to show her just how much he loved her. He pulled her into his arms and kissed her, tasting the salt of her tears in that kiss that bound them together.

When he pulled away, they sat on the sofa in the living room, her body touching his. He didn't know if he'd ever want to let go of her. He'd almost lost her, and he'd never let that happen again.

"Can we keep the dogs?" he asked. "Our dogs? They could be the pack leaders for the rest of the fosters. Help them out, get them comfortable. How would you feel about that?"

She laid her palm on his chest. "I like that idea. Let's do that."

"We'll build a life together, Hazel," he said. "With both of our input. I won't make assumptions about what you want or need. You'll tell me."

She reached up and swept her hand across his jaw. "Maybe we'll start with house shopping? Something with a small amount of land. I've already got a line on a job as a sous-chef at a nice, trendy restaurant. I'm kind of excited about cooking there."

"That sounds pretty great."

"Then let's work on our future together."

He smiled down at her, brushed his lips across hers. "Yeah, I can't wait to get started."

They sank into the couch together and started making plans, and Linc felt settled. Happy. And utterly in love.

Life was good.

Photo by Claudio Marinesco

Jaci Burton is the *New York Times* and *USA Today* bestselling, award-winning author of more than eighty books, including the Play-by-Play, Hope, and Brotherhood by Fire series. She has been a Romance Writers of America RITA finalist, and she was awarded the RT Book Reviews Career Achievement Award. Jaci lives in Oklahoma with her husband and dogs.

VISIT JACI BURTON ONLINE

JaciBurton.com
🅕 AuthorJaciBurton
🐦 JaciBurton